Murder by the Waters

BY ROBERT LEE HALL

A Benjamin Franklin Mystery

Murder by the Waters

Further Adventures of the
American Agent Abroad

by
ROBERT LEE HALL

St. Martin's Press
New York

Library of Congress Cataloging-in-Publication Data

Hall, Robert Lee.
Murder by the waters: a Benjamin Franklin mystery / Robert Lee Hall.
p.   cm.
"A Thomas Dunne book."
ISBN 0-312-13568-8
1. Franklin, Benjamin, 1706-1790—Fiction.   2. Government investigators—England—Bath—Fiction.
3. Americans—England—Bath—Fiction.   4. Bath (England)—Fiction.   I. Title.
PS3558.A3739M84   1995
813'.54—dc20   95-30626
CIP

First Edition: November 1995

10 9 8 7 6 5 4 3 2 1

For my oldest friend, Larry

Murder by the Waters

🙰 1 🙰

*IN WHICH a journey is proposed
and wax discloses a secret . . .*

M
r. Benjamin Franklin turned from the bow window
of his chamber overlooking Craven Street. "Shall we
to Bath, Nick?" This on a fine April morn but a
week after he had brought the murderer of Cranbourne Street
to earth.

The year was 1758.

I sat by the hearth with my Latin. Wanting a holiday from
murder—needing a holiday—I looked up eagerly at the stout,
sturdy gentleman framed by an open casement. Behind him
the rooftops of London were a jumble of brick and slate
against a blue, blue sky. "I should be happy to go to Bath, sir,"
said I. "But what is it? And, if I am not too bold, why do we
go?"

"You are never too bold, Nick—if you temper boldness with
a watchful eye." Hands at his back, he rocked on his square-
toed shoes. "Bath is a market town some hundred miles from
London: a shrine of hope, where the lame and halt creep to
ease their pains, a palace of greed where mountebanks scramble to line their pockets, a watering place where the quality
flee to game, gossip, make love. As to why we go"—he took a

letter from his desk—"this is the answer."

"Who writ it?"

"A fellow investigator. As you know, I have some small reputation amongst the Natural Philosophers." (This was modest, for men as far away as Italy called themselves "Franklinists.") "This is from one of that company, Mr. Arthur Brown. I met him at the Royal Society last December, where he listened to my view of Earth's age and in turn gave out his speculations on the ancient Celts and Romans who once inhabited Bath. We spent two hours rummaging amongst Time's debris."

"Happy hours?"

"O, yes."

"And became friends?"

"After a fashion. He wishes to show me his artifacts and to continue our discourse. I have long wished to test Bath's waters (I doubt their efficacy, but the experiment must be made). Too, I possess letters of introduction to Ralph Allen of Prior Park. Further, I should like to meet Richard Nash, the famous Beau." He flung a hand toward the open casement. "And it is spring." His brown eyes behind his small round spectacles lit. "Shall we taste of the country in spring?"

"I should like that, sir."

He beamed. "I thought that you should." It being Sunday morn, bells began to peal over London. At their sound Mr. Franklin's expression sobered, and he tutted softly. "My invitation is not without its mystery, however." He held out the letter. "What do you make of this?" I took the thing. Hearing a wary note in his voice, I examined it closely. It seemed nothing out of the ordinary, a common fold of paper, its instructions in a neat, clear hand directing it to *Mr. Benjamin Franklin, Craven Street, the Strand,* and telling that it had been sent by *Mr. Arthur Brown, Orchard Street, Bath.* Mr. Franklin often tested my perceptions, and I turned the letter back and forth, peered, stroked, coaxed. I even sniffed the paper—it smelt of the leather of the postbag in which it must have been carried—but I could discover nothing out of the ordinary.

"Make of what, sir?" said I at last.

"Why . . . the seal, of course."

I squinted at the reddish wax, rubbed it with my fingers. "I still cannot perceive what you mean."

"Someone opened it before I did. And resealed it."

"But how can you tell?"

"Aha!" Beckoning me to his desk, he bade me peer through his quizzing glass whilst he held the severed halves of the dark red puddle of hardened wax together. "Look you, here is the line where I broke the seal—but here, at the edges almost opposite one another"—he pointed with the tip of a quill pen—"two small indentations, which show that the wax was previously sundered."

They were small indeed. "But—?"

"I have made a study of the effect—no very great one, done whilst I waited upon the Board of Trade. Yet it was enough to see how the thing might be managed. And repaired."

I looked at him: a little under six feet, barrellike in his plain brown suit of clothes. He smelt of tobacco, witch hazel, freshly ironed linen. A round, unremarkable face, a mild expression— yet how probing were his eyes! I could not forget that his square, blunt fingers and workman's hands had fashioned a kite that had astounded the world by demonstrating that lightning and electricity were one. Too, he had made studies into fingerprints and handwriting, so I was not surprised to learn he looked into wax seals, for he was expert at ferreting out discoveries which might appear useless to the common run of men.

But could this signify?

Sounds of our landlady rose from below: a clatter of pots, a cry as she subdued some rebellious implement of huswifery.

"I am quite certain the seal was broke before I opened it," persisted Benjamin Franklin. "Observe." Again I was bid to peer through the quizzing glass, to see how the entwined A and B, pressed into the wax, were well-formed at top and bottom but seemed to have been blended with some heated metal point at the middle. "Repaired, see? After the thing was opened."

"But might not your own tearing of the wax have produced the effect?"

"You might ask more. Did Mr. Brown himself break the wax for the purpose of adding some last-minute thought? Was the seal broke in the post? But in either case," his eyes narrowed, "why trouble to repair it so artfully?"

I took his point. "I do not mean to doubt—"

He clapped my shoulder. "Nay, you are right to do so, for one must always doubt. As for myself, does my ill reception by the Penns—that suspicion with which I am treated by so many on these shores—lead me to suspect they open my letters before they arrive?" He waved his hands. "We shall pay no heed. Brown's letter is a fortnight old; I have already concluded arrangements with him. We travel by coach day after tomorrow, so ready yourself, lad, to partake of the pleasures and perils of Bath."

*IN WHICH we grow to six in a coach
and set off for Bath . . .*

W hen Mr. Franklin settled upon a thing, it was as good as done. Thus we were up at cock's crow Tuesday morn and upon the stoop of number 7 Craven Street by half-past six. It was barely dawn, mists rising from the Thames at the bottom of the lane, though at the top traffic already surged, carts and drays clattering. A poulterer hung capons by his shop window. The last of the nightsoil men trudged by with his stinking load.

Mrs. Margaret Stevenson stepped upon the damp cobbles with us. She had been Mr. Franklin's landlady since he arrived in London nine months ago, providing him four well-served rooms on the second floor of her tidy house. Now she stood in her white apron with her daughter Polly to bid us good-bye. Gravely, hands arub, she eyed our boxes as the hired coachman strapped 'em to the back of his hackney. "You are quite sure you have ev'rything, sir? Your fine Holland shirt? Your worsted stockings? Your new calfskin shoes?"

Mr. Franklin patted her hand. "Our stores have been well seen-to, dear lady; I am sure we take more than we need. Bath is not the South Seas, you know."

Mrs. Stevenson looked as if it might be the Canary Islands, whilst Polly, her honey ringlets bobbing, planted a kiss upon the gentleman's cheek. She kissed me too, a quick peck that made me flush, after which Mr. Franklin and I climbed into our coach. As its straps sank under us, I glimpsed a dusky face at an upper window: Peter, Mr. Franklin's blackamoor servant, whom he had brought with him from America. Seeing him, Mr. Franklin touched a finger to his tricorn hat, and I saluted, too. Peter had once saved my life, and leaving him behind stirred regrets in my breast.

Yet leave him we must, for our hackney set off, its mare clip-clopping, Mr. Franklin and I swaying against one another in that rocking jostle which ev'ry soul who travels London's rutted ways must know. At the Strand we turned west, past Northumberland House; from thence to Charing Cross with its pillories and looming equestrian statue of Charles I. Soon we were past Spring Gardens and into the Haymarket.

Thirteen years old, I gazed with eager interest at London, as I always did when Mr. Franklin took me about. Yet, never having traveled farther than Deptford, this caused me to reflect on my narrow upbringing: the drudging life of a boy of work at Inch, Printer, Moorfields. What good fortune that I had been rescued by Mr. Franklin! Since then a great kindness had fortified me under Mrs. Stevenson's roof. How should I fare without that good woman's ministrations, her daughter's courtesy? I should sorely miss them in Bath, and I began to miss even William, Mr. Franklin's twenty-eight-year-old son, who had come from America with him to study law at the Inner Temple. William treated me with sneering hauteur, but I would have been glad just then for one of his barbs.

Yet these misgivings dissolved as morn began to gild the Tudor half-timbers and Palladian brick along our way. Was I not by the side of Benjamin Franklin? He might be sorely beset—the task for which the Pennsylvania Assembly had sent him, to wrest taxes from the sons of William Penn, went hard, and many a Tory spat upon him for a dangerous republican— yet he had friends amongst philosophers and Whigs, amongst common folk too, such as Mrs. Martha Clay, whose brother's murderer he had brought to justice when he had discovered soon after arriving in London that I was his natural son.

We never spoke to others of his paternity, but stealing a glance at his round, bespectacled face, I felt no shame. I was Nicolas Handy, and Benjamin Franklin was my father.

Mr. Franklin had informed me that there was more to Arthur Brown's letter than he had first told. A young lady of Brown's acquaintance, Miss Emma Morland, would also be traveling to Bath, it seemed. She would be in the company of her aunt, Mrs. Fanny Snow, and would thus be "tolerably in hand," Brown had writ. "Yet he wishes me to guard her from footpads." Mr. Franklin had laughed at this—though I had not, for I trembled to think on the villains who lurked with bludgeons and pistols upon Hounslow Heath, which we must cross. " 'Would it discommode you, sir, to travel with Miss Morland and Mrs. Snow, to protect 'em if need be?' " the gentleman had read from Brown's letter. "Ha, does he take me for some troop at arms? Yet as I commanded three hundred fifty militia in Pennsylvania, I suppose I can face down a brace of English pistols. Hum. Arthur Brown displays a very great interest in Miss Morland. She is 'a most lively young woman,' he says." A wink. "Is there some spark of romance?"

Our hackney rattled on.

Burlington House came and went. Devonshire House. The City of Westminster ended at Hyde Park; countryside lay beyond. Many a traveler left London by means of the Thames, taking a wherry upriver to Isleworth before encoaching; but we would to depart from the great inn hard by Shepherd's Market, the Bell and Crown. Thus, at half-past seven, we pulled under its wide arches into a broad rectangular yard. Triple stories rose in a U-shape about us, a stables at one end, and all was abustle at this hour: hackneys leaving off passengers, workmen strapping boxes onto the great machines that would make the journey west, ostlers prodding horses, postboys scampering in a great din that was pierced ever and again by the sharp toot of the wayfarers' horn as the latest conveyance set out: *Godspeed!* Curricles and gigs waited. Single riders pranced about on their steeds; and one such fellow, jaunty in a bright scarlet coat, skittered so near us on his roan that he nearly knocked Mr. Franklin down. Tipping his hat, he cried, "Beg pardon, sirs!" before he set off in a scattering of stone.

Mr. Franklin gazed about at the tumult. "Well!"

The sky was cloudless blue. Our coach was to depart at eight, so there was no time to lose. We discovered it, a six-passenger behemoth twice as tall as I, just to the right of the arches, four thick-bodied bays just being led to its traces. Already other boxes and trunks had been strapped onto its back and top, so we presented ourselves smartly. The coachman was a burly fellow with a large squarish face. Peering at our tickets, he directed two boys to transfer our boxes. "Look smart!" The boys leapt like mice.

This done, we had some time to see if we might discover Mrs. Snow and Miss Morland. Many women moved amongst the crowd, some who might be aunts and some young women who might by a stretch of the imagination be judged "lively," but polite inquiries did not uncover our quarry, and Mr. Franklin frowned. "I sent a note to Berwick Street, where the aunt resides, to say we should be pleased to join 'em, but there was no reply. If only we knew what they looked like." He snapped open his watchcase. "Nothing for it. We must board."

We found one of our fellow passengers waiting at the coach. Of middle age, he stood by its great rear wheels looking about in some dismay, as if he were unused to such bustle. He was of medium height, thin-lipped and thin-nosed, with salt-and-pepper brows above mild eyes of a wintery gray. He wore a dark green suit, well-pressed though not of the newest cloth, and he carried a small black leather bag.

Mr. Franklin touched his hat as we came up. "You ride the Bath Coach, sir?"

"I do."

"We travel together, then." A crisp bow. "I am Benjamin Franklin. This is Nicolas Handy, my indispensable boy."

The man bowed in return. "Dr. James Woolridge." He looked at me. "Indispensable, eh? How fortunate to be indispensable," I sensed regrets in his life, but his manner was pleasant. "Pleased to meet you both. Do you know what others travel with us?"

"We know of two. Nick and I have been seeking 'em."

Mrs. Fanny Snow and Miss Emma Morland arrived just then.

They came from the direction of the inn, two women in traveling dresses. Introductions were made, bows deployed, curtseys offered. They had been inside the inn, Mrs. Snow informed us in a chattering way, the hat upon her head bobbing like a small boat upon a sea. She had a narrow face with darting eyes. "We took some small refreshment. The journey is so tiresome that one *must* take refreshment whenever one can. Dear me, two whole days in a coach! Have you traveled this road before? You will not like it. Bath is not worth the effort, but my husband's aches must undergo the regimen, he says. He has gone before us, to prepare rooms." A great sigh. "I have sorely missed him this week, but I have made do. You are a friend to Arthur Brown, Mr. Franklin? I believe you sent a note to that effect. Dear me, I meant to reply to it, but cannot recall if I did. (Do you not think that meaning to do a thing is nearly the same as doing it?) Such a peculiar man, Mr. Brown. Those old things he keeps about—faugh!—dusty bits of clay and coins one may never spend because the people who made 'em are long dead. I cannot approve it as a proper occupation for a man."

"Perhaps he does not seek your approval, Aunt," came Miss Morland's light, dry voice.

"What is that you say?" Mrs. Snow sniffed. "I tell Emma she must not speak out of turn, but she never listens."

"O, I always listen, Aunt. It is *my* occupation."

Mrs. Snow emitted a high, nervous laugh. "Whatever can she mean? I frequently do not understand what she means. Yet,"—she touched the cheek of the girl, whose lips were pursed in quiet irony—"I dote on her. But we must board, I see, for here are the stairs." Three wooden steps had been pulled up by a yardboy. "Will you help me, Mr. Franklin?"

"My pleasure, ma'am." He held her hand as she mounted. Miss Morland's trim figure climbed up next, then Dr. Woolridge with his small black bag. Mr. Franklin and I entered last.

The coach rocked as we settled. Having never rid in such a conveyance, I was much dismayed to see how crowded we would be. Two rows of three seats faced one another, so narrow that our shoulders pressed together and so close that our knees bumped. Mrs. Snow and Miss Morland sat facing front, whilst we sat across from 'em, our backs to the driver, Mr. Franklin opposite Mrs. Snow, I betwixt him and Dr. Woolridge, who perched his little bag on his lap.

Mr. Franklin snapped open his watch—"Near eight A.M." We all gazed at the empty seat next Miss Morland. Would anyone occupy it?

A long, sallow face with a flattened nose and a sullen mouth suddenly thrust itself in at the window. It was topped by a thatch of tobacco-colored hair. Was this the answer to our question? Miss Morland emitted a cry, and I myself was taken aback by the insolent eyes which peered into each face, as if to fix it in memory.

"Beggin' yer pardon," our intruder drawled. Dressed in brown livery, he withdrew his head as abruptly as he had poked it in. The coach dipped, a booted leg swung past Dr. Woolridge's window, and the man sat perched on the roof.

The doctor turned to Mrs. Snow. "Your serving man, ma'am?"

She fanned herself breathlessly. "Dear me, no."

"Nor mine," remarked Mr. Franklin. "Whose?"

But we left this, for a commotion sounded outside, and we all turned to watch a small molelike fellow in a coat much too large propel himself from a hackney which had just pulled up across the yard. He scrambled toward us in almost-comical haste; yet such was the tangle of vehicles that in darting amidst 'em, he spooked a bay. This steed reared, causing three or four others to skitter in their traces, which set up a hullaballoo. Curses sounded, fists were raised, but the man plunged on. Puffing, he scrambled through our door to fling himself amongst us just as the yard boy came to whisk away the stairs. Dr. Woolridge rose to accommodate him; in the confused grappling that ensued, they exchanged places, the newcomer sinking down by my side. Something hard beneath his preposterously large coat dug into my ribs, and I was alarmed to glimpse the handle of a pistol before he snatched the coat shut.

He was small, with a bushy mustache and damp, cast-down eyes. He panted rapidly. He had stubby hands on which the nails were bitten to the quick. "You very nearly missed us, sir," said Mr. Franklin whilst the fellow hunkered lower in his seat.

11

No reply.

"I am Benjamin Franklin." Mr. Franklin presented the rest of us.

The newcomer sent an unwilling half-look into each face.

"And you, sir?" invited Mr. Franklin boldly.

The voice came small and unwillingly. "I am Mossop. F. J. Mossop."

Mr. Franklin smiled. "You are welcome, sir."

The door was abruptly slammed, the coachman cried *Haw!*, the tin horn tooted. "This is our company, then," said Mr. Franklin, beaming round as we jerked with a creak and a jingling into motion. We should travel together two whole days, and I was not unhappy to know it, for the prettiest girl I had ever seen sat opposite me. My sketchbook was in my right-hand coat pocket. Might I draw her? I felt only one brief misgiving as we passed under the arches and out upon the way. Glimpsing a postboy with his leathern bag, I thought on Arthur Brown's letter. Mr. Franklin had imagined its wax seal deliberately broken. Had it been? Who might have secretly read the thing?

No matter. I settled back. How could a broken wax seal mar a fortnight in Bath?

❧ 3 ❧

*IN WHICH we learn the dangers of
Bath and a pistol shot rings out . . .*

Six great roads run out of London: the York, the Dover,
the Portsmouth, the Holyhead, the Carlisle, the Bath.
Upon the Bath Road our coach now set its wheels.

Tyburn Lane opened to our right, where rose the terrible
gallows upon which criminals gasped out their lives; Hyde
Park lay ahead. We halted at a gate, our coach paid its toll, and
we were within moments amongst numerous other conveyances upon the Knightsbridge Turnpike.

The sky remained blue, only a few puffs of cloud, like thistledown, blooming far to the south. Through our windows
April wafted a scent of herb and flower, a bouquet that made
me thrill. The road was well-maintained, and we progressed
for the present at ease.

Mr. Franklin had not done with F. J. Mossop. "You were in
such a hurry," said he to the molelike little man, "that I pray
your baggage was not left behind in the hackney."

" 'Twas sent yesterday by carrier."

"Your journey to Bath, then, was planned for some time?"

"As you say."

"The manservant atop is yours?"

"I have no manservant, sir."

"He belongs to no one, then?" Mr. Franklin gazed round. "How singular." He turned to Mrs. Snow. "But you asked, ma'am, if I were a friend of Arthur Brown. Truly, I hardly know him, for we met but once, at the Royal Society. Yet we who pry into Nature's secrets love to talk, so he has asked me to Bath to talk some more. Pray, how do you know the gentleman?"

Mrs. Snow wore a traveling gown of indeterminate hue, with a little mustard-colored cloak about her shoulders. Her eyes lit at this invitation. "La, we have known Mr. Brown so long," replied she in her singsong voice, "that I cannot recall when first I met him. He is a friend of my husband's."

"A good friend?"

"Quite, though I have never understood why. Mr. Brown is far too grave. I do not care for a grave man. I like a man to smile now and then."

"*I* have seen him smile, Aunt," her niece put in quietly.

"Nonsense, child. He never smiles."

" 'Tis an amazing thing, never to smile," remarked Mr. Franklin.

"Perhaps I go a *little* far," agreed Mrs. Snow. "And now I think me, he does smile—though not often, mind."

"On Tuesdays? If the sun shines?" proposed her niece with her own little smile.

"Do you rally me, child? O, I know a jibe when I hear one!" The aunt smoothed her skirt. "She has been ironical from a babe. I can do nothing with her."

"Ah," was all Mr. Franklin's reply. "You know Mr. Brown too, then?" inquired he of the girl.

"He dandled her upon his knee when she was young," interposed Mrs. Snow.

"Allow me to speak for myself. But that is right, sir. I have

14

known Arthur Brown since I was a child." Mr. Franklin nodded whilst I stole glances at the girl. How old? Eighteen? She wore a peach-colored camlet dress with a white satin front-piece and ruffles at her wrists. Her figure was trim, her bosom full despite its confining bodice, which flowered in lace at her throat. Her long neck was crowned by a firm-chinned face. Her lips were pink, her eyes sea-green, her brow forthright, her hair a rich red-brown. She was as ripe as May, and my breath came quick.

But Emma Morland paid no heed to a thirteen-year-old boy. She peered out the window whilst bird song accompanied the rattle of our wheels. "I hear that there are highwaymen upon Hounslow Heath." came her sigh.

"You have heard aright," murmured Dr. Woolridge.

"O, how I should like to see a highwayman!" burst out the girl.

Her aunt stared. "Child, what ideas come into your head!"

Emma turned. "Highwaymen are not so bad, Aunt. I have read all about highwaymen."

"O? May we hear what you have read?" proposed Mr. Franklin.

"Truly, sir?" Breathlessly the girl unfolded tales of galloping steeds and narrow escapes. In them, Jack Dash, a Robin Hood amongst thieves, always gallantly returned a brooch or ring or pearl necklace if the lady he had taken it from protested that it was dear to her heart. Murders spotted her narrative, often grisly, but they seemed only to spice it in her mind—they could never happen to her.

"Well!" protested Mrs. Snow when her niece was done.

"You read the penny papers, I see," commented Mr. Franklin.

"Pray, what is wrong with the penny papers?" Miss Morland lifted her chin. "May a girl not read the penny papers?"

15

"O, I do not say that anything is wrong with 'em. Only that one must know how to take 'em."

The girl sniffed.

"Mr. Franklin is right," Dr. Woolridge joined in. "Thieves are not heroes, Miss Morland. They cut holes in the backs of coaches to snatch travelers' wigs. You must not make 'em better than they are."

The girl fell into a pout but was all the prettier for it, and I longed to tell her that I too should like to see a highwayman—at a safe distance. F. J. Mossop had remained silent in his putty-colored greatcoat, sitting far back, his brow jutting over his eyes. But those eyes watched Mrs. Snow, Miss Morland and Dr. Woolridge who sat opposite him. What did he make of them?

"Pray, what takes you to Bath, doctor?" inquired Mr. Franklin.

"A need for change."

"O?"

"Quite. I was a country doctor many years, in a village near Chelmsford—Butcher's Cross it is called—where I ministered to the rude and humble. You spoke of talk." His smile flickered ruefully. "There is not much talk in such an out-of-the-way place; I have been famished for civilized conversation. I have no wife; my dear Agnes died four years ago. The cobwebs were growing on me, but I had saved a bit of money. 'Twas now or never to start afresh. Bath seemed the perfect place, for where is there so much talk as in Bath?"

"Much of it is gossip, I hear."

"Butcher's Cross's gossip is of pastures and poachers; Bath's must surely be better. Too, the ill and infirm flock there. It wants doctors."

"Might it not already have too many, amongst whom a new one may find it hard to make his way?"

A lift of hands. "Perhaps. But I have cast my lot. And I may do some good, for many of those doctors are quacks, which I am not. I want more than talk. I should like to help my fellow man."

Mr. Franklin patted Woolridge's arm. "I admire a fellow who battles quackery. But Mrs. Snow, you chaff your wrists."

"Pains bedevil me."

"Why, then, may not Dr. Woolridge prescribe for you?"

She turned her narrow face upon him. "Why, I suppose . . . would you?"

"Indeed, I should be honored, ma'am. I should also be pleased to prescribe a regimen for your husband, if he would allow."

"You see?" smiled Mr. Franklin. "Already you make your way."

Miss Morland had heard something of more interest to her in the doctor's words. "You have been to Bath, then, sir?"

"But once, to take its measure for my remove."

"O, please tell about it, then! Is it truly thrilling and gay?"

There was a charming ardor to her outburst, but the doctor's reply was measured. "There is certainly much gaiety. But you must remember that Bath is a place to which many come because they are unwell; disease walks its streets. It is an odd town, too, the most peculiar in England, for the social classes mix there as nowhere else. Lords quaff ale with corn chandlers, earls dance with tradesmen's daughters, ladies chat with publicans' wives. The quality condescend to people they would cut dead on any London street."

"I think I shall like this Bath," proclaimed Mr. Franklin.

"I tell you, it is dangerous!" put in Mrs. Snow. "Especially to young girls. Why, I heard just last week that the Marquis of Dorcester carried off a poor young woman of little fortune from Bath."

17

"And *married* her, Aunt," amended her niece.

Woolridge pursed his lips. "Such things happen."

"Pay 'em no mind!" burst from F. J. Mossop. At this we turned to the little man, who had remained silent for so long that we had near forgot he sat amongst us. He stared back, his damp gaze proclaiming that he was as amazed at his outburst as we. "I only meant . . . that is . . . you must forgive . . . " He subsided into his greatcoat once more.

"And yet you are right," put in Mr. Franklin. "It would be error to imagine ev'ry fellow with a laced coat a gentleman. There is much preying upon women in Bath. Shall you hear a story I was told? Captain Gunnerson wished to wed a rich widow, but though she would entertain his company, she would never listen to his proposals of marriage. Growing desperate, he insinuated himself one eve into the dame's rooms when she was unawares. Next morn all the fashionable world upon the South Parade saw him prominently in her window in his nightcap, and she accepted his hand by noon."

The gentlemen laughed, but Mrs. Snow remained severe, and her niece made a face. "I do not care how you warn me," said she pertly. "For every Captain Gunnerson there is a Marquis of Dorcester. I know that there is."

"And a Jack Dash?" inquired Mr. Franklin. "It is well known that London spies send daily reports to their Bath confederates as to who will arrive, the amount of their fortunes, the nature of their ills and their vices, so that the quacks and gamesters may prey upon 'em."

"Thank goodness no such London spies paid heed to *us*," exclaimed Mrs. Snow, but a sudden doubt furrowed her brow. She opened her mouth to say something, then thought the better and remained silent. Mr. Franklin's eyes gleamed with interest, but he did not press her.

"You wish to affright me, I see," flung out Miss Morland,

"but I shall not be frightened. Besides"—she looked down-cast—"Aunt is right: I am a girl of no prospects—or of very remote ones." She bit her pretty lip. "No one will pay attention to Emma Morland."

There was silence at this, for what man who breathed would not pay attention to so ravishing a girl? Conversation flagged, and as our coach swayed, reins jingling, hooves clopping, I peered out at the ripening fields passing by our windows. How different from London, forever smudged by smoke! Larks swooped, and little farmsteadings stood out like toys amongst the distant hedgerows. Many others rode toward Bath: a gouty squire in a pair-horsed post; a chapman, his packhorses laden with broadcloth; a grand lord's coach, the *Beaufort Hunt*, flanked by liveried postilions. Drays groaned with goods.

Yet the road changed. We had gone in relative ease, but as we neared Hounslow, the ground grew treacherous, marked by damps and ditches, boggy from winter, and all the convey-ances began to spread farther apart to seek better paths. As we slowed, I thought again how fortunate I was to sit by Benjamin Franklin's side. Though we had agreed never to speak of the fact that he was my father (he did not wish to vex his son, Wil-liam, nor to fret his goodwife, Deborah, who remained at their home in Philadelphia, nor his beloved daughter, Sally), he gave me all the attentions due a son, teaching me numbers and catechising me in Latin, *ope et consilio*. He encouraged my drawing. He gave me books: John Bunyan and John Locke and *The Parallel Lives of the Noble Greeks and Romans*. Only yester-day he had presented me with *Roderick Random*, "so you may know the motley crew of rogues and mountebanks and strum-pets we shall also meet in Bath. . . . "

Yet life with him was not all study. There could be danger, and I felt a flutter of alarm as I recalled the broken wax seal. Could there be anything to it? Souls in distress were drawn to

19

Benjamin Franklin, and his few short months in England had delivered him Cassandra Fairbrass who had begged him to exorcise a ghost, Lady Shenstone who had sought to retrieve a stolen gem, and the great David Garrick himself, whose playhouse had been threatened with ruin. The consequences had been spying, chases, and murder. Mr. Franklin had found an ally in John Fielding, the "Blind Beak" of London, Chief Magistrate for Westminster, who policed the huge city—but he had also made a dangerous enemy, the dark presence known only as Quimp, who lurked behind much London crime. Mr. Franklin had thwarted Quimp thrice. What would happen if they crossed paths once more?

But the day was fine; we rode far from Quimp's malevolent grasp—surely he could not reach to Bath. I consoled myself with glances at Emma Morland. The coach swayed her provokingly whilst her slender fingers stirred in her lap and her lips formed eager little smiles as if, despite our warnings, she thought on the joys that must come to her in Bath. Inevitably, my thoughts turned to another girl: Annie, the housemaid of Cranbourne Street, who had initiated me into love's secrets. We had lain on her narrow bed whilst she taught my body and my hands. Annie had been a simple girl, but Emma Morland had bright, intelligent eyes and a strong will. Could her aunt restrain such a niece?

Knightsbridge and Kensington were left behind. Shortly we passed Chiswick and the facade of Syon House.

"You keep a journal, do you not, Miss Morland?" asked Mr. Franklin.

The girl blinked out of her revery. "Why . . . yes, sir. How did you know?"

"Tut, by no very great effort. A small spot of ink upon the middle finger of your right hand. You wrote something in the inn, I guessed. Not a letter; you should have no time to post it.

A jotting in your journal, then. Indeed many keep the little books these days; it is the fashion. I myself write in one. Nick, too. It is a very great thing."

"*I* have never seen any need to keep a journal," sniffed Mrs. Snow.

Mr. Franklin ignored the aunt. "Do you read Mrs. Budthorne, as well?" he asked Emma.

The girl's breast heaved with excitement. "And Mrs. Orne!—she is wonderful! Do you read 'em too, Mr. Franklin?"

"Alas, no. But I have heard they make a great romance of life."

Her countenance fell. "You do not approve."

"Nay. Ev'ry soul must have romance." He peered over the tops of his spectacles. "Yet ev'ry eye ought to strive to see things as they are. But we arrive upon Hounslow, I see."

All looked out. The way had grown yet broader, the landscape wilder, a desolate expanse of windblown copses and rude little rises behind which ruffians might hide. Most chilling were the gibbets, from which corpses dangled in chains. "You wished to meet highwaymen." Mr. Franklin flung out an arm. "Here they are. They hang 'em in London, but they bring 'em here to rot. They are meant to warn us all."

Plainly this was not how Miss Morland had meant to meet such fellows, for she gasped. "You see, child?" her aunt rang out, whilst I swallowed my gorge. The sight of severed heads on Temple Bar was bad, but this was worse. We passed near one of these "warnings," twisting like a withered stick whilst a small black bird pecked at the leathery remains of a face. Dr. Woolridge's steel-gray brows drew together, and the taciturn Mossop shrank even further into his greatcoat. I did not know how the odd manservant on the top of our coach took the sight, but I felt ill.

We were distracted from our grim contemplation by a sudden lurch, followed by an alarming tilt of our coach. Mrs. Snow shrieked, F. J. Mossop emitted a mew, and Mr. Franklin gripped my arm.

We had slid into one of the many lakes of mud.

We pulled free—just barely—by the skillful handling of our coachman, but we advanced slowly now, at great peril. The conveyances which companioned us began to spread even farther apart to avoid falling into a hundred treacherous sinks. A continual squelching could be heard, and sev'ral men by a mud-caked stile struggled to right a toppled waggon whilst daffodils mocked at their feet. Rabbits darted and rooks turned in the sky as we sought our own path, shuddering along. Soon we could glimpse only a string of packhorses in the distance; then we were alone in the wild.

Dr. Woolridge wore a deepening frown. "I do not like it." He leant out. "Halloo, too marshy that way, sir, do you not believe?" He thrust a finger south. "Better there, I judge."

Our coachman must have judged so too, for we began to bear that way and in a few moments were on higher ground. It was drier here, safer, though where the true road might be—if there were any true road hereabouts—could not be seen. We had strayed onto a trackless, rocky waste; and though we did not stick in mud, we were jostled violently about. Mrs. Snow clutched at her little hat, but Miss Morland seemed to delight in the new sensation, for her white teeth laughed.

Her pleasure did not last. A horseman burst in an explosion of leaves from a thicket fifty yards up a rise. Galloping toward us, he brandished a pistol, which he discharged with a *Pop!*

Gray smoke flew up. The coachman's "Whoa!" rang out, and Miss Morland was propelled into my lap. I felt the softness of her, smelt her apple scent—but I could take scant pleasure in 'em, for she pulled free as the horseman reined up in a noisy clatter. Pushing his discharged pistol into his belt, he thrust a second into our window: "Out at once, or I'll spill yer blood!"

❧ 4 ❧

IN WHICH *a hero rides to the rescue and blood is spilt . . .*

In dire moments, I looked to Mr. Franklin. His brown eyes behind their small round spectacles were grave, and he gave me a little nod to say, *We must do as we are told.* But he was ready to fight, for his knuckles had whitened on the shaft of his stick, with which I had seen him lay low more than one ruffian.

F. J. Mossop scrambled upon the turf, Dr. Woolridge following. Mr. Franklin stepped down next, then I, the ladies debouching last to the sound of Mrs. Snow's whimpers. We stood in a weedy declivity, the men forming a phalanx before the women. Wind keened, and the air was chill; clouds had blown up into a lowering gray mass. A twisted beech marked the nearby rise.

Our coachman was ordered to stand down, too. Grumbling, he clambered to the ground.

I frowned. Where was the long-faced servant who had rid on top of the coach?

Our attacker leapt from his steed, which began to crop the grass by its dropped reins. Regarding him, I chid myself. Why had I ever thought I should like to meet a highwayman? There was no romance to this one. He was as lean as a ferret and wore an ill-fitting coat and greasy breeches, and his unkempt hair was stuck with so many bits of straw that he must have slept in a haystack. His restless eyes squinted; his mouth was a cavern of blackened teeth. A stench of sweat and gunpowder rolled off him.

He rattled a laugh. "I *knowed* if I waited long enough someone'd stray hereby. They does this time o' year. I got me a young dandy three days ago—tho' he were not so dandy when I finished with 'im." His jaw set. "Now, I mean ter have my way, so yer'd better do as yer told. My pistol is just a-longin' ter shoot some'un."

"You have but to tell us what you wish," replied Mr. Franklin staunchly.

The man wiped his mouth. "I mean ter. First thing"—he jerked his pistol at the coachman—"unstrap them boxes and push 'em down."

"But they will *break*," moaned Mrs. Snow, eyes rolling.

Her niece wore an expression of righteous indignation. "You are no gentleman!" pronounced Emma Morland scornfully.

The highwayman yawped. "I ain't one for airs!" To the coachman again: "Them boxes, hear? Wait!—some'un's ahidin' amongst 'em!" He raised his pistol. "You there—down afore I shoot!"

The long-faced servant had been crouched behind a box. Wriggling to the ground, he crept behind Dr. Woolridge. "There, now," said the highwayman as our coachman unstrapped the trunks and boxes from the roof and tipped 'em down, two bursting open as they struck. The ones at the rear of the coach were brought forth, too, and we were forced to unlock 'em all.

The highwayman poked a toe amongst some tumbled

25

goods. Unfastening a large leather bag from his horse, he tossed it to me. "You. Start afillin' these with wot I tells ye." Mr. Franklin gave me a nod, and I began to sort amongst spilt and opened boxes. There were tortoiseshell combs, lace handkerchiefs, fur muffs, a silver flask, brooches, rings. "Nay, nay, leave that . . . take that!" ordered the highwayman, his eyes darting from me to his other prisoners to the low rises about us. The wind whipped. My hands scrambled. The saddlebag grew fat. "Enough!" barked the highwayman at last. "Drag the bag to my horse."

Doing so, I rejoined the others.

"Now," the man jerked his pistol, "yer pockets, gen'lemen. Empty 'em. Ladies, yer purses too." Dr. Woolridge complied, tossing down a clinking leathern wallet and a snuffbox (he had left his black bag within). Mr. Franklin peered coolly into the highwayman's face as he drew his watch from his waistcoat pocket.

But before he could relinquish it an outburst stopped him. I had heard Emma Morland muttering in fury behind me. Now she cried out: "I shall give you nothing, sir!"

I turned. She had taken a heroine's stance, her perfect little chin outthrust whilst the breeze stirred her auburn curls like some young goddess's. Her green eyes glowed.

"Miss Morland—" warned Mr. Franklin.

"Not a thing!" persisted the girl.

The highwayman scowled. "Who are ye to say me nay?"

"Someone must."

A sly look of satisfaction grew upon the man, as if he should have more pleasure of this than he had supposed. "O, brave, eh? Come 'ere, then. I dare ye t'say it to my face."

She strode past us in a flash. "What shall you do, shoot a defenseless woman?" Back straight, she stood not three feet from him. "You are a brigand. Ride off and leave us be."

The man laughed through his blackened teeth. "P'rhaps I *will* ride off." He thrust out a finger. "With *you*." He snatched her arm, at which she struggled. "Yer a pretty prize, more sovereign than any trinket. Ha, ye'll be my queen!"

She struck him a blow. It could not have harmed him much, but it kindled his fury—"Damn ye, cat!"—and he tightened his hold, at which the girl screamed. I felt Mr. Franklin stir at my side, and I, too, longed to rush to her aid; but she and the man were at least a dozen feet from us, and he easily bent her to him with one hand whilst keeping his pistol trained upon us with the other. "Emma!" wailed her aunt as he began dragging the girl toward his horse as if he would ride off with her. Filled with alarm, I cast about. Was help nowhere? Mossop's head had popped from his overlarge coat like a turtle's, and Dr. Woolridge called, "Stop!" He took a step forward, as did Mr. Franklin, his bamboo stick half-raised; but the pistol swung meaningly, and they halted.

And then the flash of a red coat. I glimpsed it from the corner of my eye.

A rider topped the rise to our left, galloping straight for us against the cloud-thick sky.

The highwayman saw the rider the instant we did, and his body stiffened. His face grew wary, and he twisted Emma Morland so he held her betwixt him and the rapidly advancing man, whose hoofbeats sounded a thudding tattoo. The slap of leather, a horse's panting, and the newcomer reined up in a scatter of dust.

It was the scarlet-coated fellow who had near rid down Mr. Franklin in the yard of the Bell and Crown.

He was young, not more than twenty-five, and his square-jawed face had a tin-soldier freshness, as if the paint were still wet on him. Gazing out of intense blue eyes, he doffed a gold-laced tricorn hat in salute to us all, as if the amenities must be observed. Then he fixed those blue, blue eyes upon the high-wayman. "Here, sir, what do you do with that lady? I cannot permit it."

The highwayman yawped. " 'Cannot permit,' ye say? Be off. This"—a wave of his pistol—"permits or does not permit, here."

The young fellow thought on this. He seemed in no great hurry as he took in Emma Morland, who had ceased to struggle. In her dishevelment, with her hair astray, her bosom heaving, her cheeks flushed, she was prettier than ever. As for the young man, he appeared for the moment at a loss, having rid hell-for-leather with no idea what he meant to do. Yet an answer came. Rising in his stirrups he sang out, "Honor takes precedence over pistols, sir! And honor does not permit you to treat a lady so. Nor to prey upon undefended travelers. Let her go. Climb upon your horse and ride off. You may escape punishment, then."

The highwayman stared. "I'll do no such," snarled he, jerking the pistol at me. "Finish yer job. Tie that bag upon my horse."

Our hero shook his head. "Nay," said he, "I cannot allow you to take your bag, for it is plainly filled with goods which are not yours. Set the woman free, and begone."

The highwayman began to sputter. "Here, now, damn you! Who be you to . . . what . . . why?"

"You must do as he says," put in Benjamin Franklin. He stood with remarkable composure, the wind stirring his fringe of brown hair, his little spectacles glinting. "Furthermore you would do well to think twice about discharging your pistol, for you have but a single shot, and if you kill one of us—or if you miss—the rest will be upon you and tie you down and deliver you to the law, and you will strangle on a string. Your eyes will pop out, your tongue will turn black, your heels will kick; you will die. Then you will join your kind, hanging about the road to Bath. Have you seen 'em, with their faces pecked away? Think on that.''

The highwayman's look clouded, and he licked dry lips, for he saw he was indeed in a bad spot.

Yet he would not relinquish his trump card.

Holding one arm behind Miss Morland, gripping her so that she gave another cry of pain, he thrust his pistol against her breast. "I'll never miss the girl. Like to see her blood, would ye?" He glared at me. "Tie on my bag, I say!"

A great soughing rippled across the grasses, whilst our coach horses stirred in their traces. Was the helpless girl aware death pressed into her breast? Whether or no, she did not swoon, but waited staunchly for what would come. As for me, I had no idea whether to obey. I looked to Mr. Franklin for help—but at that moment the young man leapt from his horse. "You may not . . . you will not—!" thundered he like some actor in a play and made straight for the highwayman, his scarlet coattails flying.

It was madness, and time seemed to stop whilst all eyes stared in transfixed horror. The highwayman looked thunderstruck to find his bluff called. Must he then murder Emma Morland?

His features writhed; they seemed about to burst. The blond young man was barely six paces from him when he made his choice.

Jerking his pistol from Emma Morland's breast, he fired it at his attacker.

Smoke flew up. A loud *bang!* echoed, at which I flinched. The coach gave a creak, and our horses near bolted. The young man's roan shied and skittered, but the highwayman's gray hardly looked up, as if it were used to such noisy discharges. Mrs. Snow emitted a wail. Dr. Woolridge moaned. As

29

for the young man, he halted, half-turned, and with a wide-eyed expression of bemusement, as if to say: *Can this truly have happened?* he sank upon his knees. Droplets from his drooping left arm began to stain the earth.

Though past fifty, Mr. Franklin was agile, and he was at the highwayman at once. The man still held Miss Morland, but with an expression of stupefaction. Mr. Franklin swung his bamboo stick, struck the man's arm, and the man fell back. In doing so, he released Miss Morland, who tumbled like a doll upon the ground.

Mr. Franklin bent to see to her whilst the highwayman scrambled backward, flung himself upon his saddle, flailed his horse into a gallop and vanished over the rise.

Full of confusion, I gazed about. Mrs. Snow lay upon the ground at my feet. She had fainted, it seemed.

F. J. Mossop's pistol was pointed at me.

I stared whilst his small, damp eyes peered back. I had forgot the pistol. How long had it been at the ready? For what? Mossop glanced about—had anyone else seen the weapon?—but none save I seemed to have, for Dr. Woolridge had hurried straight to the fallen young man and the coachman had rushed to calm his horses. As for the manservant, his long, sallow face was absorbed in thought. Glad his skin had been saved? Mossop's gaze returned, and I was startled to realize that he might be a confederate of the highwayman. Had he meant to use his pistol on us if need be? I peered into those reticent eyes. They blinked, I blinked back, and in an instant he had plunged the pistol into his coat, buttoned the cloth, and was once more his seemingly innocuous self.

Having settled his horses, our coachman came to help Mrs. Snow. At the same time, Mr. Franklin got Miss Morland to her feet. Trembling, she fluttered a hand across her brow. "Would he have shot me . . . *really* shot me?" murmured she.

"He might very well have, miss."

I helped him walk the young woman to one of the trunks which had been flung upon the ground, where Mr. Franklin bade her sit 'til she recovered. "Stay with her, Nick." Going to fetch Woolridge's black bag from the coach, he brought it to him where he knelt by the young man. The heroic, foolish fellow wore a look of comically pathetic chagrin upon his pale face.

"I m-meant to save her! I did!" protested he.

"I cannot approve your methods," said Benjamin Franklin. There was a blackened tear in the fellow's left sleeve. From his bag, the doctor took a pair of scissors and cut the sleeve up from the wrist. A good deal of blood had flowed, but after carefully dabbing it away and probing the bruised flesh, Dr. Woolridge proclaimed him in no danger. "The ball struck your arm just above the elbow. It entered. But it excited, too, fired at close range. You are fortunate—no joint shattered, no bone splintered. What is your name?"

"Edmund Darly."

"I shall stanch and bind up your wound, Mr. Darly—but at the first stop we must wash and dress it properly." He patted the young man's good arm. "Clever of you to choose to be shot where a doctor was present. Nay, do not attempt to rise 'til I have done my work. Perhaps you might see to Mrs. Snow, Mr. Franklin?"

"Gladly." He went to her, but there proved little to see to, for the coachman had roused her, and together they brought her to sit beside her niece on the trunk, where the two women huddled with their arms about each other, Mrs. Snow whimpering, whilst Miss Morland stroked her shoulders as if it were the aunt who had been wrestled by a highwayman.

We surveyed our disaster of spilt and ransacked boxes. At Mr. Franklin's instructions, I emptied the saddlebag, replacing its goods where they belonged. When I was done, the manservant, the coachman, Mr. Franklin, Mr. Mossop, and I contrived to close and relock everything. As we strapped the last of the boxes upon the coach, Dr. Woolridge led Edmund Darly to us. The young fellow came reasonably steadily on his feet though his left arm hung in a sling. He was well-dressed I noted; thick golden hair hung across his brow. "Terribly sorry," murmured he sheepishly to Miss Morland, "I feel a great fool. I should not have been shot."

"Indeed, when the ball flew at you, you ought to have jumped out of its way," replied the girl.

The young fellow blinked. "Do you make fun of me, miss?"

She touched his arm. "Forgive me. You were very brave. You meant only the best. And as you see, the rest of us are unscathed. Therefore—"

"Therefore, all's well," supplied Mr. Franklin.

Emma Morland withdrew her hand from Edmund Darly's arm, but she gazed at him a moment, he at her, she charmingly disheveled, he handsomely chagrined—until Mrs. Snow stepped betwixt 'em. "Come, Emma," said the aunt pointedly, though she fixed a look of speculation upon our unknown savior. Did she note the quality of his dress? Did it imply some wealth? For my part, I envied his broad shoulders and his forthright face.

"Plainly you cannot sit a horse, Mr. Darly," said Mr. Franklin. "You must ride in our coach. We shall tie your mare to the back."

"No need. Noakes can take her."

"Noakes?"

"Albert Noakes, my manservant." Darly gestured at the long-faced fellow who had traveled on top of the coach. "I sent him with my baggage, but he rides quite well."

We all turned. The manservant bobbed his head. "I should not say *well*, sir," replied he.

"Nonsense, I have seen you go like the wind!" retorted Darly amiably. "Mount up. Ride on." He waggled his good arm. "In a quarter of a mile, you shall find the road."

Pulling his forelock, Albert Noakes climbed upon the saddle, flicked the reins, set out. Why had he not run to his master's side when he saw him shot?

"We shall be crowded with Mr. Darly amongst us," said Dr. Woolridge.

"Shall you ride atop, then, Nick?" proposed Mr. Franklin.

"Gladly, sir." I mounted aloft, clinging to a box strap, for there was no seat. The others climbed in below, our coachman remounted his forward perch, and with a creak and a jingle we set out in the direction which Albert Noakes had taken, the tumbled mass of clouds scudding south. As we climbed a little rise, swaying, I looked back to where our drama had played: the declivity, the rocky ground, the copse. There by a lichened boulder lay the abandoned saddlebag, like the flayed skin of a rabbit. Would our highwayman seek to retrieve it?

It was a new and pleasant sensation to ride atop, though I was disappointed that I could not hear the talk within. But we all breathed; I must be grateful for that. Still, I continued to be troubled by F. J. Mossop's pistol. The torn seal on Arthur Brown's letter haunted me, too. Was there more to what had occurred than we knew?

❧ 5 ❧

*IN WHICH bread is broken
and histories heard . . .*

In ten minutes we had found the road and in twenty more, by skirting muddy sloughs, we arrived at the posting inn at Hounslow, where we would take our midday rest whilst the horses were changed. The White Hart was awash in comings and goings, for near ev'ryone who traveled the great Bath Road stopped here. A continual clatter of metal-rimmed wheels sounded in the yard, and the milling of ostlers, postboys, and travelers made an antic commotion. Once more blue skies reigned.

I jumped down. F. J. Mossop popped out the coach door first, scurrying away without meeting my eyes. Mr. Franklin clambered out next, followed by Dr. Woolridge and Edmund Darly. Our young hero looked hearty, given his ordeal, though when Dr. Woolridge asked him if his wound pained him, he winced, proclaiming that so pleasant had been the company— this with a particular nod to Miss Morland, who was just stepping prettily down—that 'til that moment he had forgot to suffer. The young woman reddened at this.

We went in to oak beams, whitewashed plaster and a jangle of drinking cans from the taproom. Dr. Woolridge led Darly off to rebind his wound whilst Mr. Franklin and I and the two women were shown upstairs to a rush-floored chamber. Here the ordinary would be served, at a table garnished with bluebells. Midday light fell through a casement window.

Mrs. Snow was still pale and vaporish, but Miss Morland looked quite gay. Her green eyes danced. "Pray, pardon me a moment?" Drawing a small book from her bag, she went to a narrow desk set with pens and ink and began to scratch in it.

"Your journal, Miss Morland?" inquired Mr. Franklin.

"Yes. I must write down ev'rything whilst it is fresh." Her quill flew.

"He truly might've shot you, you know."

The young woman turned. "Do you mean to frighten me, sir?"

"I mean only to remind you that you do not write a romance, child. You must take care."

She gazed at him. Then she laughed, as musical a sound as ever I heard. "I believe I know what is real and what is not."

Mr. Franklin spread his hands. "Then you are cleverer than I. Forgive me for seeming to chide."

"I forgive you." The girl turned back to her pen.

This was saucy, but Mr. Franklin seemed not to mind. The girl's pretty figure bent over her task. How little we knew of Emma Morland, I reflected. Where were her parents? Why did she travel to Bath with an aunt? Seating myself at the table, I slipped my sketchbook from my pocket and began to draw her. She had a fresh, impudent beauty. Could I capture it? I was sketching the auburn curls at the base of her neck when Dr. Woolridge stepped in with his patient. We made room for 'em at the table, Emma joined us, and within moments a repast of veal chops was borne up by a maid.

Our young hero looked pale, as if the re-dressing of his wound had proved painful, but he wore a brave face. His arm was still in its sling, and seated to his left, Miss Morland offered to cut his meat. "O, thank you!" he said. As she bent near I saw his blue eyes gaze upon her arms, her bosom, the ivory column of her neck.

"I have informed the landlord of the attempt to rob us," reported Dr. Woolridge. "I writ out a description of the highwayman."

"Which the landlord will pass on to the law, I presume," said Mr. Franklin.

"If there is much law in these parts."

"But how are *you*, Miss Morland," inquired Edmund Darly. "How terrible your ordeal must have been."

The girl blinked her eyes. "Ordeal? Pooh, I was never *really* frightened." Our adventure reminded her of incidents she had read in books, she told us. This led her to other books, which treated of a dozen species of romance. As she went on about 'em, her chatter made a charming gloss on unlikelihoods, and her countenance glowed as she told of elopements, secret flights, clandestine marriages. "Do you not think an elopement must put the cap on a marriage, Mr. Darly?"

"Why . . . how so, Miss Morland?"

"I mean that it must be a guarantee of the most felicitous happiness," she sang.

His blue eyes grew large. "I am no philosopher, but perhaps a good beginning does not guarantee a good ending. I beg your pardon for disagreeing."

She laughed. "Too timid, then, to carry off the woman you love, Mr. Darly?"

There was a silence. "Child!" Mrs. Snow chid. 'Mr. Darly was shot in the arm to save you. Surely you cannot call him 'timid'?"

The girl reddened. "O . . . I am very sorry . . . why, you are

36

not timid at all, Mr. Darly . . . I am a very foolish girl." She hung her head in chagrin.

But Darly patted her hand. "Do not trouble yourself." He bent nearer, as if he would devour her. "Never trouble yourself over anything on my behalf, Miss Morland."

We averted our gazes whilst Mr. Franklin watched a fly buzz by as if it were the most fascinating object in the world. An apple tart was delivered, which we ate in silence, and very shortly we were called to continue our journey. As I scrambled atop our coach, I glimpsed F. J. Mossop under the jutting roof of the inn. He appeared to talk to someone, but I could not ascertain whom, for deep shadows prevented my seeing clearly. In any case he soon trotted up, our conveyance dipped as he got in, and its door slammed.

I gripped the box straps. We set out.

I was as eager for new experience as Emma Morland, but within an hour I had experienced enough of coach roofs to make me despise 'em forever. Wedged amongst rattling trunks, I must cling fiercely to avoid being bounced into the road. My fingers ached, dust flew in my eyes, the sun beat mercilessly. The birds in the sky seemed only harbingers of more punishment to come and I was deprived of all human commerce, for the coachman never looked back once.

Yet all tortures end, and by six we had reached our mid-journey stop some sixty miles from London: The Cock's Crow. This was a collection of vine-covered lodgings and stables amongst horse-chestnuts. The trees spread a welcoming shade as I slid gingerly from the coach roof and began to revive, though for a quarter of an hour the ground persisted in lurching beneath my feet. This was a much smaller inn than our previous stop, only one of many hereabouts which travelers might choose. I was glad for its peace. No noisy commotion filled its broad, earthen yard, where a dun-colored mongrel nipped at fleas by the stoop. Blue smoke curled from the kitchen chimney as we were shown into a large, low-ceilinged parlor whilst our rooms were made ready and our necessaries carried up. F. J. Mossop looked as if he should like to flee once more, but there was no eave under which to dart, no hole for his small self, so with a wary look he followed along.

Soon enough we were allowed up. A landing ran the length of the inn, overlooking the entryway. Mrs. Snow and Miss Morland were lodged in a chamber near the head of the stairs, Dr. Woolridge and Mr. Franklin were midway along, and Edmund Darly had a chamber of his own, as did Mr. Mossop, at the farthest end. Mossop popped into his room like a mouse into its burrow.

I would sleep under the eaves with Albert Noakes.

Mr. Franklin gave me a glance as we stopped by his door. *We must speak soon*, it said, and I nodded; I longed to tell him of F. J. Mossop's pistol.

There were more stairs at the end of the landing, steep, and I dutifully mounted to the third floor. This was the attic: bare wood planks, blackened beams, a smell of sun-warmed thatch and vermin. Six narrow pallet beds were tucked against its musty walls. As I chose one under the steeply angled roof, I heard a sound.

I turned. Albert Noakes rose into the chamber.

I had glimpsed the liveried man at the stables with Darly's mare. Now his sullen look fell upon me. "Here, now, that's my bed!"

"If you please," said I, backing away, perfectly willing to let him have whatever he liked.

He bowed, in a mocking fashion. "No, young sir, I forget

myself. I am only a servant. You rid *in* the coach. You must choose wot bed you please."

Dim light came through the one small window at the end of the room. "I do not mind where I sleep," said I.

He barked so loud that I jumped: "Choose!"

"I shall take this, then." I pointed to a bed far from the one in dispute.

"So be it." Noakes marched upon me. "Wot's yer name?"

"Nicolas Handy."

His features twisted. "A young gen'leman, eh?"

"I accompany Mr. Franklin."

"Which one's he?"

I described him.

"That 'un." A laugh. "But the girl—sweet as honey, eh? Should you like to roger her?"

I drew myself up. "I do not think you should talk of her so!"

He thrust his long, saddle-jawed face into mine. "A gen'leman's boy does not think such thoughts, eh? But just how much of a gen'leman is *your* gen'leman—tell me that? Does *he* never think such thoughts?" He flung a small brown leather bag upon the bed. "To the devil with gen'lemen—but God praise their purses; that's reason enough to tolerate 'em. Do not touch my bed. I have biz-ness at the stables." He went down.

I stood in dismay. Must I share the night with this fellow?

Needing company, I descended to discover Mr. Franklin by the front door of the inn. He made a little silencing motion, and I gazed out to where he looked. The stables lay to our left, amidst the horse-chestnuts. Evening light sifted through their flickering leaves; dust-motes danced. Edmund Darly stood beneath the great trees with his servant. He seemed to be expostulating with him, in some pique it seemed, though the distance muffled his words. He poked at Noakes's chest, at which the servant flung up an arm. I caught my breath. Did he mean to strike his master? It would have been an astonishing act— but at that instant the servant caught sight of us, scowled, and wheeled away into the stables.

Darly strolled toward us. "Damned fellow," said he in his easy way, as if what had occurred meant nothing. "Noakes has his fits of rebellion, and he's not the prettiest fellow in Christendom, but he's served me well for half a dozen years, so I put up with him. He's good-hearted at bottom, and it is a man's heart that counts; do you not think, Mr. Franklin?"

"A right mind signifies too."

For my part I found it hard to trust either Albert Noakes's heart or mind. Would his master speak so forgivingly if he had heard what I heard his man say in the attic? But it was hard to find fault with Edmund Darly. Despite his injured arm, he stood at ease in fawn and scarlet, a breeze lifting the locks of golden hair upon his dewy brow, whilst his eyes gazed frankly. Were they too frank, of too little depth, too shallow to spy the wickedness in the world?

One must be wary, Mr. Franklin had taught.

Darly glanced once more at the stables. A frown troubled his brow. Yet the look vanished in an instant, replaced by cheerful nonchalance, as if the world, too, must be good-hearted, despite highwaymen. He patted Mr. Franklin's arm, out of sheer good will it seemed.

A curtseying maidservant called us to supper, and we went in.

A half-dozen other travelers lodged at The Cock's Crow. They were seated at three or four small round tables in the dining parlor, whilst our band of seven had a long trestle table to itself, near the fire. I sat betwixt Mr. Franklin and Mr. Mossop,

40

the others opposite us. I had learned that during the journey from Hounslow Edmund Darly had said little—his wound had troubled him, and solicitous discretion had silenced inquiry, so no one had learnt his particulars, though ev'ryone must have wished to—but as he now seemed well enough to speak, Dr. Woolridge called him to account. "Tell us of yourself, then, Mr. Darly, if you please."

Darly sent his blue gaze round. "Why, my father is the third Earl of Hendon, did I not say?"

Silence. Then a stir. Woolridge cleared his throat. "You are a lord, then?"

"I confess it."

"Are you the eldest son?" put in Mrs. Snow bluntly.

"The only son. But I have a sister, Caroline, whom I dearly love."

"Then, you are—or will be—the fourth Earl?"

"I fear I shall."

"O, my!" Mrs. Snow was clearly taken aback—I saw her gaze flash to her niece—but Mr. Franklin was not.

"A peer o' the realm," said he with a smile. He lifted his glass. "How d'ye do, my lord. We are honored. But are the earls of Hendon in the habit of charging at highwaymen unarmed?"

The young lord colored. "No. My family *does* boast a long history of bravery—but my father distinguishes betwixt bravery and rashness, and he has often rebuked me for the latter." A rueful shrug. "I do not entirely please him, I fear."

"What? Should he prefer a cowardly son?" demanded Mr. Franklin.

"No-o. But I am not what the heir to a title should be. I am frivolous; I am thoughtless. He finds many dissatisfactions."

"You seem an excellent young man."

"I do not know my place, my father says; I do not act like a

41

lord. I fear it is true. I was raised in the country, you see. My mother died when I was young, and father was often in London, so there was no one to guide me in what I ought to be— what he should like me to be, that is. I slept in a grand house, true, but I spent my days amongst servants and tenant farmers. The blacksmith taught me to shoe a horse, the plowman to plow a furrow. Their sons were my playmates, you see—we fished together, we pretended to be soldiers. I learnt to treat these lads as my equals; it is a habit I find it hard to shed."

"An egalitarian lord!" proclaimed Mr. Franklin. "Would that there were more of you." For my part, I began to see why Darly might endure insolence from a servant. A thought struck me. Was Noakes entirely Darly's man? Might he report back to the father?

"If your so-called 'failings' make you a more genial companion for our humble company," pursued Mr. Franklin, "I am sure we never mind."

"Hear, hear," seconded Woolridge.

Darly flushed. "Thank you, sirs. And, truly, I heartily wish your good will and hope that none of what I have said shall diminish it."

Miss Morland had been observing him out of her green eyes. "I shall not let it affect *me*. I shall treat you like a tradesman; and if you forget yourself and attempt to command me, I shall remind you that it goes against your nature."

Her aunt glowered at her, but Darly was gallant. "I should prefer *you* to command *me*," said he to the girl.

Emma only smiled, as if this was her due. "You may count upon it, I will."

"But tell us, my lord," said Mr. Franklin, "what takes you to Bath?"

"To pay my respects to old friends of my father's, Mr. and Mrs. Valentine. Too, all the best society gathers in Bath, father says. He wishes me to mingle in it, to learn to be a peer."

"He sends you to school, then."

"I have many lessons to learn."

"Bath teaches bad lessons as well as good ones," warned Dr. Woolridge.

"I pray I shall know the difference."

A course of pigeon pie arrived, and we set to it. "But, do not call me 'my lord' or 'your grace' " urged Darly as we ate. "I could not bear it. I prefer to be another gentleman amongst gentlefolk. And I should like to know more of each of you. Miss Morland, your aunt travels with you to Bath. Do your parents, then, await you there?"

"They are deceased."

"O, I am truly sorry to hear it!"

"It happened many years ago," put in Mrs. Snow. "My sister died when Emma was four and Emma's father did not live long afterward." Her tone seemed to express some disapproval of her sister's husband. "Mr. Snow and I have no children, so we have brought up poor Emma as if she were our own."

"Poor Emma, indeed!" sniffed Miss Morland. "An orphan, alone in the world. You may all pity me now." Her lower lip pouted.

"Emma, you have never been alone!" protested her aunt. "You have me. And you have Mr. Snow; he is devoted to you. Well . . . and then there is your other uncle, of course—"

"Uncle Titus?" Emma emitted a bitter laugh. "Indeed, there is Uncle Titus, though there might as well not be."

"Titus Morland?" came F. J. Mossop's soft voice at my side. Emma turned to him. "My uncle is named Titus Morland."

"Wealthy Titus Morland?"

"Rich as Croesus, I hear—though little good it does me. You know him, sir?"

"No. But I know *of* him. Who from Gloucestershire does

43

not?" Mossop licked his small, pursed mouth. "If I had one tenth of ev'ry groat old Titus Morland possesses, I could buy me a kingdom. I hear that he is ill."

"Ill?" Mr. Franklin said.

But Mrs. Snow interrupted. "We need not fret ourselves over *that* man," proclaimed she. "He is a very devil, and I do not care to upset my niece. Is this not a rather poor pigeon pie?" She chewed vigorously. "I am sure our cook in Berwick Street makes a much better one."

We ate quietly for a time, in earshot of the nearest table, at which a fat gentleman was complaining fulsomely to a thin one of "the gnomes and salamanders" who frequented Bath. "I shall lodge by the Cross Bath—anything to avoid the Pump Room!" said he.

"Indeed, I shall not gad about when *I* am there," Mrs. Snow echoed his theme.

Her niece's fork stopped in midair. "But how am I to go about if you do not? O, Aunt, it is too unfair!"

"Emma, you must acquiesce. My nerves are bad, and surely you cannot expect—"

"May I help?" offered Edmund Darly. "If your aunt will allow. My father's friends, the Valentines, go about a great deal—Mrs. Valentine does, at any rate. She is a thoroughly respectable woman. And she knows Bath well. I am certain she would be happy to show such a charming girl the delights of the town."

Emma brightened. "That is very kind, Mr. Darly. Is it not kind, Aunt? The very thing to please us both?"

We waited whilst Mrs. Snow relished a great bite of the "poor" pigeon pie. We did not wait long, however. "I shall speak to Mr. Snow on the subject, thank you, Mr. Darly." The aunt formed a smile. "I believe we may look forward to meeting Mrs. Valentine."

Her niece stroked her arm. "Dear aunt!"

Mr. Franklin had been peering at F. J. Mossop. "You come from Gloucestershire then?" asked he as a sweet pudding was served round.

Mossop started. "Did I imply so? I did not mean to."

"From where then, may we know?"

"Why . . . from Cornwall. Cornwall, yes."

"Cornwall, it is," replied Mr. Franklin, though he did not ask how F. J. Mossop of Cornwall knew of Titus Morland, who lived far away in Gloucestershire. Instead he drummed his fingers. "Our encounter this afternoon," mused he, looking round. "Our highwayman was not a very good highwayman, was he?"

"What can you mean?" protested Mrs. Snow. "There cannot be a school for such creatures."

"I mean only that they customarily travel in twos or threes. Our man ventured against us alone."

"Surely there are many sorts of highwaymen," proposed Dr. Woolridge.

Mr. Franklin smiled, as if what he had said made no matter. "You are right." He turned the talk to the sea life he had observed on his voyage to England: the dolphins, the sharks, the hawk-billed turtles. He evoked the ship, the waves, a tossing storm—he could paint a picture well—and our company seemed glad to escape reminders of robbery. Did only I wonder what he had meant about the highwayman?

An unsettling note sounded when we rose to go up half an hour later. As the others walked ahead, F. J. Mossop stood briefly in my way. I halted, experiencing a chill as his damp little eyes met mine. As if by accident, his coat fell open. No pistol to be seen. *See, I am unarmed?* he seemed to say.

His coat shut like a door, and he crept off.

❧ 6 ❧

*IN WHICH blows are struck and
a gentleman vanishes . . .*

W hat errors Mr. Franklin and I made. How little we saw of what was happening around us. But that is hindsight. We could not know, and Mr. Franklin was not wholly deceived. As the others went up, he bobbed his head to say he wished me to remain below. Eager to talk over the events of the day, I followed him into the taproom. This was a broad, low-ceilinged chamber, deserted save for a potboy just now lighting the lamps. Night lurked beyond the bottle-glass panes of the windows.

We sat at a small, round table in a corner. Mr. Franklin called for a glass of port for himself, a syllabub for me.

He leant forward. "We begin well, do we not, Nick?" asked he.

"Do we, sir?"

"You have misgivings?"

The gentleman always liked me to speak my mind. "Beg pardon, but our highwayman might have shot Miss Morland— or any of us. Is that 'beginning well'?"

He pursed his lips. "In truth he did shoot someone—though

fortunately not fatally. I meant it is *interesting*, is it not, our little band of travelers?"

I agreed with this. Yet despite his words, Mr. Franklin's brown eyes behind their small, round spectacles appeared weary. Had our journey overtired him?

I told him in as lively a way I could about Mossop's pistol. "After supper he seemed to wish me to know he no longer carried it."

"You observe well, Nick. A pistol? What, then, do you make of F. J. Mossop?"

"Could he have been in league with the highwayman?" Their confederates sometimes ride in coaches, I have heard. They signal their fellows. They help in the robberies if they are wanted."

He pulled his lip. "Did Mossop signal, that you saw?"

"No."

"Did he play any part in diverting us toward the lonely spot where the highwayman waited?"

"No."

My discouragement must have shown on my face, for Mr. Franklin patted my arm. "Your idea may prove right nonetheless. Without doubt the man is a puzzle; I should like to get to the bottom of him. One thing is certain: he is no Cornishman, for he has not their manner of speech. But what is he, then, damn the fellow?" He changed subject. "Miss Morland is a sprightly girl, is she not?"

"Yes, sir."

"Pretty?"

"Why . . . tolerably so."

He laughed. "Come, Nick, name me a prettier! She has a brain, too—but does she have judgment? She is ardent and willful, not bad qualities in themselves; but they may provoke

an inexperienced nature to danger—to herself and to others."
He yawned. "Dear me, I am almost too weary to think. Yet I
cannot forget how Arthur Brown asked me to accompany Miss
Morland. As if he foresaw danger? I look forward to putting
questions to him in Bath."

Our drinks came. Mr. Franklin sipped his betwixt more
yawns, his head near dropping upon his chest. It was unlike
him to flag in the face of mystery, but it had been a long day.
Gazing round at the taproom's smoke-smudged plaster, I
thought once more on the broken wax seal; did it signify?

I found no answer in the bottom of my glass.

At nine-thirty Mr. Franklin roused himself, and we carried a
candle up. All the doors along the second-floor landing were
shut; ev'ryone retired, it seemed. The landlord snuffed lights
below.

Mr. Franklin's feet dragged. "How I want rest! Sleep well,
Nick." As he opened his door, I glimpsed Dr. Woolridge
propped in bed with a book. He sent a flickering smile from
under his nightcap, and I wished both men good-night and
moved on. Fretted by a growing conviction that the day por-
tended more than I knew, I mounted to the attic. Snores
greeted me. Cautiously I lifted my candle. Not six feet away
Albert Noakes, arms dangling, mouth slack, lay fast asleep.
Creeping past him—I had no wish to rouse the mean-spirited
fellow—I set the light on the table by my bed, slipped out of
my clothes, pulled on the nightshirt Mrs. Stevenson had laun-
dered only yesterday. Was I already sixty miles from the good
woman's ministrations? Dear Mrs. Stevenson! Stretching out
on the prickly horsehair pallet, I read *Poor Richard* for a time,
pocket-sized, my frequent companion:

Who is wise? He that learns from everyone.
Who is powerful? He that governs his passions.
Who is rich? He that is content.
Who is that? Nobody.

I smiled. Of all men Benjamin Franklin, who had writ these lines, came closest to learning from everyone; and was closest to wisdom. Might I, Nick Handy, be wise some day too?

Yet I could not read long. Our journey had taken its toll, my lids fluttered, and though the many vivid experiences of the day—Mossop's pistol, the highwayman, Emma Morland's dancing eyes—clamored to be thought on, I was asleep within moments of snuffing my candle.

I awoke with a start. What hour was it? Sitting up, I scratched. Bedbugs, the bane of travelers, had feasted well, for I was plagued in a dozen places, but it was not bedbugs that had roused me. Something else. What? Slipping from bed, I crept to the window at the end of the room. It was past midnight by the angle of the moon, an icy orb, brilliantly full, bathing the yard and stables and fields in pale parchment-colored light. Bats swooped for insects under the huge chestnut branches, and somewhere a small animal screamed as it gave up its life. The air felt heavy and still, and Mr. Franklin's lassitude as we sat over our drinks returned to trouble me. Had I ever seen him so drowsy?

I resolved to go down. I did not know what I intended, but I could not stay where I was.

Pulling my breeches over the tail of my nightshirt and tugging on my boots, I crept past Noakes's bed—yet, to my surprise, his coverlet was thrown back; the man was not there. I shivered in the pale light that sifted through the window. Was he elsewhere in the room, observing me out of those mean yellowish eyes? But a panicked glance told me he was truly gone. Where? Why?

Hoping not to encounter him, I started down.

The attic descent was more a ladder than stairs, but I did not stumble, for my eyes had accustomed to the dark. Arriving at the landing, I paused but could hear nothing save the creak of old wood. F. J. Mossop's chamber was at my back, Mr. Franklin and Dr. Woolridge's three doors ahead. Creeping with no fixed plan, I glanced over the railing. Below, the entryway lay deserted in long black shadows, though a glow that seemed more than moonlight seeped from under the taproom door. A lamp? Someone awake?

I arrived at Mr. Franklin's door. It was open a crack—no surprise, for the gentleman liked fresh air. Thinking I heard a stirring within, my spirits rose. Was the gentleman awake after his bout of torpor? Did he pace? Might he be happy to whisper his ruminations into a willing boy's ears?

I pressed gently on the door.

It was well-oiled, making no sound as it opened farther than I had intended, so that in an instant the entire room was revealed. I could see quite clearly, for moonlight flooded through the open casement in the opposite wall. Dr. Woolridge's bed sat to the left, Mr. Franklin's to the right. I frowned, for the first thing I observed was that like Albert Noakes—indeed, like myself—the doctor was not abed; but this was jarred from my mind by a more dire sight: two figures lurking in the center of the room.

Their backs were to me. They crouched menacingly.

Plainly they had not heard me, and my blood turned cold as they took three stealthy steps to the side of Mr. Franklin's bed.

They carried bludgeons.

50

Lifting 'em, they began to pummel his sleeping form.

At the first sickening thud, a great anguish overwhelmed me. Mr. Franklin! The men were bigger than I—surely I ought to run for help—but I did not.

With a cry of *"Stop!"* I leapt upon the back of the nearest intruder.

Wrapping my arms about him, I dug my fingers into his face. I tugged, I kicked. With a curse he shook me off, though my desperation lent me a furious tenacity, and I was at him again in an instant, striking out. I hit a lucky blow to his eye, for he yelped, clutching his face, stumbling back, but the other man had wheeled, club raised. He was no more than a black form against the window, but the moonlight fell upon Mr. Franklin's bed, and I felt a surge of joy.

Their blows had dislodged the covers. Only bunched pillows and a knot of clothes lay beneath. Mr. Franklin was not there.

I had no need, then, to be a hero. With no time to think what those pillows meant, I made to flee—but a chair tripped my ankles, and I toppled. Anger at being thwarted surged through me as the rough wood of the floor struck my cheek. There came the scrape of boot by my face, a rude snarl of triumph: "Got you!" Flattening, I heard a terrifying whoosh as the second man's bludgeon swung so near my skull that it ruffled my hair. A splintering crash told me the chair was its victim.

I scrambled up, but strong fingers clutched at my nightshirt. I twisted, fought, struck blindly. Cloth ripped, and I tore free, dashing into the corridor. "Help, help!"

As I stumbled toward the stairs, the taproom door flew open below, a glow of candlelight spilt out, and Dr. Woolridge and Edmund Darly hurried into view, Darly's wounded arm hanging free of its sling. Both stared up. "What? Who?" Darly called.

I came pell-mell along the upper rail. "Murderers! Bludgeoners!"

In an instant Darly was thundering up the stairs with all the blind determination with which he had charged our highwayman. "Good God, man, your wound!" came Dr. Woolridge's cry after him, but the young lord never faltered. As I reached the head of the stairs he charged past me, and I stopped and turned.

No one pursued me.

Darly halted in the middle of the landing, plainly dismayed that there was no villain against whom to test his mettle. "There!" cried I, pointing at Mr. Franklin's open door, and he dashed through. I heard a curse and a commotion. There followed a panting silence before he rushed into view once more, clutching his wounded arm as if only now did he feel the pain where dark blots of dried blood stained its sleeve.

"They have gone out the window," cried he. "What has happened?"

"They struck at Mr. Franklin's bed," gasped I. "They meant to murder him, I believe."

Darly stared. "But . . . Mr. Franklin is not there."

I lifted my hands. "Nonetheless—"

Darly drew himself up. "I will stop 'em in the yard." With hardly a breath, he tore past me once more, clattering like a stallion down the stairs.

Emma Morland's door flew open just as he bounded out the front of the inn. She stepped onto the landing, her aunt behind her, chalk-white in the light of the candle she held tremblingly. Her niece clutched the collar of a pale blue dressing gown about her throat. She gripped my arm. "What has happened? Tell us, boy."

I did, as best I could.

"We are cursed—that is what it is!" moaned Mrs. Snow.

"That is foolishness, Aunt."

Just then other travelers began to poke out their heads: the fat man, the thin man, an old woman with a face like a shriveled apple. "What? What?" she keened into the night. "Some trouble, ma'am. But it is over," I assuaged her. "You need not fear."

The fat man drew himself up as if to rebuke all such outrages, but he thought better of it. The trio exchanged a silent, fearful colloquy, then darted back into their rooms and clicked their latches.

So much for danger to *them* on the road to Bath.

Emma Morland's hair hung loose about her face; for an instant her green eyes glowed, as if to say what a fine bit of news this would make for her journal—but the import of my story struck home and she pressed my arm even tighter. "*Two* men, you say? And Mr. Darly has gone after 'em alone?" Her eyes grew large as saucers. "Why, he may be harmed!"

He was not, however. Dr. Woolridge had run out after him, but the pair now returned, and the two women and I descended to receive their report. "Good morning Mrs. Snow, Miss Morland," said the doctor gravely. "You have heard the story? Alas, our two villains climbed down the vines at the back of the inn, as they arrived, it seems. They are nowhere to be found."

"I laid hold of one at the window, I did!" burst out Darly. "But this useless arm, curse the thing—" He stamped his boot in frustration.

Woolridge frowned at the arm, which Darly held close to his chest with his good hand. "I hope you have not done it more damage."

"It is nothing."

"I am heartily glad you were downstairs, sirs!" exclaimed I.

"Fortunate we were," replied Woolridge. "Mr. Darly woke

me to say his wound plagued him, so we came below to see to it. I had just removed the sling and was about to re-dress it when we heard your cries."

"Was Mr. Franklin abed when you left your chamber?"

"Why . . . I believe so. Why do you ask?"

I explained what I had seen: the blows to the pillows.

The doctor's brow furrowed. "Pillows? But—?" He looked thoroughly bewildered.

Emma Morland asked me forthrightly, "Did you know the two men?"

"No, miss," said I. "That is, their backs were to the moonlight. I could not see their faces."

"Why should they seek to harm a gentleman like Mr. Franklin?"

"I *knew* that we should never travel to Bath," put in Mrs. Snow. "Did I not say so many times?"

Her niece ignored her. "I ask again: why Mr. Franklin?"

"Perhaps they did not seek him in particular," Woolridge replied uncertainly. He clapped a hand to his mouth. "Dear me, I hope that it was not *I* who put him in harm."

"How could you?" asked Darly.

"By leaving our chamber door unlocked when I came down to see to your arm. I thought nothing on it at the time."

"They were burglars, then?" said Darly. "They crept about, tried sev'ral doors, and entered the first they found open?"

Mrs. Snow uttered a shriek. "They may even have tried *ours?*"

Her niece stood firm. "You still have not answered my question. If they came only to rob, why not simply do so? Why strike a sleeping man?"

"To silence his outcries, foolish girl!" snapped her aunt.

"Before they began?" Emma's green eyes still doubted. "The boy here says the pillows were placed to make it appear a man slept there. If what you say is true, how do you explain that?"

An unenlightening silence followed whilst a case clock ticked.

"It is a mystery indeed," murmured Woolridge. "But there is a greater: where is Mr. Franklin now? That is what I wish to know."

"Did he go to sleep at once, after he came to your chamber, sir?" asked I.

"Fast asleep. He appeared exhausted."

Mr. Franklin's drowsiness grew more ominous than ever, and I frowned up to where his chamber door stood open. Yet the door at the end of the corridor remained closed: F. J. Mossop's. Why had ev'ryone been roused by my cries save he?

At this moment the landlord straggled in, tucking his nightshirt into a pair of hastily-thrown-on breeches. He peered anxiously into our faces. "Is there some trouble? Did I hear cries?"

Dr. Woolridge told what had occurred.

The landlord clutched his chest. "In *my* inn? But . . . but—!"

"Please, let us find Mr. Franklin!" pled I.

"Nicolas is right," Dr. Woolridge concurred. Calming the landlord, we held counsel. It was decided that the ladies must return to their chamber—this was for safety, in case the attackers had not truly run off—whilst the men would divide into two parties: Edmund Darly and I in one, Dr. Woolridge and the landlord in the other.

Emma lifted her chin. "I can search as well as any man."

Her aunt groaned. "Will you never listen to reason? If those two men return, you cannot fight 'em."

Her niece sniffed. "Very well. But sometimes I wish that I were a man!" This appalled Mrs. Snow even more, but Emma allowed herself to be led upstairs, whilst Dr. Woolridge and the landlord set off to search the inside of the inn: its travelers' chambers, kitchen, corridors, closets, stillroom—all.

The yard and stables being left to Darly and me, we slipped out into the night.

We paused a moment in the yard. The air was scented with mist and earth, and the moon hung large and bright over the great Bath Road. A ringing stillness reigned. We looked ev'rywhere about the grounds, even to the fence that rimmed the area, our feet whispering on packed earth or pressing through grass. The landlord having provided a bull's-eye lamp, we shone it in cribs, outbuildings, stables, but came upon only drowsing animals. An ostler roused from his pallet said he had seen or heard nothing, as did the ragged boy who slept in a mound of straw by the horses. Peering from his chamber next the stables, our coachman proved no more help, grumbling that whatever had happened we must be on the road by nine next morn. "We can wait for no one, sirs."

"Does your master often go off like this?" asked Edmund Darly as we returned toward the inn.

"No, sir," said I in deep discouragement.

"He is from America, eh? He said so in the coach. A fine fellow! He hopes to persuade the Pennsylvania proprietors to pay taxes, I hear. I wish him well."

"He succeeds at much."

"He has other business, then? What?"

Bringing blackmailers and murderers to justice, thought I. Recovering stolen gems.

And saving one small boy, Nick Handy, whose life had near been lost.

"He is a kind of philosopher," said I, feeling near tears. "He studies Nature. He is famous for his electrical discoveries."

Darly's big, honest hand drew me to a halt. "I do not know what 'electrical' signifies, but I like your Mr. Franklin. We shall find him." I looked up at the fellow. His locks of hair shone in the moonlight, his teeth gleamed in a smile meant to assure me and I tried to smile back. Though he was very different from Mr. Franklin, I liked Edmund Darly very much. "Do not fret," said he, giving a sturdy squeeze to my shoulder as we resumed our way to the inn. "I tell you, we shall discover your master."

But we did not discover him, nor had the others when we met after three-quarters of an hour in the entryway; they had seen nor hide nor hair of him. We shuffled our feet. What to do? Return to bed, it was decided; hope for the best. I was cast down by this, but what else was there? Our landlord retired to his chambers, whilst Dr. Woolridge beckoned Darly into the taproom to finish seeing to his arm. "It aches dreadfully," Darly confessed with a grimace.

Going upstairs, I rapped on the ladies' door, calling my name, and they opened. I told our bad news, and Mrs. Snow moaned, more in fear for herself than for Benjamin Franklin, I thought—but Emma Morland sent me a look of genuine sympathy from her long-lashed eyes, and I saw that she, who had lost both parents, understood. "Thank you, miss," said I.

And then their door was closed, and I was alone.

My candle flickered as I moved along the landing. I peered into Mr. Franklin's chamber, hoping against hope that he might be there after all, but I saw only the disheveled bed. Moonlight fell upon its tangle. How strange. Had its two pillows been deliberately configured to simulate a man? Had Mr. Franklin known he might be in danger? More bewildered than ever, I returned to the landing. Was not F. J. Mossop's door open a crack? But drawing nearer I found it shut, and I heard the click of its latch. So the odd little man was awake after all. Why had he not so much as peeped out?

Dread wracked me as I climbed the attic stairs. Let Mr. Franklin be well!

As I came up into the attic, Albert Noakes leapt at me, snatching my arm so hard that hot wax from my candle spilt upon my hand. He pushed his long face into mine. "Here, why're you acreepin' about?"

I was so startled I could hardly find words. "I—I am not creeping," stammered I into his stale breath. I told of the bludgeoners, our search. I blinked, remembering: "Why were you not here when I went down?"

His grip tightened. "Wot d'you mean? I have always been here."

"No. You were not. Your bed was empty."

He laughed. "I was pissing. Do you not piss? I was at the chamber pot." He jerked his head to the white porcelain pot against a wall. His yellowish eyes warned. "The chamber pot, I tell ye."

"The ch-chamber pot. Y-yes. I mistook because of the dark."

He nodded meaningly. "Much may be mistook in the dark. Your master 'scaped beating, did he? Pillows, ha!—what a cleverboots." He pushed me away. "Get to bed."

Snuffing my light, I curled up on the prickly pallet. But I could not sleep, and when I heard Noakes's ragged snores begin, I slipped to the window to peer out. The moon had dipped lower, but its light was still bright. Doves cooed. A wolf howled far away. There was no Mr. Franklin as I had hoped— but there was something. Mounting to the edge of the casement rose heavy vines, a mat of 'em. They covered the side of the inn. Albert Noakes—or F. J. Mossop, come to think— might thus have made their way with easy stealth.

❧ 7 ❧

IN WHICH I glimpse an old enemy,
and bells ring out over Bath . . .

I woke to sunlight and stirrings from the yard below. Having promised myself to renew the search for Mr. Franklin at first light, I cursed, for dawn was plainly past. But I had lain awake hours after creeping to bed, sleeping only fitfully; exhaustion had thwarted my plan.

Rising, I found Noakes gone. Good riddance. Hurrying to the window, I peered out. Let Mr. Franklin be there! I saw nothing of him however, only a lone horseman in the yard. The fellow's manner arrested me, and I kept watch. Tall, swathed to the ankles in a long, dark cloak, he sat on a powerful roan mare which I had not seen in the stables last night. Just arrived, then? He wore a wide-brimmed hat that hid his face, and he sat very still, regarding the inn in a speculative and (I thought) disgruntled fashion. His gloved hand flicked impatiently; then, decision reached, he wheeled his mount toward the gate—but in that instant, I caught a glimpse of his features. They were enough to make me blanch.

Quimp?

I gripped the sill as the stranger galloped off, cloak flying. I must be mistook. Shortly after Mr. Franklin's arrival in London, Quimp had accosted me in one of his many disguises to say I must warn Mr. Franklin to cease meddling in his business; thus I was one of the few who had seen the villain close up and lived to tell. But how could a glimpse months later, at twenty yards, be sure of that thin nose and the hooded eyes that brooked no crossing? Besides, London was Quimp's realm. Surely his reach did not extend here. Imagination works upon you, I told myself as a more urgent sight banished the man from my thoughts: an ostler leading our team of horses to the traces. Our coach was being readied.

I backed from the window. What was I to do if Mr. Franklin did not reappear? The coach would not wait upon him; it would set out for Bath. Should I go with it? Stay? Seek to return to London? Pulling on my clothes, tugging my boots, I struggled to form some plan.

Dr. Woolridge was kind and reasonable. I would seek advice from him.

I hurried downstairs to do so—but my dilemma was swept away by joyful news. Edmund Darly stepped from the dining room as I reached the entryway. "Can you guess?" Smiling broadly, he swept a lock of golden hair from his forehead. "Mr. Franklin is returned. He sits even now to breakfast."

My heart seemed to burst, and if I gave the young lord thanks I do not recall, for in an instant I had dashed past him into the dining room. I halted by its door. There was the same plain, long, low-ceilinged chamber, rush-floored, in which we had supped yesterday, and there sat Benjamin Franklin, large as life, at the head of a table at which Dr. Woolridge, Mrs. Snow and Emma Morland sat, too.

The familiar round, bespectacled face looked up. The little jots of eyebrows lifted, and the warm voice spoke: "Nicolas, I am glad to see you. But you have slept late. Tut, do I not tell you that early rising is best?" He stood as I came to his side, to gaze into his plain, good features, longing to pour out how much I had feared for him—but his brown eyes behind the twin lenses of his small, squarish spectacles sent a warning: *Make no to-do.* I glanced round the table. Expectant faces were lifted to us, Edmund Darly's, too, for he had followed me into the room and stood rocking on his heels just behind Miss Morland, beaming at our reunion.

I turned back to Mr. Franklin.

He shook his head, as if to dismiss all mystery. "I have been told there was some fuss last night. A search too? Foul play in my chamber? Two men, would-be thieves, curse 'em! But they were roundly foiled by you, I hear. Brave lad! But what is this mark upon your cheek?" He felt of it.

I had hardly known it was there. "I bruised myself when I fell," said I numbly.

"I am glad your injury is small." Sitting, he motioned me to the place beside him. "As for myself, I am unmarked. I was just telling our company that I was in the inn all the while."

"But where, sir?"

"In this very chamber. Your expression says you doubt, but it is true. Feeling a dizziness in the night—most strange—I came down to seek the air of the yard. But I could not get so far. Turning into the nearest door—this one—I sat down upon that low bench near the fire, meaning to stay only a little, but I fell asleep. I lay just below the edge of the gate-legged table." He pointed to it. "Dr. Woolridge tells me that he and the landlord passed through, seeking me, but the table must have hid me from view."

"But we searched thoroughly!" protested the doctor.

"Did you look behind the table?"

"I thought that we did, but—"

"—for I was surely there, sir, fast asleep! I woke in the same place not an hour ago." Mr. Franklin shook his head. "Dear me, I cannot recall feeling so drowsy in my life."

"I am happy the explanation is so simple," said I.

"Simple?" Emma Morland's voice was sharp, her green eyes fixed upon the gentleman. "If 'twas all so simple, sir, why did you arrange your pillows into the semblance of yourself before you came down?"

Mr. Franklin blinked. "Pillows?"

"Made to look like a man."

"Why . . . who says this?"

"Your boy."

He turned to me. "Nicolas?"

I flushed. "I thought—"

"That I had planned it?" A dismissing chortle. "But you know how I toss when I sleep, pulling my pillows here and there."

I knew no such thing. Whenever I found him asleep in Craven Street, he lay as straight as a board, his pillow square under his head. "I must have forgot me," said I.

He laughed some more. "What a joke upon our robbers, to be fooled by dim light into thinking those pillows were me."

The moonlight had been far from dim.

"And, doctor, what a good thing you were not abed," Mr. Franklin went on. "Why, they might have set upon you."

The doctor blanched. "Dear me, yes!"

"I tried to catch 'em," Edmund Darly put in impetuously, "and near did, curse the luck. I longed to get my hands on 'em, Mr. Franklin."

"Would you had, to keep 'em from troubling other wayfarers. But our breakfast is here, I see." A maid had carried in a tray. "Why, I am as hungry as a bear!"

Darly sat, and we fed on platters of country bread, meat, and cheese, the travelers who had poked their noses from their rooms last night staring at us from nearby tables, as if the trouble were all our fault. "At this rate, our throats may be cut before day's end!" Mrs. Snow wailed, but no one paid heed. Edmund Darly gave his attention to Miss Morland, who invited it by doing nothing more than dropping her dark lashes against the pink bloom of her cheeks. Dr. Woolridge told stories of the rustic life in Butcher's Cross whilst Mr. Franklin smiled and listened, and I struggled silently with truth and lies.

We rose to depart shortly before nine. I had hoped for a few moments alone with Mr. Franklin and was glad when just outside the door he bent near. "I shall relate what truly passed soon, Nick, for there is more to this than I have told." Squeezing my shoulder, he walked on, climbing with the rest into the coach whilst I mounted atop. F. J. Mossop scrambled out the inn door at the last moment. He had not joined us at breakfast. Did he carry his pistol? His voluminous coat hid that secret. "My man has rid ahead on my mare," Darly proclaimed.

A brusque *"Ho!"* from our coachman, a jingle of reins, and we were on our way once more.

Bath lay eight hours ahead. At one o'clock we stopped at yet another inn for a brief repast and a change of horses; we then rattled on. The weather was pleasant, no rain to drench me, and my previous day aloft had made me adept at hanging on despite the dips and bumps of the road. We were in sight of other conveyances once more: curricles, post chaises, a coach, and four with liveried postilions. I was troubled by many questions, but they did not prevent me taking in the sights: the little villages and stone fences of Wiltshire, coal barges on the rivers, farms tucked about, sheep, buttercups, the nodding wildflowers of spring. We had struggled through quagmires near Hounslow, but as we went farther west a new mischief plagued us: dust, so that I must breathe through a handkerchief whilst our coachman rid muffled to the eyes. All the while I wondered what my fellow travelers talked on. Had Miss Morland ensnared Edmund Darly's heart? How I despised being thirteen, despised being poor.

We came at three o'clock to a landscape of flat-topped hills cut by river valleys: the Cotswolds, and the dust began to be tamed, for a series of pumps appeared at the side of the way, manned by minions with numbered brassards who watered the road. And then the sparkle of the Avon. And then Claverton Down, the very anteroom of Bath. The down was infested with footpads, I had been warned, and the hair at my nape pricked, but we were not molested.

A little rise, and Bath lay before us beneath the blue afternoon sky.

At sight of it I forgot all the aches of the journey, for it was an elegant dream of a town: a bowl of houses of mellowed golden stone set in a deep curve of the river. Round it spread hills and parkland in which ladies and gentlemen strolled as if in Elysium. It seemed a painting of paradise. Could danger truly lurk there? To titles and purses and hearts?

We crossed the Avon into Bath.

Amongst the Brobdingnagians, Lemuel Gulliver had learnt that seeing a thing near at hand gave a perspective that the farther view did not afford. I learnt the same as we came within Bath's walls, for crippled souls hobbled about its outer lanes, reminding me that the town was a place of sickness as well as a place of pleasure. Bold young whores and stout bawds plied their trade, whilst sly-eyed felons squinted at our passing coach like pirates at a rich merchantman. A stink of coal fumes tainted the air; this, too, was Bath.

But there were glimpses of noble facades as well, and the air grew better the higher we rose in town, the *ton* mingling in fashionable coats and dresses. At a quarter past five our driver drew our horses to a halt before The White Hart off Stall Street. At once bells began to peal. "The four-and-twenty of the abbey," Dr. Woolridge informed us. "They greet ev'ry coach."

Fresh visitors were arrived, fresh company, fresh pickings.

As we got down, the city waits crowded round to serenade us, another custom it seemed (it signaled that we must open our purses). Doctors scurried up to offer their services. Guides thronged to lead us to the baths. Beggars crept to relieve us of coin, whilst a bevy of tittering maidservants flocked to know our names so their masters and mistresses might learn if we were worth calling upon. Much interest was shown in young Lord Edmund Darly, less in Mrs. Snow and her charge, less still in Mr. Franklin and Dr. Woolridge, who had neither fortune nor title to recommend 'em, and none in F. J. Mossop, who had scurried away. As for Nicolas Handy, I was raddled by the clamor, but it soon subsided so we might look to the business of settling in.

Two gentlemen had been kept from us by the throng, but as postboys unstrapped our baggage, they approached. First came a sober, stoutish man of about forty-five: Mr. Edgar Snow, it proved, pinched about the eyes, with a goutish hobble. He greeted his wife as if she were a letter that bore ill news, and once he had delivered his stoic peck upon the cheek, he found he had been right, for she unfolded a flood of woe, all about our highwayman, his threat to Emma, the mysterious attack at the inn. "The intruders might have *murdered* me, Mr. Snow!"

"Dear me!" He patted her hand with a dry little squint. "I see that they did not." He turned a warmer eye upon his niece.

"I am happy to find you unharmed, Emma." He gestured to the man who had waited with him. "But here is Arthur Brown. You remember Mr. Brown?"

This man had hung back but now stepped forward, his tricorn hat atwist in his hands. He was of medium height, lean, and plainly dressed. I could not tell his age: past thirty but not yet fifty. There was no great vigor in him (his shoulders had the scholar's stoop), yet there was a nervous excitement in the manner in which he took us in. His features were taut as parchment, his cheekbones prominent, his lips thin and wide, his brows pale wisps over deep-set eyes, his nose a great, awkward beak. His steel-rimmed glasses caught a glint of light above a restive smile.

A small bow. "I *h-hope* you remember me, M-Miss Morland."

"I do, sir." She gave a restrained little curtsey.

He fixed lugubrious eyes upon her. "I am d-dreadfully s-sorry to hear you were s-set upon. And so p-pleased you are safe!" He blinked round at the rest. "I mean, of course, I am p-pleased that *all* of you are safe."

"It is entirely due to Mr. Darly," said Miss Morland crisply. "He saved us." She gestured toward the magnificent young man by her side.

Brown made a bow. "Arthur B-Brown, sir, at your s-service. We have m-much to thank you for."

"I should have done more!" proclaimed Darly, puffing his chest. "I should have trounced the fellow!"

"He w-wounded you, I see. How dreadful."

Darly glanced at his arm, in its sling. "It is nothing." He gazed ardently at Miss Morland. "Why . . . I should give both arms for *her*!"

Silence greeted this, broken by Mr. Snow, who presented himself to the young lord. "Your servant, sir. I, too, thank you for what you have done and hope that we may meet again so we may thank you better. But for now—come, wife, come, Emma. Your adventures must have tired you. Mr. Brown has found us excellent rooms near his own."

Darly's great blue eyes shot wide. "But let us not part without saying where and when that meeting shall occur. At my lodgings? Tomorrow? Luncheon?" He addressed this mainly to Miss Morland, though his glance said that of course Mr. Franklin and Dr. Woolridge and any who wished must come as well. By then servants had loaded bags upon carts, and sedan chairs stood waiting. "I am in the South Parade," Darly said, "number five. I have a view across the Avon—Miss Morland, you may then meet the Valentines. You will surely want Mrs. Valentine to take your niece about, Mrs. Snow."

Emma sent a begging look at her uncle, and it was agreed. Pleased, Darly kissed each woman's hand, bid the gentlemen a flourishing *au revoir* and bounded into his waiting chair. Mrs. Snow plucked at her husband's sleeve as the chairmen set off. "Just think, a young lord! He will one day be the Earl of Hendon!"

Mr. Franklin had stood aside, whilst this business was concluded, but he now presented himself.

Edgar Snow bowed. "I am happy the robbers did you no harm in the inn, sir." He met Doctor Woolridge, too. "How fortunate that you were present to see to Mr. Darly's wound. I am happy we may talk at more leisure tomorrow. But for now"—he took his wife's arm—"we must go, my dear, for the evening does my pains no good. Your bags have preceded us, and your indispensable maid, Harriet, has made all ready. Come, Emma."

Mrs. Snow sank against her husband as if her journey had drained her of will, and they turned away. As their niece made to follow, she sent one last glance back at Arthur Brown. It seemed to tease the beak-nosed scholar, who reddened, crushing his hat against his chest as if it were his heart.

The Snows beckoned Emma into a small open carriage. It set off, and Dr. Woolridge walked away with his bag.

Evening was coming on, shadows lengthening. Our coach retired from the square—other travelers would take it tomorrow, back to London or on to Bristol, but for now it must be put away with the horses. Arthur Brown greeted Benjamin Franklin at last. "So, s-sir, you are here. M-Most p-pleased. I did not th-think . . . that is, until I saw you s-step down—"

"I promised to come, and I have. This is my boy: Nicolas Handy." He gestured at me, and Mr. Brown vouchsafed a nod, though plainly Mr. Franklin was his interest.

"Let me s-say again, sir, how g-gratified I am that you regarded our meeting last winter highly enough to consent to visit."

"And to accompany Miss Morland, as you requested?"

"Why . . . y-yes; that, too. I thank you for your part in s-saving her from the highwayman."

"O, Edmund Darly did the saving—after his fashion. You take a particular interest in the girl?"

"N-nothing out of the ordinary. I am a friend to the Snows and thus, naturally, of M-Miss Morland."

"I see."

Arthur Brown removed his spectacles, peered into 'em, and returned 'em to his prominent nose. "Shall we to our l-lodgings? Yours are just above m-mine, in Mrs. Finching's house. Will you walk? It is not f-far, and the cart can f-follow with your bags."

"I should like to walk through Bath."

Arthur Brown led the way. He had large feet and a storklike gait. Though his suit of clothes was neat and clean, it was frayed about the elbows, and I wondered if he lacked the coin to pay a coach's hire.

In any case, I too was happy to walk. We marched south, down Stall Street, the backbone of the town, which bisected it into east and west. Mr. Franklin had told me somewhat of the history of Bath. Like many cities—like London herself—it had burst its ancient Roman boundaries, though we now stayed within the old walls which until half a century ago had been sufficient to contain the town before it became England's most fashionable watering place. We passed many Tudor half-timbers, blackened by time, but there were also buildings in the new Palladian style: facades of golden Bath stone; plainly, the city remade herself. We walked by the Pump Room, where chairs came and went and elegant ladies and gentlemen strolled. It was now past six, dusk mantling the city in day's dying glow. A gossamer murmur hung in the air, making me think that Emma Morland might indeed find the romance she sought.

"Tell me of the Snows," proposed Mr. Franklin as we neared Southgate. "How do you know 'em?"

Brown bobbed along with his long-fingered hands behind his back. "To tell of that is to t-tell of m-myself. My father was of that d-despised profession, the schoolmaster. He taught in a small day school in a parish of Wiltshire. He l-loved l-learning, but the boys drove him mad, so the parish drove him out. He b-brought his family to London, where he found work in a bindery. He was adept with his hands—he l-liked anything to do with books—and so he made a decent l-living. He sent me to Westminster School, then to St. John's College, Cambridge, but I never received my degree, for he d-died when I was seventeen. This left my mother with l-little for herself and nothing for me." Brown shook his head. "I was ill-prepared for the world."

69

"A man who could read but could not mend a shoe, eh?"

"As you say. Fortunately Mr. Edgar Snow helped me. He had been a friend of my father (they both loved books), and he s-saw my s-straits, for he himself had started from inauspicious beginnings—he was a l-lawyer's clerk, you know, putting by enough to purchase a thirtieth share in a merchantman. That was the beginning of his rise; he is now well off, trading s-sugar from the West and timber from the East."

"I admire a self-made man."

"Mr. Snow took me on as a clerk in his office," Brown went on. "He taught me its ways. I was not the b-best clerk, for my mind would not fix on ledgers and numbers (I longed to s-study the p-past; I am a rather f-fusty f-fellow, you see), but Mr. Snow kept me for three years, out of his friendship to my father."

"Thus you made your fortune?"

"Dear me, no!" A rueful laugh. "I do not think I could m-make threepence to save my l-life. No, I was left a small annuity when I was twenty-two—a great aunt unexpectedly died with no one else to leave it to—and that has set me up in a s-small way, free to pursue my interests. I have published two papers in the Royal Society's *Transactions*."

"Excellent. But how I envy you! Though I need no longer work for a living, I have been unable to pursue my scientific interests. Politics has got its grip on me, you see. But I keep my hand in, I keep my hand in."

"Why, sir," Brown gazed sidelong, "you have done m-more than many do in a lifetime!"

"Have I? How kind of you to say so." We strolled past a crumbling wall that might have been left by the Romans. A scrofulous old man huddled in its shadows whilst a workman rattled by with a barrow. "Emma Morland was raised entirely by the Snows?" asked Mr. Franklin.

"Very nearly. Her mother was Mrs. Snow's sister; she d-died before Emma was five. Her father was Joss Morland, of Hereford. He was (I am told) a man of many schemes for making a f-fortune, but no l-luck in bringing 'em off. After his wife passed on, he fell into some bad business—I do not know what—but one day he was found dead, a s-suicide it was given out. Emma came to live with the Snows when she was six. They have r-raised her as their own."

"But she has a very rich uncle."

"Titus Morland, her father's elder brother."

"She does not care for him?"

Brown sucked his lower lip. "He is a v-very wicked m-man, Mr. Franklin."

"Her aunt thinks so, too. Is it true that you dandled Emma on your knee when she was a child?"

"That was l-long ago," murmured Arthur Brown.

71

❧ 8 ❧

*IN WHICH we sort through mystery
and unknown eyes watch under the
moon . . .*

We had came to a crossing near Southgate. To our right lay the street of Lower Borough Walls, to our left the small church of St. James. Turning past its stone facade, we came in sight of Ham Gate, which we passed, too. This delivered us to Orchard Street, a short, unprepossessing curve of cobbles below Bull Gardens. On the south side crowded three wood-framed houses, two of brick, the third wattle and plaster, the upper stories leaning out. All were slate-roofed; all displayed many-paned windows that glowed softly in the last light of day.

They appeared well-kept in spite of their age: lodging houses, Arthur Brown informed us. "My rooms are on the g-ground floor of the one on the left, quite s-satisfactory for my n-needs (I have had 'em two years). I have engaged the top floor for your stay. I h-hope it will suit." The Snows were lodged in the house next ours, he informed us as we watched the cart which had carried their things rattle away in the gloom. "I s-secured the house for 'em when Mr. Snow wrote to say he would be coming with his wife and niece. The r-remaining

72

house is recently let to another lodger, Mr. Hobhouse, I believe, though I have not met him."

We went to number three.

We were met in the entryway by Mrs. Dora Finching, a brisk, ruddy woman whose manner seemed to take it on account that we should have nothing to complain of. She had one walleye, but the other regarded us keenly. The cart which had brought our things had come and gone, she said, and her maid of work, was waiting to put 'em into wardrobes for us. Accordingly we were led up to two adjoining rooms lit by candles, where we were curtseyed to by the maid under the unremitting gaze of Mrs. Finching's fixed eye. Mr. Franklin told the maid she might unpack our trunks as she saw fit. "I do not travel with a great deal of impedimenta, you see."

"Shall you wait with Mr. Brown in the parlor?" inquired Mrs. Finching.

Mr. Franklin agreed to this plan.

This disappointed me, for I should have preferred to stay to hear the truth about last night; but, Mr. Franklin lifting a brow to say that that truth must keep, I resigned myself and we went down. The parlor lay to the left of the entry, as agreeable as the rest of the house, with sprigs of lavender on the walls, little pewter pots on shelves, crisp white curtains at the windows. Arthur Brown sat with his knees stuck up like a grasshopper's. Unfolding himself as we came in, he stammered that he hoped we were content.

"Excellent rooms!" pronounced Mr. Franklin. "We could not do better."

Mrs. Finching swept in to announce that supper would be served within the half hour, then swept out, and we sat by a fire, well-laid, upon which Mr. Brown tossed occasional sticks of wood with his long-fingered hands. I guessed him about thirty-five, not as old as I had at first supposed. His hair was light-brown, tied back with a black ribbon, his brow broad. Though his nose was large and ridged, it was not ignoble—in truth, it was rather aquiline. If he could not be called handsome, he was at least less severe than I had judged him. And though he had the scholar's air, he had not the pallor, for he was as brown as a nut.

Pulling my sketchbook from my coat pocket, I began discreetly to draw him as he and Mr. Franklin conversed.

They recalled their meeting at the Royal Society, when Brown had told Mr. Franklin of the old Roman artifacts which he had unearthed round about Bath. "I too like to learn of the past," agreed Mr. Franklin, leading Brown out. "But tell me," said he after a quarter hour's disquisition on old marble tombs, which had begun to make him fidget, "is Bath truly so corrupt a place as I am led to believe? A den of rogues and mountebanks and fortune-hunting dastards who will do anything to obtain a lady's love or a place in a wealthy man's will?"

Brown looked pained. "I cannot say that I d-do not hear s-such things, and it is true that life here is decidedly more l-lax since the Beau lost much of his authority. Private assemblies used to be s-strictly forbidden, but now they grow without number, and who knows what g-gaming and intrigues go on at 'em? Still, I do not l-like to judge what I have not examined with my own eyes. I am afraid I do not go about much; my compass is narrow."

"Come, you range over the whole age of the earth!—that is not narrow." Mr. Franklin tilted his head. "But to another subject. Was there any special reason you wished me to accompany Miss Morland to Bath?"

"Why . . . no."

"Yet in your letter you used the word *protect* . . . "

Brown began to look alarmed. "M-merely a manner of speaking, I assure you."

"Then she is in no danger?"

"How could she be? Only the d-danger which ev'ry inno-cent person is in, that is. She d-does not know the w-world, you see."

"Perhaps she knows it better than you think?" Mr. Franklin watched Brown stir uneasily, whilst a settling log sent up sparks. "The girl is the ward of your benefactor. For this reason alone, you seek to see that she keeps well?"

"Who w-would not?"

"And marries well, too?"

Brown's Adam's apple bobbed. "If she ch-chooses."

"You yourself have never married. Why, may I ask?"

Brown looked as if he would like to laugh but could not. "How you question me, Mr. F-Franklin! But the answer is simple. M-my books, m-my studies—"

"Come, sir, you are an eligible man. One many a woman might be happy to catch. Should you not like to marry one day? But here is Mrs. Finching. Supper, ma'am?" Rising, Mr. Franklin rubbed his hands. "I look forward to it."

Arthur Brown only stared.

Supper was a cold collation of meat and potatoes, followed by a sweet flummery. As we ate Brown regained some equanimity, for Mr. Franklin asked no more of personal matters, keeping strictly to the paths of natural philosophy and history. Brown grew voluble on the topics: "Though my compass is not b-broad, I grant you it is deep. Because I keep just this little curve of the Avon under my eye, I know it exceedingly well. I have d-dug up m-much around town."

"If earth flies, look for Arthur Brown, eh?"

A half smile. "The townspeople m-make japes at me for it: 'There goes Brown with his spade.' But I s-seek truth, you see. To combat the lies about Bath's past.

"Lies?"

"O, there are m-many. The B-Bladud story, for one. You have not heard it? Allow me to tell you, then." He adjusted his spectacles. "Some t-two thousand years ago (they say) one Hudibras, descended of Aeneas, ruled as king in Britain. His son was handsome and virtuous; all the court l-loved young Bladud. But he fell ill with leprosy and had to flee for fear of spreading his disease. He wandered sad and alone. Coming across a farm, he offered to herd its p-pigs. The farmer agreed and Bladud began to t-tend the animals, but after a time he gave 'em leprosy too. In shame at what he had done, he t-told the farmer he would d-drive 'em across the river in search of food. They crossed this very Avon, where the pigs plunged into a morass. Bladud lured 'em out with a b-bag of acorns— but when he washed the mud from the animals, he was amazed, for he found that the waters had c-cured 'em! Soon he was likewise cured. He returned in joy to his father but vowed he would come b-back to clean the springs and erect a city. And that is how Bath came to be."

"All untrue?" asked Mr. Franklin.

"Ev'ry word. Bladud is said to have d-died trying to fly like a b-bird, by wings he built himself."

Mr. Franklin laughed. "I am no lover of lies, but whether he walked the earth or no, I like this Bladud!" He winked at me. "I have sometimes wished to fly. Shall I build me wings, Nick?"

"Only if you do not jump off a tower with 'em, sir," said I.

Brown told some of Bath's real history, too. As he did, he appeared another man from the awkward, diffident soul who had greeted our coach. Fire burnt in his deep-set eyes, and his hands carved an eloquent story whilst his great nose gleamed. So Arthur Brown was a man of feeling after all. For old pots and dead souls only?

We rose from table at ten. Before we went to our rooms, Mr. Franklin asked one last question: "By the by, the letter you sent—you sealed it well?"

"With the s-strongest w-wax. Why do you ask?"

"It received some ill care in the post. Come, Nick." We went up.

In our chambers, Mr. Franklin turned to me. "And so . . . ?"

"I have been longing to hear what truly befell you at the inn!" said I.

"And I to hear what your story too." He gestured. "Is this not a perfect pair of chairs before the hearth?" We sat in 'em, he lacing his fingers over his belly. "Now. You recall how we parted at the chamber which I shared with Dr. Woolridge. He was deep in some medical book; we spoke but little. Getting into my nightgown, I looked into my Addison, but I could not keep my eyes open. Such drowsiness, Nick! My fingertips felt cold; I seemed to drown. My book slipped from my hand, and I fell fast asleep.

"That might have been the end, but agitating dreams crept upon me. Alarms seemed to ring—I must wake! Somehow I did, by a great struggle. Finding it dark, I fought an inner darkness, a black tide. If I had sunk into it, I have little doubt I should now be gravely injured, perhaps dead, but I fought the pull, rolling from bed, ending on the floor on my knees. This cleared my head enough for me to conjecture that someone had drugged me. A dram in my drink? Who had put it there? Some servant at the inn? One of our party? All I knew was that I must escape, for surely the miscreant had done it in order to harm me.

"Finding my feet—how I wobbled!—I pulled on my breeches and coat. As a last measure, with nearly my last strength, I pushed the pillows into the semblance of a man under the coverlet—if they could trick me, I could trick them! Only then did I note that the doctor was gone, but I could not seek the why of it, for I felt consciousness slipping away. I staggered into the hall, all dim, yet with enough light to see the attic stairs at the end, by Mossop's door. I went there, crawling into the small, cramped space beneath 'em. It was ignominious—poor Ben, like a mouse in a hole—but I was hidden and safe. Curled there, I fell asleep. The drug must have been strong, for I heard neither your cries nor the search that followed."

"So I walked near you, sir—*over* you—twice?" said I.

He nodded. "You must have, coming down and going up."

"I wish I had known. I would not have fretted so horribly."

"Yet my secrecy kept me alive. (It is not so easy to do in Ben Franklin.) As for the following morn, I thought it best to say nothing to the others of my suspicions."

"Because one of them—?"

"Perhaps. Now, tell your tale."

Taking a breath, I described all I had seen and heard last eve: my encounter with Noakes as I went to bed, my waking, my creeping downstairs, my near-escape, our search. "I may have been wakened by the rustle of the intruders climbing those vines that grew up the inn."

"Noakes was gone when you woke but had returned when you came back to bed, you say?"

"Yes, sir."

"It is a pity you did not see the intruders' faces. You were brave, Nick."

"I must save you, sir."

He looked at me long. "I am happy you are my son." He

shook his head. "But if I had known there would be danger—"
He bent forward. "Listen well: we must both keep our eyes
and ears alert in Bath."

"But what is it all about?"

"Some great matter. Otherwise why such elaborate plans?
Mossop, you say, never poked his nose out his door?"

"Not that I saw—though I have forgot to tell you: his door
was open a crack when I returned to the attic. He closed it, but
I heard the latch."

"And he sometimes hides a pistol in his coat? And does not
say who he really is? And a highwayman stopped us. And
sneaking devils sought to bludgeon me."

"And the broken wax seal on your letter," added I.

He pulled at his lip. "Why should someone wish to read a
letter to Benjamin Franklin from Arthur Brown? Then there is
Brown himself . . . " Mr. Franklin sighed. "These numbers
will add to something, Nick—but not tonight. Let us sleep."

"Yes, sir." The chamber was large, with a high, canopied
bed. A writing desk faced a tall casement window looking
north over the town. Rising, Mr. Franklin set about preparing
himself, whilst I withdrew through the door by the fireplace.
This led to a sitting room containing two large mahogany
wardrobes, where most of our clothes had been disposed. A
truckle bed had been made ready against a wall. Setting my
candle on the small round table beside it, I hung my clothes
over a rush-seated chair and slipped into my nightshirt.

Returning to Mr. Franklin, I found him already abed, a book
on his knees. He glanced from under his nightcap. "Never
fear, I have latched our door." A small smile. "I have looked
out too; no vines climb the walls of Mrs. Finching's abode. We
are safe, I believe. Sleep well."

"Sleep well." I went back to my room, but I was in no state
of mind to rest. I picked up *Roderick Random*, dropped it. I

wandered to the window. Its casement stood open, and resting my palms on the sill I leant out into cool night air. Before me stretched a shadowy rise of rooftops. The towers of Bath Abbey dominated the town; above 'em the sky was star-flecked, the moon little diminished since last night, a vapor of cloud like a fairy ribbon strung across it. Bath. Was Nick Handy really here? It was still, but I could hear faint music uphill, laughter like the tinkle of glass, and I pictured a ball, dancers, the carefree pairing of the rich. I thought again on Emma Morland. Arthur Brown had called her innocent. Was she? She had a contradictory nature: despite her ironical turn, she sought romance. What of Edmund Darly? Recalling his rashness, I wondered if he might be even more innocent than the girl, in his way. Could a man like Darly remain in love with an ironical woman, however pretty? Could a woman as clever as Emma Morland love a man like Edmund Darly, though he be handsome and a lord?

I leant out more. Orchard Street curved, so that I could see the fronts of the two houses to my left. Lights shone in the upper story of the nearest, where the Snows lodged. Did Emma Morland also gaze out, wondering what Bath would bring? I glanced down. But one dim lamp lit the street, where a chair came and went. A tipsy man wobbled, reeled, vanished. Then all lay deserted.

Beginning to feel the weight of our journey's long hours, I yawned and was about to pull in my head when I glimpsed a new figure below, furtively skirting the light to end in deep shadow with only his boot toes showing. Who was he? What did he watch? Our rooms? The Snows? The Hobhouse lodging? I blinked, the boot toes winked out, and no amount of peering could discover 'em; the man seemed made of smoke. I closed the casement. How much Nick Handy had observed from windows of late. Had one of the devils who had wished to harm Mr. Franklin followed him to Bath?

Surely not Quimp, prayed I.

❧ 9 ❧

IN WHICH we hear of old Bath
and visit a young lord . . .

M r. Franklin and I were launched into all the difficul-
ties and dangers of a two weeks' residence in Bath.
Hoping there should be pleasures as well, I was
heartened by the sunbeams that greeted me when I flung
open my casements at seven. No watcher watched. Only ladies' maids and vegetable sellers scurried below, whilst a fid-
dler squeaked a tune. Rooftops glimmered with dew as the
bells of the Abbey pealed out.

Dressing, I went to Mr. Franklin's chamber; I found him
shaving at his basin, "to avoid the dirty fingers and bad breath
of a barber," said he. Silently I trailed a finger along a chair
back. Ought I to tell what I had glimpsed out my window last
night? Would he think me foolish?

I determined to speak.

He scraped the last lather from his face as I finished my tale.
"Nay, Nick, it is right that you tell all. The man seemed to
sneak, eh? And watched for a time? It may have nothing to do
with us—but, then, it may. I am pleased you follow my instructions to keep your eyes peeled."

This encouraged me, and I told him of the rider at the inn, who might have been Quimp. At this Mr. Franklin looked deeply grave and questioned me close, but I could still say only that it might-have-been.

"Still . . . the devil!" His brown eyes narrowed. "We must watch close indeed."

Breakfast was served on the ground floor, in a small parlor giving upon a tidy yard. Mr. Franklin stepped into this garden for a moment, I following. We found lady's smock, gillyflowers, and a chestnut pink with bloom. The area was connected by a low brick wall to one next it, where the Snows resided; a similar low wall led to the house next that. A portly, elderly gentleman stood in this third yard, hands behind his back, taking the air. Hobhouse? His pouchy old eyes turned our way—surely he saw us—but he made no acknowledgment, only turning and making his halting way indoors. Drawing a breath, Mr. Franklin sucked in fresh spring air—"Ah, Nick!" We went in and seated ourselves just as Arthur Brown arrived.

He tucked a voluminous white cloth at his throat. "Did you sleep w-well, sirs?" The sharp bridge of his nose gleamed like bone. "I hope that I m-may show you my treasures today."

"I look forward to 'em."

Brown regretted to inform us that we must wait upon his return. A man digging in his cellar in Barton Street had come across some potsherds; he had sent round a note saying that if Brown wanted 'em he must collect 'em before ten or they should be thrown out. " 'The D-Dustman of B-Bath,' they call me! Nonetheless some folk know what I s-seek and t-tell me if they find it." Three bites of bread, a sip of ale, scattershot regrets, and Arthur Brown was gone.

Mr. Franklin gazed after him. "A devoted scholar, Nick?"

* * *

The leisure was not unwelcome. Back in our rooms Mr. Franklin sat at the desk to write letters to the persons whom he wished to meet whilst he was in Bath: Ralph Allen of Prior Park, the builder John Wood, Dr. William Oliver who had founded the Royal Mineral Water Hospital, the actor James Quin, whom Mr. Franklin came to know when he exorcised murder at Drury Lane. "Perhaps I may also meet Lord Chesterfield," mused he, tapping his chin with his quill. "Spiteful old Horace Walpole? Pitt the Elder, Bath's man in Parliament?" Benjamin Franklin had a great gift for friendship—but I also knew that if he could win any of these to Pennsylvania's cause, he would, for he was profoundly pragmatical as well. "Naturally, we must meet Beau Nash," added he, the rims of his spectacles glinting as he scribbled yet more.

About ten, having posted these letters, we went out to subscribe to the pleasures of town. "Bath does not yield her favors for nothing," Mr. Franklin said.

We gave two guineas toward the balls, a guinea toward the music in the Pump Room, half a crown for the private walks beside the Assembly and the same to a bookseller so we might remove books to our lodgings; last, a subscription to King's Coffee House in Westgate Street for pens and ink and a bench to peruse the newspapers. We rested at King's just past eleven, looking over the *Bath Chronicle*. Its stories were rife with gossip: a young woman of Maidenhead had eloped with a man of Wells; a gamester had been thrown from a second-story window for cheating at faro ("He should've played on the ground floor," proposed Mr. Franklin wryly); a French adventurer, the Vicomte de Barre, had fatally shot a man in a duel on Beechen Cliff. Mr. Franklin tutted. "Does not Beau Nash forbid duels? But, see?—they write of the arrival of Edmund Darly. Prompt, these newspaper men! 'The handsome young lord,' they call him, 'the future Earl of Hendon.' 'Eligible,' they might add—though ev'ry unmarried young woman within a fortnight will know that without being told. But where is Ben Franklin? Am I of no interest to Bath? Come, let us to Orchard Street. Surely Arthur Brown has returned with his booty."

He had returned, barely, when Mr. Franklin rapped upon his half-open door.

We were called to come in.

Brown's rooms were two, the rear containing a bed which I glimpsed through the connecting door, though this chamber was small, a mere afterthought compared to the large front room, crammed with tables and tall shelves crowded with the detritus of Bath's history: cracked pots, bent implements, flint shards, bits of marble, mosaic, beads, and bones. A toothless skull gazed out of black sockets on a high shelf opposite the door.

Brown's dun-colored coat had soil on both sleeves. What he had retrieved from the Barton Street cellar was unimpressive, I thought, fragments of broken clay; but with great gravity, as if they were hallowed, he fit together the bits to show how they had once made a small round vessel. "Celtish," said he. "As to its age . . . I must s-study that." Placing the shards upon a shelf after carefully lettering upon a paper where he had got 'em, he said, "Now, may I sh-show you about?" Beckoning us to the far end of the cluttered room, he began to speak of a mysterious age before the Romans, when the ancient Britons had crept about the Mendip Hills. "We know so l-little of 'em . . . yet I hope to shed some l-light . . . " He gestured, as if parting a curtain. "Imagine 'em: savage, w-worshiping gods with pagan rites. What did they make of this place when they f-first f-found it beneath the darkness of thicket and shade, a morass stained r-red by salts from the spring? The city is genteel now,

the old spring is covered over by m-manners and m-marble—
but what sacrifices were made here in olden times, what r-rites
observed in the name of the old goddess, Sul? I s-sometimes
w-wonder if the savagery of a place can be entirely suppressed.
Will it well up? Break out?" I thought on the duel of which we
had read as Brown opened a drawer. "The ancient B-Britons
may've been savage, but they had great skills. See?" He took
out a circle of beaten yellow metal, paper-thin, about three
inches across: an ornate sunburst, so fragile that he must hold it
with great care. His voice whispered over it: "Beautiful . . . "

"Beautiful, indeed," agreed Benjamin Franklin.

Brown showed many other finds: bronze spoons, Celtic
coins, a jar with wavelike designs. He gave us more history,
too: "In A.D. 43, the Roman army c-came to subjugate Bri-
tannia. They stayed four hundred years—imagine! They built
r-roads and c-camps. Bath was called *Aquae Sulis* then. The Romans saw the w-wonders of our w-waters, they tamed the
spring, they built a great bath; it became known worldwide.
They even brought a goddess with 'em—Sulis Minerva, she
was c-called. See this head?"—he showed a small bronze of a
woman with an emblem of an owl. "I b-barely rescued it from
a sewer in Stall Street. (Dear me, what if it had been l-lost?)
We do not yet know all about the Roman baths—they were
l-long covered over—but when the Abbey House was torn
down three years ago, in 1755, much of the old p-precinct was
unearthed. William Hoare made a drawing." He unrolled a
copy, which showed a great excavation containing a rectangular bath amidst the severed feet of long-gone Roman buildings. It looked vast, and I began to catch some of Brown's fer-
vor. What had it been like when ancient legionaries walked
and talked here far from Rome? For a moment whispering
voices in that long-dead tongue seemed to rise up around us.

There were other sorts of romance than Emma Morland's, I saw.

"And so I d-delve, Mr. Franklin," said Arthur Brown. I heard real voices now, the scrape of feet, but Brown seemed not to, so absorbed was he. "After the R-Romans withdrew, their r-roofs and walls collapsed and their baths silted up. A long d-darkness followed. (It is d-difficult to pierce, though I hope to write its history some day.) King Edgar was crowned here in 973. From the tenth century on it was a m-monastic borough. The town fell on hard times under the Normans; yet though it was d-devastated by invasion and n-neglect, its fortunes turned when John of Tours transferred his see from Wells to Bath—"

"—which occurred in 1088," came a new voice, "after which Bath became a prosperous cathedral city." We turned. Emma Morland stood in the doorway in a pale violet dress that set off her remarkable green eyes. Just behind her waited her uncle and aunt.

Arthur Brown visibly swallowed. He bobbed his head. "M-Miss Morland."

She strolled in, looking about. "So this is your precinct, Mr. Brown. As to King Edgar's being crowned here you neglected to say that that is the beginning of Bath's custom of electing a king ev'ry Whitsuntide."

"How well-informed you are, Miss Morland," said Mr. Franklin.

"Mr. Brown informed me. You have writ me many letters on the history of Bath, have you not, Mr. Brown?"

"I did not know you r-read 'em so well."

"I must be too caught up in the fashion of today to care for the past?"

He paled. "Why, n-no. I have always respected your c-capacities, Emma."

"So, it is 'Emma' now. That is better. But have you quoted Geoffrey of Monmouth? Solinus? The *Gesta Stephani*? You ought, for you quoted 'em to me. He gives you short shrift, Mr. Franklin. Make him tell all."

"I shall insist upon it. Good day, Mr. Snow. Mrs. Snow."

"Good day, sir." The uncle sent his niece a chiding look. "Do not rally Mr. Brown, Emma. He has been most kind to us, most accommodating."

Mr. Franklin glanced at his watch. "But it is time to set off for Lord Darly's. History must wait, Mr. Brown." He offered his arm to Miss Morland. "I look forward to the gathering of our company."

And to investigating our mystery, said his glance at me.

The South Parade was only a little distance, and the day remained fair; we would walk. As we stepped outdoors, I glimpsed the portly old gentleman whom we had seen earlier, leaning on a servant's arm. He headed the opposite way. Did he note us? Again I thought he must, but he averted his eyes.

Dr. Woolridge arrived at this moment from the other direction, and we set out.

Within a quarter of an hour, we stood before a row of tall, stately buildings made of golden Bath stone. Black iron railings stretched below, balustrades above, and courses of fine, tall windows marched like soldiers in a line. "John Wood the Elder's design, completed j-just ten years ago," Arthur Brown informed us. "The South Parade is the h-height of f-fashion." Just beyond flowed the Avon; beyond it Bathwick Meadows led to undulating hills under a clear noon sky, where parasols twirled amongst the broad green swards.

Edmund Darly's house lay nearest the river. Mr. Snow

rapped at a white fanlight door, and we were admitted to a spacious marble entry by a liveried servant—not Albert Noakes, I was glad to see. The servant said he would inform his master we were come, but the young peer prevented that by dashing amongst us, dismissing decorum. Laughing, he clapped backs with an easy air—his father might have disapproved his lack of restraint, but it put us at our ease. He paid special court to Miss Morland, clinging to her fingertips long after he kissed 'em, at which she colored. Her aunt gazed with unabashed satisfaction upon these attentions, but her uncle merely watched. Arthur Brown stood awkwardly by.

"I hope you do not mind my bringing my boy, Mr. Darly," said Mr. Franklin. "He is quite indispensable."

"He is as welcome as you," replied Darly graciously.

We were led about the house, the young lord showing us niches and mantels and painted ceilings, all grand. I started as we turned a corner. Albert Noakes peered down from the top of a stairs. He was as before, with his long, sallow face and arrogant yellowish eyes, though his black thatch of hair was capped by a servant's gray wig, producing an oddly sinister effect. He darted back as if he did not care to be observed, and some impulse made me glance at Darly. The young lord checked himself at sight of his man; I almost thought he feared him. Had I been mistook? He chattered gaily on.

Mr. Snow observed that his arm was no longer in a sling.

"You are better so soon?" inquired Miss Morland.

"All thanks to Dr. Woolridge," said Darly. "He stopped by early this morn to see to his patient—he is a good man. My arm is healing well, he said, no doubt due to his quick and excellent ministrations; and though it must still be dressed (I wear a bothersome bandage under my coatsleeve), it pains me very little. Barely a scrape."

"There was a deal of blood for barely a scrape," observed Mr. Franklin.

"Our young hero is fortunate that the ball passed straight through," Woolridge replied.

Darly led us into the parlor, very fine, with yellow brocade curtains and Turkish carpets upon a parquet floor. An elegant woman perched on a sofa holding a dish of tea. She rose with a rustle of satin as we entered.

"Mrs. Sophia Valentine," Darly presented her. "I told you that I should introduce you. This is Emma Morland. Is she not as charming as I promised? And this is her uncle, Mr. Edgar Snow. Mrs. Fanny Snow. Dr. James Woolridge. Mr. Benjamin Franklin. His boy, Nicolas. And . . . forgive me, sir—?"

"Arthur B-Brown."

"And Mr. Brown, who digs old things out of the ground, I am told." Darly beamed.

Mrs. Valentine regarded us. She was a handsome woman, perhaps forty, with a splendid carriage, a sharp chin, and a way of looking straight at you with a glittering little smile that was both knowing and reserved. Meeting so many might have occasioned awkwardness in a less confident soul, but she greeted us with cool, appraising ease, holding out her hand to each gentleman, nodding to the ladies. "Mr. Darly has indeed told me of you, Miss Morland," purred she, examining the girl as if she were a piece of goods. She touched Emma's chin. "Yes . . . you are quite as pretty as he described. You will make a great success at Bath, and it would be a shame if you did not see the town—and it you. Decidedly you must go about. I am given to understand that your aunt does not care to accompany you?"

"I am of a nervous constitution," twittered Mrs. Snow. "I may walk now and then, naturally, for who does not in Bath, but—"

"Then you must allow me to take your niece in hand," Mrs. Valentine pronounced firmly.

Emma begged. "Do allow it, aunt, uncle . . . "

"Mrs. Valentine is exceedingly respected," urged Darly.

It was Mr. Snow's decision. "I had hoped to meet your husband, Mrs. Valentine," said he.

Her smile was as brittle as flint. "He is of a retiring disposition. You will meet him someday, I am sure. But as to your niece—?"

Edgar Snow thought a moment. He bowed. "Naturally, since Mr. Darly recommends you . . . "

"O, thank you, uncle!" Emma cried, and having won her point, Mrs. Valentine took the girl aside to instruct her in the sights and pleasures of the town. I heard murmurs of bathing, walks, balls.

At one we went in to luncheon, in a room with tall windows that looked out over the Avon. At the far end of the table, Emma sat *tête-à-tête* with Mrs. Valentine, but she glanced now and then at Arthur Brown, who appeared wholly out of his element, dirt on his coat sleeves. Doubts seemed to cross the sprightly girl's face. Yet after a time, as he stayed with his beaky nose over his plate looking as if he would prefer to be digging shards out of a bog, she ceased to regard him. She was well distracted, for seated on her other side, Darly was charming; he made her laugh. How well they appeared together, I thought: the handsome young swain, the pretty nymph. Yet what might come of it? Emma had no title, no money. Could Darly think of marrying her? Such unions were sometimes made in Bath, we had been told, and Mrs. Snow plainly began to wish for this one, for I saw her glance from the lord to the maid, as if she counted the days 'til he proposed. But could it be? Did Emma calculate her chances? I watched her lips part in a gay little laugh—she must see that if she played her cards well, she, an orphan, might one day be Lady Hendon. Yet I remained troubled, for I knew that young lords could also play games; and when the last hand was down, no matter the cards, they always won.

Darly was pleasing—but was he sincere? Did he make eyes at Emma only to see how far he might go with an innocent girl?

As for Benjamin Franklin, he observed the lively scene through the small twin lenses of his spectacles. Emma's laughter pealed like the tinkling of glass that might easily be shattered, and I thought I read his mind: did the answer to the broken wax seal, the highwayman and a skirmish at an inn sit at table with us?

❦ 10 ❧

A s luncheon drew to a close, Edmund Darly exclaimed,
"Tomorrow is Friday, a ball night. You all must attend."

Mr. Snow pursed his lips. "Nay, sir. My gout."

"My nerves," seconded his wife promptly. "They will not
bear such excitement so soon after arriving. Decidedly I must
stay home with Mr. Snow. But you will be there, Mr. Darly?
Why, then . . . Mrs. Valentine—?"

Mrs. Valentine smiled her thin smile. "Have I not said I
should see to Miss Morland?" She patted the girl's hand.
"Never fear, you will be well taken care of, child."

Emma emitted a purr of satisfaction. She shot a look down
the table. "And what of you, Mr. Brown. Shall you attend the
ball?"

Arthur Brown ducked his head. "As I d-do not d-dance, I
had best stay at home, too."

The girl frowned. "Do you suffer from gout as well? I think
you might go to my first ball at Bath. I should like *some* old
friend about me."

Brown blinked. "Why . . . I s-suppose I may give dancing a try."

Darly looked from one to the other. He laughed. "Excellent!" He rubbed his hands—too vigorously it seemed, for he winced and clutched his wounded arm. Dr. Woolridge noted this, and Mr. Franklin took it in too, though his quick gleam of eye died soon. Fine crystal shone upon the tabletop, and two underbutlers waited to see to any need. "I do not know why I think of that little man, Mossop," Darly mused, leaning back, turning a glass of wine, "but I wonder if *he* shall be at the ball?" He smiled, but no one answered.

"Before you all arrived," said Mrs. Valentine, "Mr. Darly had begun telling me of your highwayman. He held you at pistol point upon the road?"

Dr. Woolridge related the story.

Mrs. Valentine gazed with particular sympathy at Emma. "How terrible for you! But how fortunate to have a brave man to save you. Is he not a hero, my dear?" She meant Darly, and all eyes turned to the golden-haired lord.

"Ev'ry girl desires a hero," murmured Emma, whilst Darly flushed with pleasure.

Mr. Franklin asked how long Mrs. Valentine had resided in Bath.

"Three years, sir, ever since my husband, Colonel Valentine, determined that we must settle here. He loves to game, and Bath provides much gaming. He is such a great friend of Lord Hendon!" The woman was beautiful in a spare, brittle way. How much older than Darly was she? I wondered. Old enough to have dandled him upon her knee, as Arthur Brown had dandled Emma Morland when she was young?

All pleasures must end, and twenty minutes later, we had gathered in the entryway. Snatching a pair of letters from a small table near the door, Darly flourished one as we made ready to depart. "You see, Miss Morland, I have already writ to my sister, Caroline, to tell her how pleased I am to know you. To know you all, I mean. I hope you may meet her someday, for she is my greatest confidante."

"I hope we may meet, too," replied Emma whilst her aunt's eager look said that knowing an eligible man's sister might give a girl a great advantage.

"I have some letters I writ just this morn," said Mr. Franklin to Darly. "Allow me to post yours with mine." He held out his hand.

Darly smiled. "O, but my manservant—"

"Nay, I shall be happy to do it."

Darly looked at Mr. Franklin's hand, at Mr. Franklin. "Why . . . most gracious, sir—but I have not yet directed 'em." A writing desk stood just inside the door of an adjoining parlor. Striding there, the young lord bent his back whilst we listened to the scratch of a pen. Returning, he gave the letters to Mr. Franklin. "Thank you, sir."

A small bow. "Your servant." Mr. Franklin tucked the letters into his coat.

Outside we discovered that clouds had come up, a lowering gray mass above the facade of South Parade. The Avon wrinkled beneath 'em, whilst trees bent their woolly heads, and a keening wind rustled the women's dresses. A chair awaited Mrs. Valentine, who lived in Duke Street, off Queen's Square, she told us. "I shall call upon you tomorrow, to make arrangements for the ball," she announced peremptorily to Emma before she was borne off by two stiff-backed chairmen.

Mr. Snow peered dourly at the sky. "We must hurry or we shall get wet. My legs begin to ache."

A last wave to Edmund Darly and we headed off, Miss Morland beside Arthur Brown, who looked more than ever like a stork with his great nose preceding him and his hands behind his back, his feet plodding one before the other.

"And how do you like Edmund Darly?" Emma asked him.

"W-well enough," replied Brown. "How do *y-you* like him, that is what I should like to hear."

Mrs. Snow scowled. "O, do not ask my niece what she likes! How can she know?" She smoothed her dress. "But she is a sensible creature, she shall come to like what she ought. Dear me, a drop of rain? Let us hurry."

As we reached number three, the clouds burst, the downpour driving us into Mrs. Finching's entryway. Our landlady was amongst us at once, insisting that the Snows and their niece and Dr. Woolridge must take shelter in her parlor for as long as they wished. We crowded in smelling of damp, and the maid lit a fire. The talk was desultory. There seemed some strain betwixt Emma and Arthur Brown. Looking at Mrs. Snow's pinched face with its busy eyes, I began to wonder if her protests against Bath's dangers were heartfelt. Had she—and her husband—conveyed Emma here hoping to find a husband?

Mr. Franklin was not one to let gloom triumph; he spoke as if the sun had not ceased to shine. Dr. Woolridge had had little chance to find custom in Bath, he supposed?

"No—although I have three or four letters of recommendation. And I hope for a good report from Mr. Darly." Mrs. Snow chafed her wrists, as she had in our coach. "They still trouble you, ma'am?" asked the doctor. "Shall I still prescribe for 'em? Perhaps you, as well, Mr. Snow—?"

Edgar Snow had been rubbing his gouty calf. "You may do some good. Come round tomorrow afternoon, at three."

The rain subsided to a pattering and in ten minutes was spent. A general stirring said the visitors must go. Arthur Brown had stood in a corner, whilst Emma perched stiffly in a chair. Neither had spoke, but as she rose, she said with uncharacteristic demureness that she hoped he would show her his collection of old things some day. "I am not insensible to their charms."

"I should be h-happy any time, Emma."

At the door Mr. Snow, his niece and Dr. Woolridge walked on, whilst Brown retired indoors. Mr. Franklin contrived to detain Mrs. Snow on our stoop. "A word, ma'am?"

"Sir?"

"Your niece is pretty," observed he.

Mrs. Snow squinted at the girl's back. "I must be grateful for that, I suppose, for she has little else."

"Surely she has charm?"

"You call it charm when she oversteps herself? She is headstrong! Neither I nor Mr. Snow know what to do with her."

"Tut, we all bear burdens. But her uncle—her other uncle, I mean; the wealthy one—"

"Titus Morland."

"Might not he do something for her?"

Fury danced in the woman's eyes. "He never sees his niece! He does not wish to!"

" 'Wicked,' you called him. Why, may I ask? (I do not mean to pry.)"

Mrs. Snow glanced about as if other ears might listen, but seeing only me, whom she appeared to judge of no consequence, she took a breath. "We rarely speak on it (my husband prefers to keep the thing buried), but I shall tell you, since you ask. Besides, it happened so long ago that there can be no harm in the story. You will promise to keep it to yourself?" Mr. Franklin placing a finger solemnly to his lips, Mrs. Snow began. "It was like this: My sister, Mary, was not a sensible woman (not such as I); she *would* marry Joss Morland. O, his family was decent enough—his father was a respectable corn merchant—but Papa had learnt enough about the younger son to know he was a dreamer. Alas, he turned out to be a schemer, too; he broke the law, you know. I never learnt exactly what wickedness he fell into, but my poor, foolish sister must have known, and I am quite certain the knowledge led to the ill-health which caused her to expire when Emma was young."

"And Titus Morland?"

"Joss's older brother, and a more different man you could not imagine! He was even then on his way to making a fortune. At first Joss was on good terms with him, though Titus was always after his younger brother to stay within bounds, my sister said. I never met Titus, you understand (having married two years earlier, Mr. Snow and I lived far away, in Cheshire), but Mary wrote of calling upon him and his wife, before the wife died. 'Titus loves my babe,' she said, 'he holds her in his arms.' Well, he may have had a tender spot for Emma, but to his servants and near anyone else he was a tyrant, my sister said, given to terrible rages. 'He takes revenge on anyone who does not do his bidding.'

"His relations with his brother grew worse; they had great rows, Mary wrote just before she died. Then . . . then"—Mrs. Snow's eyes puddled—"she was gone, and within six months Joss was in disgrace. They would have had him before the magistrate—he might've been hanged—but he escaped."

"He took his life, I understand?"

"How did you learn that? Did Mr. Brown tell you? O, it is indiscreet of him, and I do not like his doing so. Yet it is true. Joss flung himself from a cliff. But he left a note. It begged me and Mr. Snow to care for Emma. Of course we took in the babe. I wrote to her Uncle Titus—I thought he would wish at the very least to see her—but he wrote back that his brother had stained the family name, and he would have no more to do with the child of such a man. The letter was strange, almost as if he regretted his words—as if stubbornness rather than inclination made him say what he did—but he has stayed true to his promise. Never in all the many years since has he made any attempt to see Emma, and for all I know, he has forgot her."

The clouds were scudding away. "A tragic story," said Mr. Franklin. "Still, his niece has turned out well."

"But can she *do* well without a dowry?"

"Titus Morland's wife died, you said?"

"Of typhus."

"Did he remarry?"

"No."

"Has he children, then, upon whom to settle his estate?"

"A son, twenty-two. Wesley Morland."

"Have you met him?"

"No. And I should not wish to!—I have never forgiven his father for forsaking Emma. Besides," Mrs. Snow lowered her voice, "I have heard dreadful tales of Wesley Morland: profligacy and vice. He was sent to India in hopes of curing him, we were told, though I hear he has recently returned. In any case none of this matters, for old Titus Morland is dying; he may be dead as we speak." Mrs. Snow looked both satisfied to've told this tale and bitter at its nature. The anger and regret at the loss of a fortune which her niece might have shared had not diminished.

She looked like she wished to rejoin her husband, who was just bidding good-day to Dr. Woolridge on the rain-wet cobbles; but before she could escape, Mr. Franklin said, "One more matter, ma'am. In the coach I talked on the spies who report on travelers from London. As I did so, you gave a little start."

"You watch close."

"It is my habit."

"But—?"

"Tell me, how long had your husband planned your visit to Bath?"

"Six weeks. More."

"Plenty of time, then, for spies to learn of it?"

Mrs. Snow paled. "We made it no secret. But you cannot think . . . dear me, I have reflected little on it, but there *were* inquiries about Emma in those days. I put 'em out of my mind, and yet—"

"Tell of 'em."

"For one, a man accosted our housemaid, Jenny, in the street to ask if Emma was the Emma Morland related to Titus Morland. (I learnt of it only because the girl had been late upon an errand, and I demanded the reason; she is a laggard!) Someone also entreated Emma's dancing master for news— Mr. Fanshawe loves to tell ev'rything."

"The same persons in both cases?"

"I do not know. I did not ask what the men looked like. I made little of the occasions." She peered in alarm. "Ought I to have?"

Mr. Franklin patted her arm. "No. I do not even know why I ask, for what Bath spy could take interest in a girl with no dowry? But your husband waits; I must detain you no longer." He tipped his hat, and she walked off.

When the Snows had gone in, Mr. Franklin murmured, "Bludgeoners, and now spies? But I have promised to post Edmund Darly's letters. Accompany me."

"You said you had other letters, sir. Must you not get 'em from our rooms?"

"Other letters? Nay, I have none." This took me aback. Had he lied? Pulling Darly's two wax-sealed missives from his coat, the gentleman gazed at each, front and rear, as if there were something he sought. "Hum, one to his sister and one to his father. He tells the sister of Miss Morland—but does he tell the father?" He tapped the letters thoughtfully. "It would be easy to find out—but though others may do so, we do not break seals." He put 'em in his pocket. "We shall dispatch these honestly."

It took but a quarter hour to do so. Afterward we strolled past the Assembly Rooms. It was four, Bath awash in chairs. Servants groaning under the spoils of shopping trailed after fine ladies, whilst gentlemen stretched out their legs in coffee shops. Card games and small private parties would follow this eve.

"Miss Morland speaks very sharply to Mr. Brown at times, sir," observed I as we went.

"Is she displeased with him in some way? Too retiring for her liking. Do you find Arthur Brown rather meek?"

"At times."

"Yet in seeking Bath's lost history, he looks for nothing less than to conquer time."

I agreed that this was ambitious.

"Let us reserve judgment on Arthur Brown, then, for we do not know all of our scholarly friend. What do you make of Mrs. Valentine?"

"I should not care to cross her."

He laughed. "She *is* formidable—one of those creatures who floats on society like a swan upon a lake. But she does not drift, she guides her course. Does she guide others as well?" We paused by Southgate. Below lay the quays, where ferries and barges delivered passengers and goods to Bath, while above the Mendip Hills the clouds wheeled away to the east. Benjamin Franklin rose and fell on his heels. "Did you observe Darly's man at the top of the stairs?" said he as a wind stirred his fringe of brown hair.

"I observed Mr. Darly, too, at the very same moment."

A sharp look. "And—?"

"The servant seemed to keep an eye on the master. I almost thought that Darly feared him."

A small smile. "You continue to observe well. As to the truth of your idea . . . what fear could a manservant lodge in the heart of a future earl? Still, you may be right, for I do not forget that the moment I was meant to be bludgeoned, Albert Noakes was gone from bed."

That night we went to a play. It was at the Orchard Street Theatre, built in 1750 by the brewer John Palmer—said, after Drury Lane and Covent Garden, to be the finest theater in England. It was *The Maid of Bath*, by Samuel Foote, in which Mr. Dancer, Mr. Fitzmaurice, Mr. Barrington, Miss Cowper, Miss Hippisley and others acted a lively comedy. Arthur Brown did not join us, preferring to immerse himself in his studies. We sat in the pit.

Afterward we strolled out with the throng but soon found ourselves alone in deserted ways. Deep shadow lay betwixt the lamps, and we heard footsteps at sev'ral turnings, though we did not see another soul. Night had been our enemy of late, I reflected—but we arrived at our lodgings without incident. Dressed for bed, I slipped to my window. No boot toes. Surely it could not have been Quimp who rode away from the inn.

Mystery would not dissolve so easily, however. There was some plan in all this. Yet, as I climbed into bed, I looked forward to pleasure, too, for tomorrow we should take Bath's famous waters.

❧ 11 ❧

*IN WHICH we take the waters
and more eyes watch . . .*

I woke to a shake of my shoulder. Sitting up, I rubbed my
eyes.

Mr. Franklin stood by my bed in muzzy dawn light.
"Up, Nick, for the baths!"

By seven we were dressed, down and out upon the cobbles.
Though it was spring, the air was chill. Morning's yellow glow
lit tails of cloud in the east.

We set out, sedan chairs flocking with us at this early hour.
There were five baths in town, Mr. Franklin informed me as
we marched uphill, "but only two are frequented by the *beau
monde.*" These were the King's Bath and the Cross Bath. "The
King's is the best, I am told. Thus we shall go to the King's."

In a quarter of an hour we were there. It lay on the south-
west side of the Abbey, a great rectangular pool open to the
sky and bounded on two sides by a stone railing over which
one might look down upon the bathers. On the west side stood
the famous Pump Room, five tall arched windows from which
the privileged could observe the bathers in the waters below,
whilst they themselves imbibed 'em.

Following the throng, we found our way to the mean lane

which led to the waters. Many chairs jostled hereabout, passengers debouching, twittering, grumbling of ills, all close-packed. From here we descended like cattle to the slips, which proved yet more unpleasant: cramped, dungeon-like tunnels sweating from the steam of the baths. Finding the undressing rooms, Mr. Franklin dropped a shilling into the palm of an attendant, who gave us our bathing costumes: loose canvas drawers and shapeless jackets. We put these on.

We set out for the bath.

Guides importuned as we went, but Mr. Franklin waved a hand: "We shall not need a guide." He might not—but I? He had often told me how he had practiced Thevenot's Motions in a Boston pond, teaching himself to swim so expertly that he could propel himself upon his belly while holding his left leg in his right hand (it was one of his favorite stories), but I was no friend to water—nor was it a friend to me, for I had nearly drowned three months ago in the icy Thames—so I felt a mounting anxiety as the end of the dank slip loomed.

We emerged at the edge of the bath.

Great clouds of steam plumed from the water's surface, and there was a nose-curling smell, like hot, acrid iron. Three shallow stone steps led down. "Ready, Nick?" With no more ado, Mr. Franklin plunged in.

Girding myself, I forced myself to follow him, taking the first step, the second, until water lapped my thighs. It proved surprisingly warm, almost hot, and I felt a terrified desire to climb out. Too, there was a turbulence beneath the surface, currents that seemed to wish to topple me. Did we hover above some cauldron which might boil us like sprats in a stew? Gritting my teeth I stepped further in 'til water lapped my breast, but panic surged, and I turned to flee.

Emma Morland stopped me.

A curtain of steam lifted, and there she bobbed, not six feet away, laughing at the waters. She wore a voluminous yellow bathing dress that billowed about her, making her look like a flower, transforming the turbid waters into a lake of delight. At sight of her, I flushed. Seeing us, she beckoned with an arm like an ivory stem. Her face was rosy, her skin bedewed by mist. And her breasts—I glimpsed the tops of 'em as her dress flowed and shifted: pale globes. Could I run before this fearless nymph?

In truth the depth grew no greater, four feet or so, with a gravel bottom. The swirls of water began to seem pleasant, my nose ceased to wrinkle at the stench, and with a growing calm—pleasure even—I gazed about at the great King's Bath.

I had seen nothing like it. Here some fifty or sixty souls danced a strange bobbing dance, as at some dream-party. Fiddlers bowed in a corner, whilst conversation buzzed, little cries popped like bubbles, laughter floated up, and all sorts of folk, from beggars to grand gents, leant upon the stone railings above us to smile at our sport. From the center of the waters rose an octagonal tower, where a statue of King Bladud himself looked down. Beside it stood a hot pump from which attendants spilt healing waters upon the scrofulous and lame, who hung their crutches upon hooks. Yet despite the obviously afflicted, most of the swimmers appeared able-bodied; this was a social rite.

How comic it was too! I had to smile at the gentlemen in cocked hats and ladies in fine bonnets. Many women were rouged and patched; but these patches forever slid off in the steam, so that small black dots, like mites, swam amongst us. Other women had floating wooden trays held to their waists by ribbons, upon which perfume bottles, handkerchiefs, and nosegays rode like passengers on little ships. Some even carried looking-glasses, forever examining themselves. There was sport too. A prankster hurled a dog into the bath; it nearly struck Mr. Franklin—but no harm, for it merely bobbed to the surface and paddled about. Other gentlemen tossed down coins, which small half-naked urchins sought to obtain by plunging like cannonballs from the railings above. A sergeant with a staff stomped round scowling at these antics, but he could not prevent any; and in truth few seemed to mind, for they only added to the amusement.

Rich and poor alike bobbed and bumped. "Is this what heaven shall be, Nicolas?" asked Mr. Franklin. "I welcome it, if it is!"

We joined Miss Morland.

"Is this not a great joy?" came her trill. "Do you like it, boy?"

"Very much, miss."

"It likes me!" proclaimed Mr. Franklin, diving beneath the water, head and all, and swimming an expert circle round us.

Emma clapped her hands. "O, teach me to do that!"

"Decidedly, no." Her aunt bobbed nearby. "It would be unseemly." She sent Mr. Franklin one of her pinched looks. "I beg you, sir, do not conspire in this fancy."

"Let me teach *you*, then." Grasping her hand, he lifted it. "You have most handsome arms, strong and well-formed. You would swim well."

"O, sir!" But Mr. Franklin had pleased her. For my part, it was hard to take my eyes from her niece. The waters, surging in equal part from our motion and the bubbling of the spring, lifted Emma's bathing dress, so that I glimpsed her ankles, her calves, a dimpled knee. She made no attempt to push the garment down, instead swayed prettily. If she wished to be looked at she was, for many men's eyes turned her way.

Edgar Snow came amongst us, red-faced. "The waters give me much relief," puffed he. "I take 'em each morn."

"O?" said Mr. Franklin, but Emma paid little attention. She looked for someone, it seemed.

Suddenly she waved, and I glanced up to see Edmund Darly leaning upon the stone railing a dozen feet above us, his golden hair shining in the morn. He beamed down. "Had I known you took the waters this day, Miss Morland," called he, "I should have sought to join you. Alas, I have business, but I hope we may meet before the ball." With a wave he was gone.

Our party drifted apart, Emma to attempt swimming, Mr. Snow to duck under the hot-water pump, Mrs. Snow to perch primly upon one of the stone niches along the side of the baths. "It is singular, is it not, Nick?" said Mr. Franklin, scooping water in a palm. "Whence come these waters? And why are they hot? Is the earth's core afire?" Pulling from his bathing-jacket a thermometer, he read it. "Forty-six degrees. Remember the number, Nick, to write down at your leisure. I shall test all five baths. Perhaps there is something to discover."

Just before eight, the fashionable began to desert the waters. The Snows joined 'em. Following, their niece paused a moment on the top step, her garment clinging so tightly to her skin that she seemed naked. "Finer than the finest mermaid in Christendom . . ." murmured Mr. Franklin before the attendant wrapped her in a cloak, and she was led like Proserpina into one of the dark slips. "We shall depart, too."

We made to do so—but just then I glimpsed F. J. Mossop in one of the niches along the wall, hiding within his bathing costume just as he had hid within his coat. He wore a hat low over his brow, under which his damp eyes met mine. *We meet again,* they seemed to greet me. *Say nothing.* Barely bobbing my head, I turned away, but I was troubled. How long had the little man sat here? He did not seem the bathing sort. Did he suffer some affliction which had brought him to Bath? 'Twas no crime to carry a pistol.

"The man has been there this last quarter hour . . . " Mr. Franklin murmured. I thought that he meant Mossop, but his eyes gazed elsewhere, and nodding upward he added, "Look—but do not crane your neck conspicuously." Obeying, I was not pleased to discover Albert Noakes leaning on the stone railing above us, picking his teeth with a stem of straw. His long horse-face was set in its customary mocking expression whilst his yellowish eyes roved. Did he seek someone? Friend? Enemy?

F. J. Mossop watched him, unseen. Spies spying upon spies? thought I.

Benjamin Franklin's voyage to England had been rigorous, but after landing eight months ago, he had made it a point to detour to Wilton to examine its curiosities before he traveled on to London. He liked to take in ev'rything, that is; thus it was no surprise that, as today had launched us upon Bath's round, we should try to see ev'rything of it too.

The Pump Room was next on the list. Returning to Orchard Street to dress, we pried Arthur Brown from his dusty shards and set out into town once more.

By nine we were there. The Pump Room was an airy, high-ceilinged room, marked by tall Corinthian columns, a gathering place. At one end sat a bar with a marble vase, from which a liveried pumper filled patrons' glasses with the curative waters. Folk I had seen in the waters stood about, but dressed now: noblemen in ribbons and stars, grain merchants, members of Parliament, ship's captains, actors, Methodists, boarding-school mistresses, doctors, gamesters, country squires, fortune-hunters. Voices babbled, eyes roved, satin whispered.

Women wore elaborate dishabille, and bumpers of the iron-smelling water flowed down ev'ry throat.

A marble statue of a stout man in a huge hat stood conspicuously in a niche. "Richard N-Nash. The B-Beau," Arthur Brown informed us as we came in.

"I hope to meet him," Mr. Franklin replied.

I looked at the grandiose figure with the fat-englobed eyes. Would the famous Beau Nash, who held all Bath under his sway, be here in person?

The Snows were present, Emma dressed in sky-blue taffeta, gazing eagerly round, whilst her uncle held his nose as he quaffed a glass of the malodorous water. His wife looked as if she might invoke her nerves any moment, but she held her tongue. We all obtained glasses, and Mr. Franklin tasted his. "Better than a bleeding," pronounced he judiciously. I found it a warm, brackish brew.

Our party made small talk. Mr. Snow ignored me, Emma looked through me, and Mrs. Snow's curious brow seemed to ask: what does the boy here? I was accustomed to such treatment. It was odd for a gentleman to drag his boy about with him, but Benjamin Franklin told me I must see the world and hearken to its discourse.

Taking out my sketchbook, I retreated for a time to one of the tall windows overlooking the bath.

Lepers and poor lame souls were all who remained below, where low and high had bathed together to cure disease and boredom. I drew an old man with a gaunt face who clung to an iron ring of the Bladud Tower. Turning my attention to the Pump Room, I limned a corpulent old dowager freighted with pearls. Though I was content to draw, I still thought on the highwayman's sally, the attack at the inn, Noakes, Mossop, boot-toes in the night. My gaze strayed to Emma Morland.

Did the answer lie in her? Her picture, which I had begun at the inn, remained unfinished, and folding back pages, I made to complete it. I sought for more than a likeness, but her nature was difficult to capture, her compound of innocence and impudence; and though my pencil could fashion her straight, saucy nose, it could not discover her heart.

I rejoined our company. Mrs. Valentine had just sailed amongst it, purring how excellent it was to meet in Bath. Her brows were perfect arches, very thin, and I saw with a little start that they were painted on. "When I come to Orchard Street this afternoon, I shall take you for a drive, Miss Morland," said she. "You must be seen."

"B-but . . . I thought you m-might care to look at my things this afternoon, as you said, Emma," put in Arthur Brown.

"As they have lasted 'til now, they must grow a little older before I see 'em," she dismissed him gaily.

"I s-suppose I must g-grow a little older, too . . ." replied he.

A young man was striding past us toward the pump. Seeing Edgar Snow, he stopped, blinked black eyes. His face broke into a gleaming white smile. "Why . . . hello, Snow!" He made a crisp bow. "So your wife has come at last?" Another bow. "Your servant, ma'am. But can this be your daughter?" He gazed with great interest upon Emma. "You did not say you had a daughter."

"She is my niece," said Mr. Snow reservedly. "Emma Morland." He introduced us all, and the young man clicked his heels.

"Tom Bridger, at your service." He made a comic face. "I was about to drink some of that dreadful water. Like rotten eggs, eh, Miss Morland? But one must imbibe it. Why else come to Bath?" The young man was lean and limber in a gold-frogged, lace-edged coat and shoes so waxed they shone like glass. He had a broad, mobile mouth and snapping eyes. His

110

hair, pulled trimly back, was gleaming black.

He appeared to wish to linger, but his gaze suddenly met three men across the room. They frowned at him. "Dear me, I shall have to forgo the egg-water. Some . . . ah . . . friends wait upon me. I must be gone. Shall we meet again soon?" He darted in the opposite direction from the men.

"What a curious young gentleman," pronounced Mrs. Valentine severely. "Pray, where did you meet him, Mr. Snow?"

"Why . . . here and about." Edgar Snow seemed not to care to talk on Tom Bridger, and I wondered who else he had met, what he had done, in his week alone in Bath.

"I shall call for you at two, Emma," said Mrs. Valentine, sweeping off, and our party set out for our lodgings. In the square in front of Bath Abbey, we glimpsed the morose old man we had sighted twice before: he who let the third house in Orchard Street. Mr. Snow exchanged a nod with him as he wheezed past us into the Pump Room on the arm of a servant. His eyes were fiercely pinched, as if he fought great pain.

As we turned south toward the crook of the Avon Mr. Franklin asked, "Who was that, sir?"

"Isaac Hobhouse. He arrived in Bath the day before you."

"What do you know of him?"

"Very little. We have spoke but twice. He buys and sells as I do, though he is not of London, I believe."

"Buys and sells what?"

"He did not say."

"Where is he from?"

"He did not tell that either."

"Plainly he does not wish to be known," said Benjamin Franklin.

❧ 12 ❧

*IN WHICH we go to church
and meet a famous Beau . . .*

Shortly after ten we were back in Orchard Street, consuming buttered oatcakes and ale in felicitous privacy, with a pot of chocolate for me. Arthur Brown ate little. Plainly he longed for more discourse, so Mr. Franklin talked on the electrical fluid, describing how he had first become interested in the phenomenon when he saw Dr. Spencer's traveling act in America. "Imagine my wonder as sparks were pulled from a farm boy's ears." This had led to Leyden jars and his "Philadelphia Machine," as he called it, which might kill a man by its powerful charge. "Hence have arisen some new terms: we say that B is electricized positively, A, negatively. Or, rather, B is electricized plus and A, minus." Mr. Franklin pronounced this off-handedly, though the formulation had made him renowned on two continents. Brown asked many questions, and again I thought how he was two men: one the awkward fellow who could hardly speak in company, the other the avid seeker of knowledge who leant across the table in passionate absorption.

Did one Brown or the other—or both—figure in our mystery?

After a time the scholar pled that he must return to his shards, and Mr. Franklin and I set out once more into Bath. Mr. Franklin was not a church-goer ("at the last day we shall not be judged by our hours at worship but by what we did," he was fond of asserting), but we would attend eleven o'clock services at the Abbey Church, he said, for that too was a stop in the daily round.

As we passed the King's Bath, we found it empty. "Its sluices are opened to cleanse it at midmorn of each day," Mr. Franklin informed me. "The spring refills the basin by eve. Remarkable, eh? I long to study its mechanism."

Bath Abbey stood across the square from the baths, its west front a huge arched window flanked by a pair of towers displaying the strangest design I had seen upon any church: stone ladders up which little carved figures appeared to be climbing to heaven. Crossing the square, we crept in amongst the preacher's intoning. The pews were all filled, so we stood by one of the massive columns near the door. High windows filtered beams of morning light, whilst the fan-vaulting made its fantastical tracery overhead.

We caught sight of the Snows, Mr. Snow grimacing— whether due to gout or Bishop Hurd's sermon I could not tell. Mrs. Snow wore a pious expression, her nerves in abeyance, it seemed. Her niece gazed about at society, blithely irreverent. Mrs. Valentine's fine lace hat showed conspicuously far in front, whilst the new young gentleman, Tom Bridger, lounged three rows behind the Snows, watching Emma with an amused, rakish smile upon his handsome lips. Old Hobhouse was there too, in the left-hand pews, his massive head down, wig askew, dead asleep, it appeared.

Mr. Franklin observed 'em all, and I understood that he did not go about solely to see how Bath's day went. A highwayman had shot a young lord. An attack at an inn had near done in

Nick Handy. This was not to be borne. Further, some plan was afoot which might lead to worse crimes, and he could not defeat such a thing without watching close.

Yet we did not stay 'til the benediction, but strolled back to Orchard Street in the blue forenoon. Amongst the chairs and fine satin suits the lame and halt made their way. Back in our chambers Mr. Franklin writ more letters, to Mrs. Stevenson to say we were arrived safe; to his son, William, to urge him to keep to his studies; to John Strahan, the London printer; to Mrs. Comfort Goodbody, too, his particular friend in Wild Street, where he supped—and slept—sometimes.

For my part I fashioned a letter to Polly, who always loved news.

Coming down around one, we found the Snows paying a call on Arthur Brown in the entryway. Emma wore her bright, polished look. "You promised you would show me your things, Mr. Brown. Shall you do so now?"

"Nay, child," protested her aunt. "You must hurry home to await Mrs. Valentine."

"There is plenty of time for that," insisted Emma. "It is the perfect opportunity. Do you not think so, Mr. Brown?"

The scholar gestured gratefully toward his workroom, and she sailed in.

Mrs. Snow seemed to wish to chaperone her, but her husband took her arm. "Emma will find her way next door safely when she is done." He led his wife out.

The door of the workroom stood open. Mr. Franklin looked at me, I at him. We followed Brown and Emma in.

The staring skull greeted us from its shelf. Brown was just gesturing round his jumble. "Wh-what should you like to be told about first?"

"O, you must say," replied Emma. "Be my guide."

Poking up his thick-lensed spectacles, Brown began with Sul, recapitulating what he had told Mr. Franklin and me. He showed Roman seals and Saxon coins. He talked on Tacitus's references to *Aquae Sulis*, and Geoffrey of Monmouth's to *Hettum Bathum*, at which Emma's clear, smooth brow wrinkled not a jot. Another young woman might've found Brown's discourse wearisome, but so well did the girl seem to follow it that she finished it for him, relating how Princess Anne's visit in 1692 had set the seal on Bath's success:

"When she returned here as Queen, her approbation of the town made it a center of fashion. You writ that in your letters too, Mr. Brown."

He pressed his hands together. "I d-did not recall I s-said so much. How t-tiresome you must have found me."

"No." She trailed a gloved finger along his worktable. "Old tales are not tiresome. Nor are old things." She faced him straight. "One ought to respect age." She laughed lightly. "At least, that is what Aunt tells me. But she is right that I am engaged to go out with Mrs. Valentine. I can stay only a moment more."

"Then s-see this." Brown took a little leather pouch from a drawer. Inside was a shining, polished disk about three inches round. "One of my g-great treasures." He turned it before our eyes.

"Gold?" asked Mr. Franklin.

"G-gold."

"How extraordinary!" exclaimed Miss Morland.

In truth the disk was both beautiful and terrible, one side of it displaying the face of a grimacing beast, mouth open, hideously malignant; it gave me a chill. "There is a Latin inscription on the other s-side"—Brown turned it—"see?"

Mr. Franklin translated: "*Vanquish my enemy.*"

"I r-rescued it from the r-rubble of the baths. It was tossed in the w-waters more than fifteen hundred years ago. W-was it a prayer? A supplication?"

"A call for vengeance, it seems," murmured Mr. Franklin.

"The R-Romans had their superstitions."

Miss Morland laughed, but with a shiver. "How grave you look as you say that, Mr. Brown! As if such a thing were more than a toy. *I* am not superstitious. But I must go. Do not forget your promise to attend the ball tonight."

Mr. Franklin and I accompanied her to her door. Outside, the sky was ruffled by scudding clouds. A pig rooted amongst cabbages at one end of the lane, whilst at the other a tired-looking pony labored up from the quays.

When we were by the stoop of number two, Mr. Franklin asked the girl how she liked Bath so far.

"O, I am in love with it, sir!"

"It likes you too, I am sure. By the by, your other uncle, Titus Morland—your aunt has told me more of him. How dreadful that he should have given you up! I suppose you recall very little of him?"

"I was so young, Mr. Franklin—but I do recall a man whom mama and I visited. He smelt of tobacco and honey, for he always had a honey-sweet to give me. Too, he held me on his lap and told me stories and petted me, so that I came to think I was his favorite. How foolish children are! I have been told he had a terrible temper, but I do not recall it. I believed he loved me (he never had a daughter, you know)—but, then, that may be only what a girl who has lost her mama and papa should like to believe for I last saw him when I was but five."

"Yet he has a son?"

A bitter smile. "Does not a man always love his son best?" She made a little fretful motion with her hands. "I must go in.

116

Thank you for seeing me to the door, Mr. Franklin." Without another word, she fled.

Back at number three, we found Arthur Brown seated at his worktable, the gleaming Roman disk with its terrible, grimacing face and vengeful imprecation lying before him as if it meant nothing.

"Ought you not to put your treasure away?" asked Mr. Franklin.

Brown blinked distractedly. "You are r-right. It is gold."

Just past two came a reply to one of the notes Mr. Franklin had writ. It was from Richard Nash, the Beau himself, saying Benjamin Franklin might call upon him. The hand was unsteady, but the letter was signed with a grandiose flourish. "We shall go at once,"

Walking up Stall Street, Mr. Franklin told what he knew of Nash, who was now near eighty. "He was born in Wales. He was sent down from Oxford in the midst of scandal. He purchased a commission in the army but quit that, tried law at the Middle Temple but quit that, too. He had one talent, it seemed, and discovered it when he organized a grand celebration for William of Orange. This made his name, but it did not line his pockets (he has always been dependent upon gaming, I hear). Yet fortune smiled upon him, for he chanced to arrive in Bath just as she needed a man to tame her. Thus he became the King of Bath, whilst Bath became the Queen of watering places. He ruled her well for many a year. I am sorry to I hear his influence has waned."

This brought us to Westgate Street. We turned left, then right into Barton Street, past Queen Square, where I could see how the old medieval town flowered in new, elegant facades of golden Bath stone. We entered a drab lane. In his heyday Nash had lived in a splendid manse in St. John's Court, Mr. Franklin said, but no more. The gaming laws of 1745 had curtailed his livelihood, and he now subsisted in a shabby house in Saw Close, in the shadow of his former glory.

We knocked, and a little woman with a painted face, elfin-locks and bird-black eyes opened to us: Mrs. Juliana Papjoy, the only one who remained to tend to the Beau. "In honor Richard Nash exceeds the common as much as the oak exceeds the bramble!" she adjured as she led us to the man himself.

He sat in an ill-furnished parlor by a cold grate, a great doughty heap of a man, swollen with age and a lifetime of strutting. He had a red, heavy face marked by pinched eyes and a petulant mouth, and his sausage-like fingers were veined near to bursting. He wore a worn lace-edged coat, his ruffled shirt showed spots of grease, and his huge wig was tatty and frayed. Only the gold-enameled snuffbox with which he toyed looked of the first water.

This was the man who for half a century had promoted order, gaiety and an unbiased mingling of the classes in Bath.

" 'Twas given me by the Prince of Wales in 1738," muttered he of the box as we walked in. "I had many more, but I have had to sell 'em, curse all tradesmen who deny a gentleman credit! You writ to say you are Mr. Benjamin Franklin. Who the devil is that?"

"An American. Of Philadelphia. We have much in common, for I, too, have done a deal for my town." Mr. Franklin described the fire company he had helped to found, the city watch, the hospital, the college, the Philosophical Society, the first of its kind in America. "In short, though I am not a 'king' I am an honest member of the Pennsylvania Assembly."

Nash regarded him. "Then you may sit, sir, for an honest man must be allowed to sit by a king." He gestured. "But who is this boy?"

118

"Nick Handy. He listens to my thoughts, he tells me what he sees. He writes and draws, too. May he draw a picture of you whilst we speak?"

Nash glowered. "Will you make me young, boy?"

"I shall try, sir."

A great sigh. "Nay, have at me as I am! Stab me to the heart with your pencil!"

As we sat, I felt privileged to sketch the famous man who had so changed English fashion that hot-blooded youths no longer wore swords in the streets. The Beau's jowls wobbled as he wheezed out his list of exploits. He talked on his glory days, when he had snatched the embroidered apron from the Duchess of Queensberry's dress because it did not please his tastes; when he had tricked the Duchess of Marlborough into subscribing twenty-five guineas toward the Mineral Water Hospital for the poor and the sick; when ev'ry person in Bath bowed to his dictates. "And I but a gamester. Well, what if I am?—I am an honest one. Why, I have lost at loo and ombre more times than won! Did I not once complain bitterly of it to Lord Chesterfield? 'Does it surprise you, my lord, that bitch Fortune, no later than last night, tricked me out of five hundred pounds?' His answer made me laugh: 'The surprise is not at your losing money, Nash, but how you come by it to lose'— Ha!"

Mr. Franklin listened to yet more tales as if nothing could interest him more, and I wondered if he saw in Nash a portrait of what he might be when he was old: a spent husk whose only pleasure was in memory.

We should all want a pair of willing ears when those days came.

"But I must go out," Nash announced after a time. "Subscriptions for charities, sir. I have collected 'em all my reign. Mrs. Papjoy!" His housekeeper ordered a wheel-chair, which arrived in the hands of an oxlike brute named Bloggs. Nash put on a great white hat like a ship in full sheet, plumes aflutter, and gave us leave to accompany him. We walked alongside as he was bounced over the cobbles. He waved a hand to one and all, some citizens greeting him with respect, some with spite, some with venom. He saw it all, without illusion. "I have made enemies in my time, but a good king must tolerate even surly subjects."

Mr. Franklin inquired after Bath society. Did the Beau know Mrs. Sophia Valentine? Was she a respectable lady?

"Ha, if you mean, is she a Bath trull (for they come in fancy dress too), she is not. As to respectable, Mrs. Valentine is one of those who make respectability their game. She goes busily about. All of 'em go about."

"And her husband, Colonel Valentine?"

"I have never met him. Some women do not like you to know they have husbands, and some husbands do not like to be known; they keep to themselves. I tell you, sir, in better times all was open, all was plain. I saw to that."

"And Arthur Brown?"

"The delving fellow. He scrabbles in ditches and hounds people for old metal they dig out of their gardens—pah!"

"I read that the young Earl of Hendon is recently arrived in town. Do you know him?"

"He has let a house in the South Parade, though that is all that I can tell you. I have not met him yet, but he will present himself to *me* if he has any honor."

"Did his father frequent Bath?"

"Not in my reign."

"What of a fellow named Tom Bridger?"

"You ask after a great many people, Franklin."

"One learns to gossip in Bath."

"Then she has got you by the throat. Very well, I have seen

120

this Bridger. He is new in town, one of your wild young game-sters. He will burn himself out faster than a rushlight."

An old man supporting his twisted body upon a stick crept near. "Please, sir . . . " He held out a hand. His eyes were gaunt hollows, his cheeks sunken, and the Beau gazed upon him in startled pity. "Why, naturally, sir, seeing you are in need . . . " He dug in one pocket after another with growing chagrin. "Hem, I seem to've come out without my purse—"

Mr. Franklin's hand moved deftly. "You have not tried that pocket, sir."

The Beau felt in the one indicated. "Egad!" Drawing forth three shillings, he dropped 'em into the outstretched paw. "All for you, sir, from Richard Nash, Esquire. Feed yourself, find lodging—there's a good fellow." He peered at Mr. Franklin. "Fancy finding three shillings. Forward, Bloggs!" Bloggs bumped the great man on, and we left him at the Assembly Rooms dunning the wealthy.

We strolled on, Mr. Franklin deep in thought. At the bottom of Milsom Street, he said, "Miss Morland is taking the air, I see." Following his gaze, I discovered the pretty girl beside Mrs. Valentine in a small black curricle. Mrs. Valentine sat with her fixed little smile, whilst Emma twisted about, looking ev'rywhere in great delight. Seeing us, she waved, and Mrs. Valentine's trim little hat bobbed at us too before they headed higher in the town.

"So, the woman's husband likes not to be known," mur-mured Mr. Franklin. "It is a theme, Nicolas, it is a theme. "But let us try the bookstores. And a dish of chocolate, before we dress for the ball? I shall dance, Nick, I tell you. What new adventures will this eve bring?"

❦ 13 ❧

IN WHICH many men dance with a beautiful girl, and we are watched again at night . . .

B alls were held Tuesdays and Fridays in the Assembly Rooms; they began punctually at six.

Dressed, Mr. Franklin and I met Arthur Brown at his door shortly past five-thirty.

The beaky fellow looked ill-at-ease in his finery, a velvet coat and ill-gartered white stockings; but having said he would go to the ball, he did not hang back. As we walked through town Mr. Franklin said, "That medallion you showed us is worth much as history, but it is also valuable for its gold. Do you come upon much of gold in your digging?"

"V-very little. The medallion is singular. No thieves l-lurk about my door."

The Assembly Rooms were on the North Parade, at Terrace Walk. We footed it there in twenty minutes. We found a throng already gathered, the streets brimming with anticipation. Emma and Mrs. Valentine had rid in chairs—we saw 'em debouch—but there were many such chairs, disgorging scores of silken dresses and fine velvet coats. An anticipatory hum rebounded off the rich Bath stone. The sun was not quite down; its fading glow shed a lingering light, and I wondered if my pencil could capture the moment, both beautiful and brittle, as if the slightest blow might shatter it.

Dr. Woolridge arrived in a suit of clothes that appeared fusty amidst the brilliance of Bath brocade, and I was pleased at my own blue velvet. Mrs. Stevenson herself had cut and sewn the cloth, and Polly had put on the buttons.

Mr. Franklin wore a small, neat tie-wig for the occasion. He asked Woolridge how his wounded patient did.

"I saw him this morn," replied the doctor. "His arm heals remarkably . . . but, then, if I were as young as he—and as rich—I should have ev'ry reason to heal quickly too."

"Wealth and title are curatives, eh? O, give me that medicine!" We greeted Mrs. Sophia Valentine. In plum-colored, silver-brocaded taffeta, she was a picture of punctilio, though her husband was nowhere in sight. Beside her Emma wore a flowered blue velvet petticoat under a white satin gown. Her auburn hair was prettily curled, her green eyes danced, and many a gaze took in this new, radiant addition to Bath society.

But she was not too distracted to tweak Arthur Brown: "You are dressed to step out, sir, I see. I did not think you capable of such show! But will you see it through? Will you dance?"

"If *you* will d-dance with me, Miss Morland," replied he solemnly.

"Why, Mr. Brown . . . !"

Mr. Franklin gestured. "Shall we into the ball?"

Tall doors stood at the top of three wide stone steps. Mounting and passing through, we found ourselves in a spacious, high-ceilinged room lit by hundreds of candles in huge wheel-like lusters. Sconces flared at the walls whilst musicians in an elevated embrasure at one end tuned their instruments. Bodies pressed, voices babbled, and I was at first overwhelmed by the crush of velvet suits and powdered bosoms. Duchesses and wealthy merchants, courtesans and artists—all were here, and there was much greeting and milling. Yet, as six o'clock drew nigh, ev'ryone moved to places at the edges of the room.

A hush fell. The Beau arrived amongst us.

He wobbled to the very center all in white, like a huge white peacock. His face was beet-red, his wheezing stertorous. Welcoming us all, he proclaimed the start of the ball. Then came a silence. Peering about as if for a victim, the Beau drew near a trembling young girl of no more than sixteen. She quailed when he grasped her hand, but she allowed herself to be led to a withered stick of a grandfather four times her age.

The flutes and *violas da gamba* started to twitter, and the pair began to dance.

The ball had begun.

'Twas a minuet. The girl's first public dance? It might be the aged grandfather's last by his gasping and tottering, I should not have been surprised if he expired on the spot. 'Twas strange and comical, and I wanted to laugh and would have were it not for the poor girl's stricken expression and the Beau's stern watchfulness. How strict and formal it was! Only one pair at a time was allowed upon the floor, selected by the Master of Ceremonies by some capricious design. A second couple stepped out, a third, a fourth, and two hours passed in this same odd manner. I shifted my feet, my back began to ache, but no one objected. Only a growing glassiness of eye said that a single soul longed for respite.

The capstone to a day in Bath.

Emma was chosen to dance with a mustachioed officer—she acquitted herself prettily, and shortly afterward a break came. How grateful I was to be allowed to graze at a supper of sweetmeats, jellies, biscuits, ham and fowl, with plenteous dishes of tea. People jockeyed for position near Lord Whatsit or Lady

Whichever, but our modest circle kept to itself: Mr. Franklin, Arthur Brown, Dr. Woolridge, Mrs. Valentine, Emma, and I, by one of three long tables groaning with food.

Emma had just begun to tell of her ride to Beechen Cliff with Mrs. Valentine—"Such a splendid view from its vantage!"—when we were joined by young lord Edmund Darly. His golden curls were tucked under a powdered wig, and his suit of clothes was port-red, but otherwise he was as solicitous of Emma's good opinion as ever.

"Is he not beautiful," said Mrs. Valentine when Darly had kissed the women's hands. "Perhaps 'tis not customary to call a man so, but I think it may be allowed that some men possess beauty. Am I not right, Emma? But you, my dear, are quite beautiful, too." She surveyed the pair. "Indeed, you are two of a kind. Do you not think they are two of a kind, Mr. Franklin?"

"Of what kind, ma'am?"

She tapped him smartly. "O, I think you know, sir. You know."

"I hope you shall dance some dances with me, Miss Morland," urged Darly breathlessly.

"Will your arm allow it?"

"It hardly pains me at all."

"Then I should be pleased to dance with you. But do we not depend upon the Master of Ceremonies?"

"No. Country dances follow next. For them you may choose whom you please."

"I am glad to hear it!" Emma turned to Arthur Brown. "But I have also been asked to dance by Mr. Brown."

Darly regarded Brown graciously. "By all means, my dear fellow. And, Miss Morland, you must dance with Mr. Franklin as well, if you like. And Dr. Woolridge." He grasped her hand. "But I hope that you will dance most often with *me*."

"Why—"

"And I hope you will dance with me too, Miss Morland," a voice interposed.

We turned. Tom Bridger stood near us bobbing on his black shoes. Smiling, he took a step that delivered him by Edmund Darly's side, and as Darly turned to look at him, I examined the young men. They were equally handsome, but Tom Bridger was cut from different cloth: darker, slimmer. Though both were of an age, perhaps twenty-four, Darly was of a sturdier build, strong as a farmboy, with a dewy look, whilst Bridger was lean and dusky, with an ironic cast to his bright black eyes. He seemed to take all our measures in an instant, and I caught Emma's small shiver as his gaze examined her with a frankness bordering on insolence—but it was not a shiver of displeasure, I thought. *I know you, Miss Morland,* his look seemed to say, *I know what you seek.* Darly saw the look, too, and a small puzzled frown marked his brow, as if he had an inkling that Bridger might pose some challenge that Arthur Brown could not.

As for Brown, his deep-set eyes seemed to sink deeper into his face, and he looked pained.

Bridger reminded us where we had met. "The Pump Room this morn, do you recall? I am an acquaintance of Edgar Snow." He bobbed his head. "Mrs. Valentine, I believe? And Miss Morland." He took each woman's hand, kissed it, then bowed crisply to Mr. Franklin, who presented him to Dr. Woolridge and Arthur Brown.

"And this is Edmund Darly, the young Earl of Hendon," said Benjamin Franklin last.

"Your servant, sir," said Bridger. He smiled at Darly. "I could not help hearing that you wish to dance often with Miss Morland." He sent a glance at her. "She is a bewitching creature, is she not?"

126

Darly frowned. "I do not know that you should talk of her so."

"What? You do not find her bewitching?"

"I find her enchanting."

"Gentlemen," Emma put in spiritedly, "I do not care to be talked on as if I were not here."

Bridger pursed his lips. "In that case I shall talk to you direct." Stepping before her, he clicked his heels. "The music has started up again. Have you promised this dance to any man? If not, I ask that you have it with me." He held out an arm.

Emma looked at the arm. She looked at us. Her expression said she did not know what propriety demanded. Darly had asked her to dance in a general way, so had Arthur Brown—but neither had requested this particular dance. Mrs. Valentine looked disapproving of Bridger's boldness, but she gave no guidance, so after a small hesitation Emma took the offered arm. "Very well, Mr. Bridger, I should be happy to step out with you." She smiled in a provoking way at both Darly and Brown. *You must be quick if you wish to have me,* said her eyes.

"I shall be pleased to dance with the prettiest girl in Bath," Tom Bridger proclaimed as he led Emma into the line.

The country dances proved to be a wholly new thing, a lively intermingling of partners. As they went on Emma was much sought after. Other men asked for her hand, but Darly and Bridger were the chief rivals for her attentions. Yet how differently they went about it. Whilst Bridger danced with her, Darly stood by restlessly, like a stallion thwarted in his amours; but when Darly took Emma onto the floor Bridger simply chose some other lady. Their dancing was unalike, too. Darly labored at his, pumping his leg, whilst Bridger moved with careless ease, and Emma seemed to fly when he led her.

Mrs. Valentine had proposed that Emma and Darly were of a kind, but out upon the floor it was Emma and Bridger who seemed matched.

"You do not care for Mr. Bridger, Mrs. Valentine?" Mr. Franklin observed as he and the lady watched Bridger lead Emma by for the third time. "Any particular reason, may I ask?"

She sniffed. "A good coat admits any man to society in Bath. That is the charm of the town—and its peril. I do not know who this Tom Bridger is, but I have looked into him since this morning—I have my methods, sir—and I have learnt that he games."

"Did you not say that your husband games?"

She returned a withering look. "That is different. My husband is a respectable man, whereas *that* young fellow—" She took a breath. "Men prey upon women in Bath, sir. O, they do so ev'rywhere but all the more here, where intercourse is so free. For a dowry, if they can. For their charms. Miss Morland does not have a dowry, I am given to understand, but she has considerable charm. I have consented to show her about; thus it is my duty to shield her."

"I see," said Mr. Franklin as Mrs. Valentine's glittering eyes turned back to the dance. She was plainly resolute, but Emma was willful. Would all the resolution in the world shield her? For the present she danced as much as she pleased with dangerous Tom Bridger.

She stepped out with Mr. Franklin, too; he was a vigorous dancer, and she cried with delight when he led her down the line. She danced with Dr. Woolridge as well, and she took the floor with Arthur Brown, who was very grave, counting out the measures as his great nose turned about Emma's pert and pretty one. "At least you know the steps, Mr. Brown," said she when they returned.

"Th-thank you, Miss Morland."

"O, I did not say you knew 'em well!" Her laughter tinkled. Brown stood very still. "You ought not to s-speak to me like that, Emma."

The girl paled. "Why . . . I am indeed wrong, Mr. Brown. Can you forgive me?"

He shook his head. "I do not know that I shall. Too many people forgive you too much." Hands behind his back, he turned and walked away.

Emma gazed after him, thunder-struck.

Mrs. Valentine tutted. "How rude of him, child, to chide you for so little a thing."

"No," said Emma. "He was quite right."

"Do not fret." Mrs. Valentine formed one of her brilliant smiles. "Here is Edmund Darly to console you." She handed Emma to the young lord, who drew his prize into the dance.

As they stepped out, the Beau trundled up to us in his white plumage. His pouchy gaze followed Emma. "A pretty girl, Franklin. I like pretty girls! But who is the fellow she dances with?"

"Edmund Darly. The young earl we spoke of this afternoon."

"What? Then I believe I know him after all."

"I do not see how you can, Mr. Nash," interposed Mrs. Valentine, "for he has never been to Bath a day in his life."

The Beau frowned in displeasure. "Has he been to Tunbridge, madam?"

"I do not know."

"I have been to Tunbridge. I have even been to London, so do not presume to tell me whom I know." His rheumy eyes continued to follow Darly. "I know him, I say. I do not recollect where or how, but I shall recall. There is much in this old brain. I am setting it down, Franklin—*The History of Bath and Tunbridge These Last Fifty Years.*"

"Ev'ryone trembles," purred Mrs. Valentine, "for fear their secrets may be published."

The Beau turned to me. "You drew my portrait this afternoon, boy. Let me see it."

Obligingly I pulled my book from my pocket. Creaking near, smelling of snuff and age, Nash squinted. "Why, that is a puffed old man! Cover it up! Let no one see!"

"Nay, Mr. Nash." Mrs. Valentine's crinkled eyes were like agates. "The boy has got you to the life."

At eleven o'clock Beau Nash took center stage once more, waved his hand, and the music ceased. There were murmurs of disappointment, but no one disobeyed, for balls always ended at eleven.

The great lusters were lowered, the musicians put away their instruments, and everyone thronged out upon the street in a milling crowd, chairs jostling, torches flaring, a waning moon looking down from a spangled sky. Emma Morland emerged with Tom Bridger; she had found him beside her when she wanted an arm, so that Edmund Darly was forced to follow behind. Plainly he did not like this. At the bottom of the stairs, I gazed across the great square. Many chairs waited, amongst 'em Albert Noakes with his master's conveyance. He watched as we emerged, and I saw his sharp yellowish eyes narrow; he started, his expression twisting in fury, before he lowered his gaze and bit his lip. What had provoked him? In confusion I glanced at Mr. Franklin, but though he seemed to have seen as I, his blithe look gave nothing away.

Shortly all who wished were in their chairs, including Mrs. Valentine and Emma. Dr. Woolridge came to bid us good eve.

"I hope some of those you met tonight will seek your ministrations," Mr. Franklin saluted him.

"We shall see."

Tom Bridger sauntered off with two or three fellows, for some "deep play," he said, whilst Mr. Franklin, Arthur Brown, and I turned in the direction of Orchard Street. It grew late—night mists curled about our feet—but not ev'ryone went home, for many slipped into houses where private parties were in progress. Beggars who had no homes crept like ghosts amongst the shadows.

In our lodgings we bid pleasant dreams to Brown, who was in a somber mood, his beaky nose pale. Upstairs Mr. Franklin sank into one of the chairs by the hearth. He tugged off his shoes, and in the glow of the candles which Mrs. Finching had sent up, we talked on our day: of the King's Bath, the Pump Room, the meeting with Beau Nash, the Assembly ball.

But we talked of our mystery as well. How elusive it was. "I have never investigated such a will-o'-the-wisp," said Mr. Franklin, "but make no mistake, there is watching and waiting. There are chance meetings, too. I have thought on our highwayman. What if we did not merely come upon him? What if he waited for us? What if Emma Morland were meant to be kidnapped?"

"But why?" asked I.

"The answer to that would tell us much. Yet she was not kidnapped. Edmund Darly foiled that. Is the plan, then, brought forward to Bath? Damn me, Nick, the girl is somehow at the heart of it." He tapped his fingers before his chin. "And then there is Quimp."

Ice set in my bones.

"There is no question that I was the object of the attack at The White Hart. It was well-planned; it was aimed at preventing my going on to Bath. Who would wish to stop me? My enemy. Who, then, is that? Whom have I foiled in the past, and might foil again?"

"Quimp, sir," I was forced to allow.

He rose, sighing. "It may not be, Nick. Yet the rider who resembled him—since you told me of him, I have feared." He shook his head. "Dear me, I did not know the man's reach went so far."

"You must take care."

"Both of us must. Yet why should Emma Morland be the object of anyone's plans?"

"What if she is not? What if it is someone else? Edmund Darly, for instance. He is rich. He is a lord."

"In that case, is Emma the lure? O, it is a web! I come to suspect ev'ryone. Does Arthur Brown play a part? Tom Bridger? Is it only chance that Bridger befriended Edgar Snow? Ah, Nick." He patted my shoulder. "The devil with speculation. Let us rest."

I withdrew to my chamber. Undressing, blowing out my candle, I went to my window. Our third night. Could I sleep? The thought of Quimp terrified me, and I prayed for some flash of insight that would make ev'rything clear. I gazed out. Beyond the casements, Bath was silvered by moonlight, a town of shapes and shadows. Laughter burst out somewhere, as the Abbey church bells tolled midnight. What solitary minion rang that sonorous tune?

And then my mouth went dry, for boot-toes poked out of the darkness once more. They had not last night, and I had prayed the first occasion had been imagination, but here they were again. I sucked air, I blinked—and they were gone. Had the man who wore 'em seen me?

132

Dear God, who watches? thought I as I shut the casement and hurried into bed.

And whom does he watch?

And why?

❧ 14 ❧

IN WHICH we meet a neighbor and a
carefree young gamester sings a song . . .

T he Bath day, then, went thus: the waters in the early
morn, followed by the Pump Room; then breakfast
(public or private), the Abbey Church, shopping, strolling, rides amongst the hills, coffee shops, bookshops, tipping
of hats, curtseys, gossip; finally a ball or a play or a game of
cards to finish the day.

In short: society.

Under the surface flowed the same currents of spite and in-
trigue which I had met in London: the watching, the jockeying
for position, the calculation masked by seeming indifference.
For here was a town where nearly ev'ryone played a game—
games of chance, games of love, games to gain a fortune by
marriage, to gain a reputation by doctoring, to gain a living by
whoring. Only the truly afflicted seemed to play no game, hob-
bling about with pain-wracked faces to reproach the world of
fashion.

Having tried the King's Bath, Mr. Franklin seemed in no
great hurry to paddle in it again, though I should have liked to,
for I longed to glimpse Miss Morland's lovely limbs beneath
her yellow bathing dress once more. On the fourth day we

went early to two others, the Hot Bath and the Cross Bath, but only so Mr. Franklin might take their temperatures. The King's Bath had been forty-six degrees; the Hot Bath proved forty-nine whilst the Cross Bath was forty. The disparity caused him much speculation as we strolled back to Orchard Street, and when we were in our rooms he spent three-quarters of an hour scribbling drawings of channels and reservoirs beneath the earth to try to make sense of it. "There is too much of this world for a man to know it all, Nick," sighed he.

I thought on other matters. I had told him I had seen boot-toes last night; it had not pleased him. Was a new attack planned? As we went to the baths this morn I had peered into many countenances. Sev'ral eyes seemed to follow us: beggars', whores'. Had some been paid to watch? Did any work for Quimp?

Breakfast somewhat assuaged me: a hearty porridge. Afterward he and Arthur Brown talked for more than an hour, Mr. Franklin on his observations of ocean currents during his long voyage to England, Brown on the promising bronze fragments which he had unearthed in a barrow last month.

I sketched the garden, visible through the half-open eating-room door.

"But how did you like the ball?" asked Mr. Franklin when scholarly talk flagged.

"I am very f-fond of music, but I d-did not d-dance well, I fear."

"Nonsense, you acquitted yourself splendidly! Miss Morland seemed pleased to step out with you. Come, 'tis not how a man dances but who he *is* which matters, eh? As to Miss Morland, I take an interest in her. In her connections, too. Titus Morland, for example. Did you ever meet him?"

"No."

"Yet you called him wicked."

135

"I only meant that I do not see how he could t-turn his back on so f-fine a girl as Emma"

"She was but five when it happened. Not that that excuses the man. He has a son, I hear. Wesley. Do you know aught of him?"

"Little. He has been gone from England m-many years—something to do with the East India Company. I have heard he is l-lately returned to these shores."

"Because his father is dying?"

"I do not know."

"The son's reputation is a bad one. Why?"

"I d-do not know that either. There are m-many ways to make a bad name, Mr. Franklin."

Mr. Franklin smiled at him. "You are right in that." He jostled the scholar's arm. "Come, in any case, *you* have a good name, sir. You should be proud of that."

Brown looked as if being proud of one's name and being happy were two distinct things, and shortly he excused himself to creep back to the past, where a good name—or a bad one—could mean nothing to ghosts.

Mr. Franklin and I went out. The day was fine, the lanes aswarm with busy-ness. We examined the shops of the upper town: the little cake-houses and chocolate-houses, the ribbon shops, the fan shops, the mercers, at one of which, Purseglove's, the gentleman paid a guinea and six for two yards of rich Florentine. "For my wife," said he, tucking the package under his arm. "How I miss my Deborah and Sally!" We met Emma Morland in pink satin just outside a pastry shop. Mrs. Valentine had bought her a jelly tart, and the girl had crumbs upon her chin. Like a watchful mother Mrs. Valentine whisked the crumbs away. "Much better, child. Let us look at some bonnets. Good day, Mr. Franklin." She led Emma off.

The day grew spotty, shreds of cloud playing hide-and-seek with the sun. "Wesley Morland must be of an age with Tom Bridger," mused Mr. Franklin as we watched a game of bowls on the abbey green. "With Edmund Darly, too, for that matter, eh?"

"I suppose so, sir." This made me think on another matter, Arthur Brown's skin. I had imagined its walnut color came from digging in the open air, but I now thought, oddly: would not a fellow newly arrived from India have brown skin, too? I chid myself for such fruitless speculation.

Mr. Franklin peered at the sky. "Edgar Snow and Tom Bridger. An unlikely pair, do you not think? Who made whose acquaintance, I still wonder? Did Tom Bridger seek out Edgar Snow?"

"Shall you ask Mr. Snow, sir?" said I.

Mr. Franklin plucked up a gentleman's hat, which a gust of wind had tumbled across the green. "I believe I shall."

Yet Mr. Snow could not—or would not—give any very satisfactory reply. We encountered him at half-past eleven in Orchard Street, just returning from town. Mr. Franklin put his question in an off-hand way.

Mr. Snow took it in some confusion. "Why . . . I cannot say. I met Mr. Bridger in the Pump Room on my very first morning in Bath, did I not? Or was it the second morn? Perhaps it was in Milsom Street. In any case I met so many congenial gentlemen during those first days, that I cannot say which of us spoke first. Hem, ah, why, sir?—does it signify?"

"Likely not. He danced a great deal with your niece last night, that is all."

"O, dear."

"The news distresses you?"

"We do not know who he is."

"Do you see him about town?"

"I do—one always sees men one knows. He nods, we speak in passing, that is all. I believe he once took me for a gaming man." Snow emitted a little laugh, as to say how foolish that was. "But here is our neighbor," said he.

We turned. Along the cobbles, from the direction of Ham Gate, trundled the old man we had seen asleep in Bath Abbey. "Mr. Hobhouse," Snow greeted him as he drew near. The man looked up from under thick white brows, as if unsure whether he wished to meet us. Deciding yes, he barked a command to the servant at his elbow and was guided our way.

Mr. Snow presented Mr. Franklin.

"Isaac Hobhouse, sir," rumbled the old man in a deep and timeworn voice. He wore a snuff-brown coat over a buff waistcoat. A huge old-fashioned wig with thick rolls of curls sat like a helmet on his head. He gripped an ancient brass-knobbed stick in one hand whilst the other clung like a talon to his manservant's arm. He was an imposing man, with a lowering look and a world-weary air, plainly closer to seventy years than fifty. Yet though he moved slowly there was a quickness in his iron-gray eyes that said his brain worked well.

The three gentlemen talked of Bath. "I do not care for a place where the height of happiness is a pair royal at cards," Hobhouse sniffed.

"Where gaming and grace
Each other embrace,
And dissipation and piety meet—

eh, sir?" said Mr. Franklin. "But why, if I may ask, do you come here?"

"For the pleasure of departing, for it does me ten times more good to bid the town good-bye than to greet it. As for its 'society,' I find one may live here at as small an expense of wit as in any place in England." The old man was a merchant who had earned a knighthood, we learnt, but when Mr. Franklin asked what service he had exchanged for the title, Hobhouse only growled, "Making money, sir," and when pressed to say exactly how he had made it, he grew silent.

"You have a fine house, then?" persued Mr. Franklin.

"Damned fine."

"Pray, where?"

"Gloucestershire. East Cornford, if you must know."

"Why, then . . . do you know Titus Morland? He resides in Gloucestershire."

There was a wary silence. "Aye, I know him."

"Your manner says you do not like him."

"He and I are at odds; I shall say no more."

"They say that he is dying?"

Hobhouse's hand tightened on his brass-knobbed stick. "I should twist the knife in him to hasten his death if the job were not better done by slow and painful degrees! Good day, sirs." Barking another order at his servant, he was led to his door.

We stared after him 'til he had gone. Edgar Snow dabbed at his mouth with a cloth. "What a remarkable coincidence that a man who knows Emma's uncle Titus has taken rooms next door to us in Bath. 'Tis a small world, is it not, Mr. Franklin?"

" 'Tis an unlikely world, that is what it is. Tell me, did you choose your lodgings solely on the recommendation of Arthur Brown?"

"I trusted him to see to us, and he has, quite well. Why?"

"Coincidence, sir; I find it is frequently not what it seems. But I am glad to learn you trust Mr. Brown. Dr. Woolridge called upon you yesterday. Do you do well by him too?"

"I like the fellow—he is not one of your Bath quacks. He

has prescribed for both my wife and me. We hope for the best. I must go in. Good day."

When the man was gone Mr. Franklin frowned at Isaac Hobhouse's door. "I should like to know why he hates Titus Morland. They all hate Titus Morland. What has the man done to be so universally despised?"

I turned over similar questions, but could conceive no reply. Shortly after noon, a reply arrived to another of the notes Mr. Franklin had writ. This came from Ralph Allen of Prior Park, a grand estate south of town, laid out by John Wood the Elder. "I am asked to call this very afternoon. You will be on your own, Nick."

"It will give me a chance to draw the town."

A smile. "Then we both shall find profit." Mr. Franklin had much in common with Ralph Allen, he told me as he dressed. Allen had also risen from humble beginnings; he had reformed the Bath postal service as Mr. Franklin had reformed the colonial service; and like Mr. Franklin he was an inventor, having devised a tramway to transport stone from the Combe Down quarries to Bath. "But it is for his character that I wish to meet him, for he is reputed to be wise and generous both. Men as varied as Pope and Pitt, Chesterfield and Garrick, sup and talk at Prior Park." Humming, he set out from Orchard Street to do the same.

I was happy to wander about Bath with my sketching book. I drew beggars in King's Mead Square, whores in Avon Street, lepers in the Cross Bath. I also gave to a pitiful crippled child by the Mineral Water Hospital all the pence in my pocket. I observed the gentleman and ladies who ruled the better parts of town. They strolled with great elegance, but dignity could prove short-lived, for when an escaped goat charged through

Westgate Street, a foppish young gent was tumbled into a heap.

I also observed Mrs. Sophia Valentine.

I came across her at the corner of the High, standing by a yellow phaeton out of which Emma gazed with her flushed eagerness. Neither woman saw me, and pulling out my book I stopped by a coster's barrow to draw Mrs. Valentine. With her high chin and adamant eyes, she was a priestess of the right thing. She appeared to be looking for someone without wishing to seem to. Suddenly Edmund Darly popped out of a haberdasher's. She greeted him in apparent surprise, yet something about her manner made me certain she had known he would be there.

There followed some dispute about the phaeton: which of 'em should get into it with Emma, for there were but two seats. The young lord protested he could not take Mrs. Valentine's place—but when they appealed to Emma, she gave a nod, at which he leapt up, took the reins, and drove off happily. I frowned. Was this right? Right for Darly to take Emma? Right for Emma to allow it? Right for Mrs. Valentine to collude in the bargain?

The woman's eyes discovered me, and she did not look pleased. Yet she made no acknowledgment. Wearing a smile which said *I have done what is best for the girl*, she strode off amongst the throng.

I returned to Orchard Street around four, Mr. Franklin at five. He gave a full account of Ralph Allen, who had lived up to all the good said of him. "He is learned and humane. And he conceded that the Penns ought to be made to pay taxes." Mr. Allen had graciously shown Mr. Franklin his house, his gardens, his Palladian bridge; they had even walked to the famous

141

tramway, to watch blocks of Bath stone proceed on their rails into town. "Would I had been at Prior Park one day sooner, for Pitt himself—Chatham, you know—visited yesterday, but he returned to London this morn. How went your day, Nick?"

I told him of sketching. I told him of Emma's drive with Edmund Darly.

"Mrs. Valentine is forward in her care of the girl. To keep her from the likes of Tom Bridger? As to the propriety of it, I am not one for vain niceties. May not a young woman ride about with an honorable young man?"

"Beg pardon, but will the town think as you do?"

"True, Ben Franklin is not the world."

"I saw F. J. Mossop accost Mrs. Snow's maid in Orchard Street, too," added I.

He grew alert. " 'Accost,' you say? Tell all."

"It happened just past four. I was coming back by way of Bull Gardens when I saw him as I rounded the corner. He was waiting for her, I am sure of it. He did not wish to be noted. He went up to her, he put some questions—but when he saw me, he scurried away."

Mr. Franklin made a face. "What is the man about? For that matter, what are *all* of 'em about, prying and spying? I shall smoke a pipe, I shall mull the thing. Later: to the Snows, for we are invited this eve."

Mr. Franklin's pipe seemed to produce little result—or at least he told me none, and he, Arthur Brown, and I arrived at the Snow's at nine following a quiet hour in which I tried to read *Roderick Random* but could not for wondering how F. J. Mossop, a highwayman, and Albert Noakes—and perhaps even Isaac Hobhouse—fit together.

The next-door lodgings were cheery ones, with many candles lit in a large parlor. Mr. and Mrs. Fiske, the keepers of the house, were accommodating, and I forgot my trepidations for the time. It was to be an evening of talk and entertainment—Emma would play and sing, and I was to make pictures of ev'ryone to pass round when I was done. Dr. Woolridge was present in his sober plainwear, discussing curatives with Mr. Snow; and after a time Edmund Darly arrived too, finely dressed as befitted a young lord, bringing his fresh-as-air manner and his large blue eyes only for Emma. Their drive together—they had rid to Widcombe Hill, they told us blithely, as if there could be no impropriety in it—seemed to have brought 'em closer together, for they smiled at one another in little secret ways. Had Darly held Emma's hand? Had she permitted a kiss on the cheek? Mrs. Snow looked triumphant, but Arthur Brown sat in gloom. Emma flatly ignored him, and I did not wonder he looked sorry that she did not care even to rally him.

The talk turned to Spring Gardens, across the Avon. "You must go there, Emma!" burst out Mrs. Snow with a coy glance at Darly, which said she hoped her niece would go there with him—when Tom Bridger strode in.

We turned at the click of his boots; we met his white, even smile. His easy swagger carried him first to Emma. Taking her hand, he kissed it with his peculiar mix of nonchalance and audacity.

She colored. "Mr. Bridger. I did not know that you would be here."

"Knowing *you* would be here, how could I refuse your uncle's invitation?"

Edgar Snow cleared his throat. "Indeed, I met Mr. Bridger in Milsom Street today. I asked him to join us." He sent a wavering smile at his wife. "Did I not say?"

"No, you did not," replied she harshly.

"Mrs. Snow," said Bridger to her. "As charming as your

niece." Kissing the lady's hand, he bobbed his head at the rest of us. "Gentlemen. How glad I am to be amongst your company, for I have been busy about town all day."

"With your gaming friends?" asked Mr. Franklin.

A smile. "As to 'friends,' they are hardly that. In truth, they are even less gamesters, for they play hazard no better than faro."

"You beat 'em, then?"

"Naturally."

"Do they like that?"

Bridger laughed. "No, they do not. But if they are gentlemen, what can they do when an honest man wins?"

"Are they gentlemen?"

Bridger looked at him. "If a man has a half a crown to bet against three kings, I take him for a gentleman." He cocked his head. "Do you game, sir?"

"I have done so."

"Let us try a hand, then, some day."

"You would perhaps lose."

One of Bridger's black brows lifted. Mr. Franklin wore a frank, pleasant expression, and Bridger merely shrugged before he turned his easy smile upon the gathering at large. "But let us not talk of gaming. It is not respectable. One must get his money in trade, like you, eh, Mr. Snow? Or," to Darly, "he must have it from his father, never lifting a finger to earn a penny of it." Darly's jaw tightened, but Bridger's voice ran on in its airy way: "Let us talk instead on the waters at eight, the sermon at eleven, the coffee houses at three."

We attempted to do so, but an awkwardness had settled amongst us. Dr. Woolridge contrived to rescue us for a time by inquiring after Darly's arm, Darly proclaiming it was well on its way to healing: "Only a twinge now and then. You performed a miracle, doctor."

"Nay, nay." Woolridge said this dismissively, but he sent almost a reproachful look, as to say: why have you not broadcast your praise wider? After all, there were many thriving quacks about Bath who had not half the skills James Woolridge possessed.

The last guest arrived; old Hobhouse. When he had been introduced round, he wheezed to a chair by Arthur Brown and proceeded to sit near silent most of the eve, though his rheumy eyes watched us all. Emma was begged to perform. Arranging herself prettily at the spinet, she strummed the keys expertly, her voice high and clear, with a thrilling quaver. Her white throat was like a swan's, and Arthur Brown gazed at her with a longing painful to see. My heart went out to him.

But he was not the only admirer. Darly's large blue eyes fixed upon Emma, too—yet it was Tom Bridger who, without a by-your-leave, strode beside the girl. Bending near, he joined a fine tenor to her sweet trills. As their voices intertwined, she looked up at him, and I saw the shiver I had noted at the ball, of alarm but pleasure too at the attentions of this dark-eyed young man. He returned her look with a careless little smile, and regaining her equanimity she sang well—better than well—and we applauded and called for more. The pair obliged with "Where the Bee Sucks." Mrs. Snow frowned through it. Mr. Franklin listened with a fixed, unreadable smile. If Mrs. Valentine were here, what would she make of this sally against the girl she meant to protect?

I did not have to wonder what Edmund Darly made of it, for he fidgeted and frowned. He could not have been more provoked if it had been planned.

❦ 15 ❦

IN WHICH we dig at dead men's doors, and interrogations are made . . .

The next day was Sunday. I looked forward to it, for at the gathering at the Snows', Arthur Brown had proposed that some of us might wish to accompany him out upon the downs, "t-to see the old b-barrows." This had been greeted as a fine excuse for an outing.

At one o'clock we set out.

The day was windswept but clear, scents of clover, apple, and thyme wafting over the vast green fields. Our company consisted of Arthur Brown, Mr. Franklin, I, Emma, Darly, Mrs. Valentine (who had become one of us) and, surprisingly, Isaac Hobhouse, who, it seemed, could walk unaided when he wished. Mr. Snow had at the last moment regretted that his aches would not permit him so arduous a venture, and his wife had remained behind as well. Dr. Woolridge had been meant to go but had sent a note begging off. This made me think on last night. Mr. Franklin had taken Woolridge aside. "Hobhouse plainly needs a doctor," he had urged. "Why not seek his patronage?"

Woolridge had been unusually silent, sitting apart. At Mr. Franklin's adjuration, he had glanced under his brows at gruff old Hobhouse, who had gone to stand like an aged bear beside Emma. "I cannot believe he wants a doctor," he had replied. "Surely he does."

"Nay." Ducking his head, Woolridge had slipped away shortly after, with hardly a word. Had he conceived an antipathy toward Isaac Hobhouse?

I could still see how Hobhouse had bent over Emma. He had murmured to her and, though I had been unable to catch his words, the girl had answered him prettily; and I felt sure, by Hobhouse's altered manner—by a solicitude that seemed to creep upon him—that Emma Morland had made yet another conquest in Bath.

As we drove into the Mendips, I wondered how Mr. Franklin took it all. Did he find clues in these moments? He continued to investigate our mystery; he had done so last night, drawing aside the maid Mossop had accosted. He had told me later what he learnt: "She had no chance to discover Mossop's intent, for he darted off as soon as he saw you, Nick. But he was not the man who asked her about Emma in London; of that she was sure. 'But what did this London man seek to know?' I asked. 'What Miss Morland was like,' she replied. 'I told him the mistress was fanciful.' Is that not curious, Nick?"

The sky was a blue dome, our horses' hooves clopping whilst reins jingled merrily. We rid in a line, in three conveyances, Mr. Franklin, Arthur Brown, and I in a small, open carriage at the rear. Darly had wished to sit next to Emma, but old Hobhouse had commandeered her, and it was they who rid just ahead of us, Darly and Mrs. Valentine making the best of matters in the most forward gig. The sun had dried yesterday's puddles, so we trotted at ease, making for the ancient Fosse Way near Combe Way. I peered ahead. Isaac Hobhouse's beetlelike back made a great contrast to Emma's bright, lively person under the parasol which Mrs. Valentine had insisted

147

she carry to keep off the sun. Hobhouse spoke to the girl, making slow, ponderous gestures. How conspiratorial the pair seemed. Emma's gay laugh floated back now and then, and Edmund Darly glanced round at her often.

Three-quarters of an hour delivered us to an outpost of the ancient Roman *Aquae Sulis*. We got down in a field of tumbled stone, and Arthur Brown began to show us about. This was his kingdom—his beaked nose held sway here—and I saw Emma regard him with interest if not admiration. Were her green eyes merely amused? In any case, she paid strict attention to all Brown said, adding now and then some bit of knowledge from the letters he had writ.

"Quite r-right, Emma. Very g-good, Emma," replied he at these moments. He showed us the tombstone of Lucia Vetellius Tacinius, half-buried in the sedge, whilst Mrs. Valentine chattered on her own theme. "Do not they look perfect together?" she insisted of Darly and Emma. " 'Twould be a pity were they not to ride together when we return."

Hobhouse growled at this.

We climbed over hummocks. Here was another half-buried slab. "An armorer of the Twentieth L-Legion, Valera Victrix." Arthur Brown pointed to the timeworn inscription on the lichened stone.

"Come, Brown," chid Darly as a breeze whipped his blond curls about his brow, "it is *old*. How can old things interest you when young ones are so much more charming?" He gazed meaningly at Emma.

Brown fell silent. He led us over a stile to an ancient Celtic earthwork. Here cows grazed, where once terrible battles may have been fought. Uncovering a long spade he had left hidden, he proceeded to dig in a tumble of earth which had previously proved rewarding, he said. Within moments he turned up a crude coin—a *denarius*, he called it.

Emma's eyes lit as he held it out. "May I dig, too?" asked she.

Darly laughed. "Surely you cannot wish to dirty your hands." But she had already snatched up the spade.

Mrs. Valentine looked alarmed. "This is unseemly, child! You will soil your dress."

Emma paid no heed. "I want to find something." She began to dig, but awkwardly. "Will I find something, Mr. Brown?"

"If you d-dig long enough. Shall I help?"

"O, please!" He joined her, and together they worked the spade. They stood close together, and it was Arthur Brown and Emma Morland who looked perfect together now. Mrs. Valentine wore an expression of barely contained disdain. As for Darly, he smiled indulgently, though he was plainly puzzled at this breathless delving.

A fragment was dislodged. It might have been tossed aside had Brown's expert eye not glimpsed it; he picked it up. "You have f-found something, Emma."

She clapped her hands. "*We* have found something, you mean."

Scraping away encrusted earth, Brown held out a broken bit of clay. It was small, no prize, but it was incised with a curved design, and Emma's eyes danced as she examined it.

"It is of ancient Britain," Brown pronounced. "Before the R-Romans came."

"Truly?" The girl turned it in her fingers. "It makes me shiver to think that hands like mine—or yours, Mr. Brown— fashioned it so long ago." She stood close. She looked up at him. "May I keep it?"

"I d-do not think that he who l-left it behind will mind."

"His ghost may haunt you," smiled Darly. "But how can you want a dusty shard?"

Emma turned. "Because Mr. Brown has writ much of such

things in his letters. Even a fragment can tell stories, which he has passed on to me since I was young. Many's the time I thought on 'em as I lay abed, and I have longed to dig in the earth as he does, to discover some old, rich thing—rich in history, I mean."

Brown gazed at her as she spoke. He was plainly moved, and his Adam's apple bobbed. "Why—"

But Darly stepped betwixt 'em. He clasped Emma's hands, he gazed deep into her eyes. "I should like to build you a room, then, with many cupboards, in which you might keep as many old things as you like, and a deep chair where you might think on history all you wish."

Emma smiled at him as the long grasses bent under a rippling breeze. "You are very agreeable, Mr. Darly." Dropping the clay fragment into the little purse which also contained her journal, she linked her arm in his and they walked off in the direction from which we had come.

We watched their backs. We made to return, too—but Mrs. Valentine discovered she was interested in old tombs after all. Did she mean to slow us? In any case, when we came to the stand of beeches where our conveyances had been left, Emma and Darly had already climbed into the smallest gig and were driving away.

Sophia Valentine rid back to Bath with Isaac Hobhouse. In our carriage Arthur Brown sat tragically glum. Mr. Franklin observed the larks swooping above the fields. "How agile they are! Does the particular forked shape of their tails, as opposed to the fanned or pointed shapes of most birds', aid their flight? I shall think on that."

We were back in Bath by four. Darly and Mrs. Valentine went their ways, whilst the rest of us rid to Orchard Street. Isaac

Hobhouse appeared sunk in thought as he watched Emma Morland step down before number two. What went on in the old man's brain?

My attention was distracted by Edgar Snow, who arrived just then at the bottom of the street. Had he not said his aches kept him at home? He was with Tom Bridger, deep in talk. Mr. Snow did not at first see us—but when he did he halted, stopping Bridger with him. Their confabulation continued, of some gravity it seemed. Bridger shook his head at Mr. Snow's expostulations; then he sent his wanton smile our way, as if he should be delighted to join us. But Snow discouraged him, and with a thoughtful look, Bridger acceded. Sending us a flourishing salute, he sauntered agreeably out of sight.

"Met him in a coffeehouse. Randal's. In Milsom Street," muttered Edgar Snow when he came up to us.

"Gaming?" inquired Mr. Franklin.

"Dear me, no!"

"I meant Mr. Bridger."

"I hear that Bridger games, but I know nothing of it. Come, Emma, we shall go in together. Good day."

"I fear Edgar Snow plays at cards with Tom Bridger," said Mr. Franklin when we were alone in our rooms. "I pray he does not lose too much. In any case, I am glad the post has come." Mrs. Finching had given him a letter, which he opened by the window. "It is from my goodwife, Nick—Mrs. Stevenson kindly sent it on. Dear me, distressing news: British troops may be billeted in Philadelphia, to fight the French and Indians! Gunpowder and barracks," he tutted. "I do not like it." He fretted on more, however, for other letters he looked for had not come. "The post cannot deliver what respondents do not write. Why do they not answer promptly?" He was agitated, and I won-

151

dered: did these tardy letters have any bearing on our mystery? Plumping down at the desk, he scribbled, sanded, and sealed for a quarter of an hour.

We went out to post these new missives shortly before five. The winds had died to a rustling stillness, but a black mass of clouds loomed; rain would come. Nonetheless Bath went on its bustling way, like an inexorable clockwork. As we strolled, Mr. Franklin reflected on the town's past. He speculated on the lost Celtic years, the Roman, the Saxon, the Norman. "We walk on history, Nick, old bones, old lives. . . . " Yet our recent chain of events was not far from his thoughts. "All hangs from that first link, the broken seal of Arthur Brown's letter, I am sure. Well, 'there is nothing covered that shall not be revealed; and hid that shall not be known,' We shall find the truth."

We came upon Emma Morland, on a stone bench by the Abbey. She was companioned by her aunt. "I have been persuaded to shop," sighed Mrs. Snow. "How exhausting it is! We have stopped to rest."

"Your husband was not so unwell that he himself could not go out today, I noted," observed Mr. Franklin.

"With Tom Bridger, too! I do not know why he must be friends with the man."

Emma had been scribbling in her journal. She looked up. "*I* quite like Mr. Bridger, Aunt."

"I forbid you to do so, child!"

Emma only smiled.

"You seem to like Squire Hobhouse, too, Miss Morland," said Mr. Franklin. "And he you, for you talked much on our outward journey. What on, pray?"

"Money."

"Money?" said Mrs. Snow suspiciously. "Whatever for?"

"Was it a happy subject?" interposed Mr. Franklin.

"No. He said that though he possessed a very great deal of it, it had bought him no joy. He seemed to wish this to give me a lesson, but I refuse to learn it. Having a great deal of money must be splendid! (It is always those who have it who disparage it.) But . . . the oddest thing—Mr. Hobhouse is acquainted with Uncle Titus, he told me. Uncle is a very wicked man, he says."

"He is right in that," proclaimed Mrs. Snow.

"And how does Mr. Hobhouse come to know your uncle?" asked Mr. Franklin.

"By a great wound, he said—fancy that!"

"What sort of wound?"

"He did not say, and I did not ask; I do not think he wished me to, for he seems a very secret man. There is something sad about him, too." The girl buried her nose in her journal once more.

When we returned to Orchard Street we found the very man we had talked on waiting for us in Mrs. Finching's parlor. Isaac Hobhouse glowered at us from a deep chair as we came in. "Mr. Franklin," rumbled he, groaning to his feet.

"Your servant, sir," replied Mr. Franklin.

The old man frowned at me.

"O, you may speak in front of Nick, for he is my second pair of ears; he serves to jog my memory when I forget what my own ears have heard. Come"—Mr. Franklin and I settled onto the sofa opposite the man whilst he sank back in his chair—"what is the purpose of your visit?"

"Edmund Darly. What do you know of him?"

Mr. Franklin smiled pleasantly. "May I ask why you inquire?"

"He pays court to Miss Morland."

"You take an interest in her, then?"

Hobhouse's liver-spotted hands twitched. "A girl such as she must marry well."

"All girls should marry well. Why Emma Morland in particular?"

The old man bit his lip. "Because I like her, sir."

Mr. Franklin rubbed the head of his stick. "You have a very short acquaintance to decide you like her well enough to meddle in her affairs."

"Meddle?"

"Do you always take young girls under your wing in this manner?"

"You grow impertinent."

"Perhaps. But I, too, take an interest in Miss Morland's well-being." Mr. Franklin spread his hands. "Still, I see no reason why you should not know ev'rything I know about Edmund Darly." Matter-of-factly he told it.

"Hum, a young earl, of good character, then," mused Hobhouse when the tale was done. "Thoughtless at times. Rash. But without the arrogance of his breed—is that it, Franklin?"

"To the best of my knowledge."

"And this peculiar fellow you reside with, Arthur Brown?"

"Peculiar? He is his own man. That may be out of the ordinary, but it is not bad. He is of good character, I believe."

"Is he not poor?"

"He does not keep a coach and four, if that is what you mean. But he has a sufficiency; he seems content in that."

Hobhouse cleared his throat. "He is fortunate, then, for though I am rich, it provides no contentment to my heart."

"Come, there are other contentments. A wife? Children?"

"As to that . . . good day, Franklin. Help me, boy." Jumping up, I aided the bearlike man to his feet. I felt a fierce, determined strength in his grip upon my arm, and in less than a moment he was gone.

Mr. Franklin stood beside me as the latch fell. "Make no mistake, Nicolas, it is no coincidence that delivered Isaac Hobhouse to Orchard Street."

❧ 16 ❧

*IN WHICH we walk in a garden
and three men duel at cards . . .*

M r. Franklin and Arthur Brown talked of philosophical
and historical matters again next morn, but Brown
was plainly downcast, his deep-set eyes troubled.
"Can Edmund Darly be good for Miss Morland, Mr. Franklin?" he blurted.

Mr. Franklin lifted a brow. "How could he not be? But do
you know of some understanding betwixt 'em?"

Brown hung his head. "No. I only w-wish—"

"You wish the best for Emma, naturally. As to your question, Darly is handsome, rich, titled. How could he be bad for
any girl?"

Brown's great Adam's apple surged, but he raised his chin; it
was an heroic moment. "He m-must be g-good for her, then.
And I shall be happy for Emma even if she marries him."

Mr. Franklin tutted. "Come, man, do not wed 'em before
they cry the banns. But I agree, it is time to ascertain the young
lord's intentions. I shall question him for both of us."

It had been settled that a party would go to Spring Gardens in
the afternoon; Mr. Franklin would thus have an excellent op-

portunity to speak to Edmund Darly. Meantime he read in the coffeehouse whilst I added to my portrait gallery of Bath denizens. The newspapers were rife with scandal, he told me: two elopements, another duel. The duel had been a farce—one of its principals had misfired before he was nicked by his opponent's ball, and both had been arrested. Mr. Franklin shook his head. "Thus is honor avenged."

Spring Gardens lay across the Avon. The ferryboat departed by the North Parade, so shortly after noon our party assembled on its landing beneath skies that were friendly once more: Mr. Franklin and I, Arthur Brown, Emma under Mrs. Valentine's watchful aegis, strapping Edmund Darly glowing like a god. Isaac Hobhouse did not join us (he had sent to say the distemper kept him indoors).

Dr. Woolridge had been asked. He had said yes only after he learnt that Hobhouse was indisposed.

Mr. Franklin took the doctor aside when he arrived. "What an odd fellow Isaac Hobhouse is, eh? He does not wish anyone to come near him." He peered at Woolridge. "Last night I thought, perhaps, that you knew the man?"

"Certainly not."

"He is a mystery, then. But, how go your affairs? Do you minister to dukes and princes yet?"

Woolridge glanced at Edmund Darly, hovering beside Emma. "I am afraid I do not."

Mr. Franklin looked that way, too. He nodded. "I quite agree that our young lord should advertise you amongst his friends. He does not? Why, you cured his arm so well that one would hardly know he had been wounded."

The ferry arrived at half-past twelve. As we boarded with the other pleasure-seekers, I glimpsed Albert Noakes at the edge of the green. Again? His sallow face and brazen eyes made me recoil, though he darted away promptly, as if he did not care to be seen. Did he spy upon his master? Us? I glimpsed another person we knew, at the opposite edge of the green: F. J. Mossop in his voluminous greatcoat. I tugged at Mr. Franklin's sleeve, and his knowing nod said he had observed 'em too. Mossop hurried away. Did he follow Albert Noakes? Did they meet?

This reminder of the odd, spying nature of our mystery cast its shadow, but I had little time to let it trouble me. The day was fresh and fine. Too, the Avon was not wide, perhaps fifty yards, so we were soon across, and Spring Gardens proved a delightful diversion, laid out in walks and parks, with parterres of flowers amongst which we might wander to breathe in Nature and observe our fellow men. We were to lunch, but not before we sampled the walks; so we joined the many other strollers who moved in little groups, like figures in a painting, their easy, elegant manner bred by wealth.

Watching 'em, I could not disagree with Emma Morland: it would be no bad thing to have money.

Darly had wrapped the pretty girl's arm in his. "I must not forget to tell you that a letter from my sister arrived just this morn," he told her, pulling it from his coat. "She says she has received my own, telling of you, and I am happy to report that she longs to meet you." Beaming, the young lord held out the letter so that any might read it if he would. I glanced at it with no very great interest, noting phrases about the delights of Lawn House, near Bristol, where Darly's sister evidently visited her dear friend, Miss Janeway. She expressed alarm over our encounter with the highwayman and prayed that Darly would not "dash into things" in his customary manner. There were a few lines at the end saying she hoped to meet "the charming Miss Morland who has so captivated my dear brother."

Mr. Franklin squinted at the paper. "May I?"

"Assuredly, sir." Darly gave the letter over, and Mr. Franklin perused it. A sharp crinkling of his eyes made me think he gleaned something of especial interest, but all he said was, "I see your sister loves you well," as he handed the letter back.

"She is the most delightful sister!"

"Do you not admire a man who loves his sister, Miss Morland?" purred Mrs. Valentine, beside Dr. Woolridge. "A man who loves his sister must make a fine husband."

Arthur Brown looked resigned at this.

After luncheon Mr. Franklin drew Darly apart. "Do you intend to ask for Miss Morland's hand, my lord?" asked he bluntly.

We stood on a little terrace beside trees hung with reddish bloom. Lapwings plunged in the fresh, blue air over our heads, whilst the Avon sparkled nearby. Darly's artless look never faltered; if anything, it became more candid, as if he were relieved to be drawn on the subject at last. "You come to the point, Mr. Franklin. How I like a man who speaks plain!" He clutched his heart. "Is it so obvious that I favor Miss Morland? I do not hide it—I do not think I could." In eager agitation, he paced the Bathstone flags. "Do you know, sir, I have met many an eligible woman since I came of age. They are thrust upon me in drawing rooms ev'rywhere, for my name and fortune. They make eyes at me, they snap their fans. Yet I have never met one like Miss Morland. She has beauty, but she has wit, too—upon my word, more than I possess. And she has truly delightful ways. In short, though I own that I have known her only a very little time, I am sure of my heart. I *do* wish to ask for her hand, Mr. Franklin. My only fear is that she will refuse me."

"But are you free to marry whom you choose?"

"My heart is not engaged elsewhere, if that is what you

159

mean. Nor have I made promises to any other woman."

"I mean, might your father make objections?"

Darly had clearly thought on this. He nodded vigorously. "Emma is not titled, it is true. And she has little dowry—curse the world which says such a thing matters! But I am on good terms with father of late; I do his bidding. And if my sister Caroline can be persuaded to my cause—as I am sure she will be once she meets Emma—and when father sees Emma's grace and good sense, I am certain all obstacles can be overcome."

"I hope your confidence proves well founded. But the girl is headstrong. That is one of her charms; yet it also might lead her astray."

"And me, too, you mean?" Darly puffed his chest. "I am honorable, sir!"

"I do not doubt it. But—forgive me for saying so—are you fully assured that Emma Morland is as honorable? Can you be certain *she* is not after your fortune?"

Darly looked thunder-struck. "Sir!"

Mr. Franklin held up his hands. "I do not mean to slander Miss Morland. I merely take an interest in you both. As for the young woman"—he chose his words carefully—"I believe she is quite sincere in what she seeks."

Darly appeared mollified. "I take you at your word, then, Mr. Franklin. You say you inquire in Miss Morland's best interest, and I believe you. I am happy, too, to've answered your questions—as I shall answer any that are made. But hear you this: I mean to make Emma Lady Darly one day." He strode off.

"What an advancement that will be," murmured Benjamin Franklin to the young lord's back.

* * *

All over Bath little parties took place each nightfall. Some were proper, but others were bumptious routs of rakes and doxies; yet others were intimate suppers where Lord M——conjoined with Lady C——despite their spouses. Ours was very proper that eve—or began so. It was at our lodgings for a change, and most of us were present: the Snows, Emma, Mr. Franklin, Arthur Brown, I sketching in a corner, Edmund Darly, the brittle Mrs. Valentine (though we had yet to meet her husband). Recovered from his distemper, Isaac Hobhouse sat with us too, like a disgruntled bear, with a rug thrown over his lap by the fire.

Dr. Woolridge had begged off.

We began by recounting to Mr. and Mrs. Snow our afternoon at Spring Gardens. This was followed by games: Hot-Cockles and Parson-Lost-His-Cloak, which Mrs. Snow and Mrs. Valentine would not play, being deep in talk (their murmurs seemed to marry Emma and Darly).

Tom Bridger arrived.

He came in with his customary swagger, his snapping black eyes taking us in. "I tell you," said he plumping his cloak into the waiting maid's arms, "I am glad to've arrived safely, for a pair of rascals who were very disagreeable yesterday at cards pursued me from my rooms. You remember 'em, Snow? Bodger and Millford?"

Edgar Snow ducked his head. "Hem, ah, why, yes, I believe . . ."

His wife stared at him in amazement.

Mr. Franklin greeted Bridger heartily. "I sent our young friend a note this afternoon," explained he to sev'ral inquiring eyes.

"Did you?" replied Mrs. Valentine coldly, whilst Edmund

Darly took a half-step in front of Emma, as to say, "You shall not come near her, sir."

But the young woman skipped past him. "We are very pleased to see you, Mr. Bridger." She gave a little curtsey. "Perhaps we shall sing some more tonight?" She beamed round, but her aunt only scowled.

Mr. Franklin, Arthur Brown, Emma, and Tom Bridger settled into a game of Questions-and-Commands. Edmund Darly watched unhappily. Old Hobhouse remained brooding by the fire, whilst Mrs. Snow quietly interrogated her husband. I sat drawing, thinking. We made a civilized gathering, did we not? Surely no one held a secret hand.

A warm punch was served, and parlor games gave way to talk of other sorts of games: cards and dice.

Darly, who had sat fidgeting and snatching at his side, where his sword would hang if he wore one, burst out, "I have played me some cards! And done well at 'em, too!"

Tom Brider's eyes turned to him. "O?"

"I tell you, I have!"

A small smile. "My dear sir, I do not doubt you."

Emma looked from one to the other, and some devil made her clap her hands. "Play, then, both of you! To see who is the better!"

A deep silence fell, marked only by the crackling of the fire. Darly said, through his teeth: "I should not mind."

"Nor I," said Bridger.

"Do not play!" urged Mr. Snow somberly. "I tell you, do not."

But Bridger was sitting forward now. "Ombre," said he, sending his smile into Darly's face. "Let us make it ombre. A very little game? For very little stakes?"

Emma's pretty brow furrowed. "I did not mean that you should play for money," said she. "I never meant that."

162

"O, I always play for money," replied Bridger. "I do not sit down to cards for nothing."

"Impudent," I heard Mrs. Valentine murmur.

"I do not mind playing for money," Darly flung out.

Bridger regarded him. "Then, let us do it, sir."

Though no one save Bridger looked pleased at the venture, no one stopped it. The landlady fetched a deck of worn cards, and a small deal table that had stood in a corner was brought to the center of the room. Two chairs being placed on opposite sides of it, the young men sat. Bridger carried bank notes in a leathern purse; these he placed carelessly on the green baize cloth which had been spread upon the table.

"I do not carry such sums about me," said Darly stiffly.

"I shall trust your gentleman's bond."

The play began.

We gathered to watch, Arthur Brown with his great nose gleaming, Mr. Franklin with his round little spectacles glittering, Emma staring at what she had wrought, Mrs. Snow squinting disapprovingly whilst making sure she had a good view. Even old Hobhouse had groaned up to join in, and his wheezing, along with the soft whir and plop of the cards punctuated the game. First Bridger won a hand, then Darly. Bridger. Darly. Then Darly won three in a row. Then four. At this he sent a beaming look at Emma, as to say: *You see, I have got him!*—but Bridger, who was by then near an hundred pounds down (larger and larger bets were made), appeared undismayed. On the next hand he bet all that had been bet before. A murmur ran round as Darly peered at his cards. "Damned if I shall not!" Scribbling a promissory note, he spread out three queens—and won.

He had, then, two hundred pounds of Bridger.

How his smile spread! Bridger did not smile. He looked long at Darly. He counted his remaining banknotes. At the next hand the bets mounted alarmingly. At last Darly pushed all he had won upon the table. "That for you, sir."

Bridger pursed his lips. "I have just enough to match you," said he, and there lay in notes and promises eight hundred pounds upon the green baize cloth.

Mr. Snow moaned as if t'were his own money at hazard.

Darly lost.

The young lord gaped. He peered at his cards, as if he could not believe they had betrayed him. For his part Bridger did not crow, only silently drew the pile of winnings toward himself, though an ironic twist of smile teased his lips. Darly glared at Bridger. Had the young lord been gulled? His fingers curled upon the tabletop. "Why . . . why—" he stammered.

"May only two play?" said Mr. Franklin into this charged moment.

All turned. The gentleman stood very still behind Darly's chair, his fringe of gray-brown hair falling from his balding crown, a look of patient inquiry upon his plain, round face. He was no stranger to cards. He had practiced 'em to learn their tricks (he liked to master many things), and he had learnt well too, for he had defeated the great sharper, Mr. Mimm, in the most notorious gaming den in London. I peered at him. What did he intend?

I turned to Tom Bridger. "My dear sir, is it not too rich for you?" he drawled. "A lord, as Mr. Darly, is one thing—what can a few hundred pounds mean to him?—but you . . .?"

"You proposed yesterday that we try a hand," said Mr. Franklin. "I should like to do so now."

Bridger shrugged. He fixed his little smile upon Darly. "What say you, sir? Shall we admit him to our game?"

Darly contrived to sputter yes, and a third chair was found.

The cards began to fly.

No doubt Darly hoped to show up Bridger by recouping his

loss—but that did not occur, for after a quarter hour's give-and-take, in which each man won and lost equally, he began to go down, as did Mr. Franklin. I felt sure Bridger cheated. Why did Mr. Franklin allow it? Had he met his match? His brow furrowed fretfully, and I understood why; for though I had no idea how Bridger manipulated the cards, the table was plainly his. Emma stood next to Arthur Brown, leaning nearer and nearer him in a kind of fascinated horror as the play progressed. At her proximity Brown looked either in pain or ecstasy, I could not tell which—and perhaps at that moment there was no difference betwixt the sensations in his heart. As for Mr. Franklin, he lost yet more, 'til he was forced to ask Bridger and Darly to accept his I-owe-yous as well. This granted, the play continued, Mr. Franklin looking increasingly distressed, 'til a great sum lay upon the table, near twelve hundred pounds.

"This is madness," Edgar Snow muttered.

"Nay, sir, 'tis gaming," replied Tom Bridger, "and he who games must be willing to pay, to prove which I shall raise the stakes. Two hundred pounds more, gentlemen. Will you follow me to that dangerous height? Have you the mettle for't?" His black eyes glittered.

Darly was provoked. "Damn you, yes!" cried he.

Mr. Franklin was silent.

Bridger looked at him. "To you, sir."

We all looked at him. "I ask myself—" said he ambiguously.

"Do not, sir," begged Edgar Snow. "You have lost too much already."

Mr. Franklin sighed. "Yet I must try." To Bridger, "I am for you, sir."

"Aha!" Bridger showed his cards: three knaves and two treys.

Edmund Darly paled. Swallowing hard, he folded his hand.

Eyes went again to Mr. Franklin.

"No?" said Bridger with his small smile. He reached out to the notes upon the table. "I am very sorry, sir."

Mr. Franklin stayed him. "Nay, sir, 'tis I who must be sorry for you."

"What?"

"He who games must be willing to pay." He showed four kings.

Bridger sat as if frozen. Never had I seen his heedless manner ruffled, but it was ruffled now. "B-but you cannot—"

"Cannot? Why?"

"Ha!" exploded Edmund Darly, thumping the table.

"O, excellent, sir!" Mrs. Sophia Valentine purred.

Bridger's mouth opened, closed, and he stared at Mr. Franklin with a narrowing gaze, in which a light of understanding dawned. Likely he could ill-afford to lose sev'ral hundred pounds; but to give him his due, he only leant back, cool as a cat. "As you say, sir, one must pay. I did not take your measure." His voice hardened. "I have took it now. 'Tis a lesson dearly won."

"As are all worthy lessons," replied Mr. Franklin. "Yet one of my principles is never to game."

"Then, why have you gamed tonight?"

"I mean, I never game in earnest. Thus: I shall not take your money."

"What?" exclaimed Edmund Darly.

"Or yours," said Mr. Franklin to him. Scraping back his chair, he held up both hands. "Nay, sirs, do not protest, in honor's name or any other. I will not take it, I tell you—though it goes without saying that, as *you* played in earnest, if you had won, I would have paid ev'ry farthing. Perhaps, gentlemen, you had best take a lesson from this."

All in the room stared. "You are too good, sir," uttered Mrs. Valentine stiffly.

"T-truly honorable," Arthur Brown declared.

"Money should be earned by honest labor," asserted Benjamin Franklin.

"Has this not been delightful!" burst out Emma with an airy laugh. "I shall set it all down in my journal." Slipping from Arthur Brown's side, she divided up the banknotes and promissory notes that lay upon the table. "There, now, you must take 'em back. I shall feel very bad if you do not, for 'twas I who I urged the game."

Bridger tucked his into his purse. "Let us play a less dangerous game." Rising, he took Emma's hand. "Let us sing a song." He led her to the spinet.

It is not a less dangerous game, thought I, observing Edmund Darly's anger provoked once more.

✺ 17 ✺

*IN WHICH we follow and are
followed, and murder is done in the
House of God . . .*

As we mounted to our chambers half an hour later, Mr.
Franklin muttered in disgruntlement, "The problem
remains: she has no money."

"Miss Morland, sir?"

He turned at the head of the stairs, by the dim light of our
flickering candle. "Who else but the provocative Emma? She
has beauty; she has enough coquetry to suffice a dozen young
women—but are they all that attracts so many men? And causes
secret interests to ask after her in London?" We stepped into
our rooms. "As to Tom Bridger, he may treat money in a cavalier
manner, but he seeks it as assiduously as anyone. He has won
significant sums from Edgar Snow, or I miss my guess—but is
Snow merely Bridger's gull, or is he the young man's pathway to
his niece?" He stared out the window. "And if so, was it
Bridger—or his agents—who asked after her in London? Pah, to
bed, lad, to wrestle once more with these troubling matters."

Tuesday morn was the seventh since our arrival in Bath. It
dawned in a gray fog, so I was glad to discover a fire blazing in
the breakfast parlor as we came down.

"An eventful eve," commented Mr. Franklin when Arthur Brown joined us over porridge and bread.

Brown peered at him. "I did not know you p-played cards so well."

"Fortune favored me."

"I do not th-think that it was f-fortune." This was uttered with great circumspection, and Brown continued to peer warily at Mr. Franklin. Plainly yestereve's events made him begin to wonder at the true nature of the man. Did he begin to regret inviting him to Bath? But what was *Brown's* true nature? O, he looked as usual the shy, gulping scholar, out of his depth in society, a kind of innocent—but could that be all of him? His brain was intelligent and methodical, a planning instrument, then. His attentions fixed on the past, but might he look to some future we could not see? Did he connive to bring it about?

What had Arthur Brown really intended when he urged Benjamin Franklin to visit him here?

As the morning passed Mr. Franklin continued to fret that the post did not deliver the letters he sought. But we had other matters to distract us, for as we strolled back from the Mineral Water Hospital, where we had gone to see how Bath succored her sick and poor, we were startled to discover F. J. Mossop, in deep converse with Isaac Hobhouse. We hurried to accost him—but true to form the molelike little man scuttled away before we could get near.

Hobhouse stood by his door, red-faced. "Damned impertinent fellow!" grumbled he as we came up. "He ran away when he saw you, Franklin. D'you know him?"

"His name is F. J. Mossop—at least that is what he gave out. He rid in our coach from London. He sometimes carries a pistol beneath his coat."

"I do not like to be asked questions, even by strangers who do not carry pistols."

"Questions about what?"

"Of no account that I could see. He had hardly begun before you affrighted him away."

"He did not inquire after Miss Morland?"

"Why should he?"

"Did you tell him anything?"

"I did not."

Mr. Franklin rubbed his jaw. "Most strange. If he accosts you again, kindly let me know, for the fellow interests me. But speaking of questions, sir, you asked me about Edmund Darly and Arthur Brown. *Quid pro quo*, I should like to ask you about Tom Bridger. What do you know of him?"

"What should I know, except that he is a sharper? I do not like the breed."

"They live as they can."

" 'Til they are taught a lesson. You gave him an excellent one last night, sir, ha! Good day." The old man trundled in.

"He and Mossop seemed most intimate to me," said Mr. Franklin as we walked to our door. "Was Mossop as unwelcome to Isaac Hobhouse as Hobhouse gave out?"

The day continued gray, with fitful rain; thus we stayed indoors. It was a time for reading and reflection and sitting by a fire. I tried to be hopeful. No irreparable harm had been done. The highwayman's shot had only grazed Edmund Darly's arm, and the intruders into Mr. Franklin's chamber had failed to harm anyone significantly. Emma might marry Edmund Darly. Was this so bad an end? It might pain Arthur Brown, but a broken heart was not a broken head, and Brown could take solace in his stones and shards. Surely the worst was past?

* * *

170

Balls occurred Tuesdays and Fridays. As this was Tuesday, we readied ourselves for our second rout, and at five-thirty joined the glittering procession that wended its way to the Assembly Rooms. A cloudburst turned the great square into a scramble of sodden umbrellas and pulled-up skirts, and one elegantly dressed gentleman slipped upon the marble steps, sending his fine wig flying. But inside all was as before: the seductive candle blaze, the huge hearths flaming, the musicians tuning up, whilst talk bubbled, eyes darted, bosoms heaved, dresses rustled, and soft leather shoes whispered on polished parquet.

We greeted Edmund Darly. Almost at once, Beau Nash tottered up to us in his gleaming white suit. "I know you, sir. I say I do," said he, waggling the end of his stick under the young lord's nose. "You have been to town before. I chastised you, I recall. For wearing your sword when you knew you were forbid to do so, eh?"

Darly made a bewildered bow. "Begging your pardon, sir, but I have never been to Bath before in my life."

Nash would have none of this. "You wore boots at an Assembly Ball, then—aha, that is it!"

"Never, sir."

"You fought a duel?"

"Dear me, no."

"Then . . . then—" The Master of Ceremonies screwed up his age-puffed features, whilst Darly looked aghast.

Mrs. Valentine arrived to succor him. "I have just spied my husband, Mr. Darly!" said she breathlessly. "You cannot miss the chance of speaking to him!"

"O, go, go." Nash waved a dismissing hand. "I must begin the ball." A shaken finger. "But I shall have you, sir. I shall recall where I know you." He trundled off.

"How the man's mind mistakes—a pity," cooed Mrs. Valentine as she took Darly with her.

"Does she not wish *us* to meet her husband, too?" said Mr. Franklin, watching 'em go. "He is another mystery I should like to resolve."

Emma had been speaking to Dr. Woolridge nearby, but he excused himself and hurried away as Isaac Hobhouse, leaning upon a blackthorn stick, made a slow progress toward us. The old man gave gruff greeting to Mr. Franklin, none to me. Watching him kiss Emma's hand with ponderous gallantry, I wondered: could Hobhouse's enmity against Titus Morland have anything to do with how Morland had treated his niece?

"That doctor . . . " murmured the old man, watching Woolridge's coat vanish round a party of men.

"Yes?" inquired Mr. Franklin.

" 'Tis of no matter, sir."

The music started up, and I resigned myself to the tedious formality of the first half of the evening. But when the country dances commenced, things livened, and Emma, in pale blue satin, stepped out as delightfully as before. She seemed made for dancing, fresh as air, and I could hardly keep my heart in check watching her small, swift feet, her elegant neck, her bright green eyes.

Tom Bridger arrived at nine.

"You are late, sir," observed Mr. Franklin when the young man sauntered to us. "Gaming?"

Bridger rose and fell on his toes. "I have gamed, I confess— and to good result, for my purse is fatter than 'twas three hours ago. Tell me, sir, have you gamed for a living? We must talk of it one day." He nodded to Emma as she whirled by on the arm of a dragoon. "Is not she a delicious creature?"

So delicious that Bridger contrived to have the next dance with her—and the next too, whilst Edmund Darly, who stood by thwarted, barely contained his ire. Bridger treated him with amused contempt, as if any young earl must be a fool, and when Bridger sought to lead Emma out a third time, I thought the impulsive Darly might strike him.

Mrs. Valentine's politic intervention prevented: "No, Mr. Bridger, Mr. Darly must have her now!"

Emma laughed. "Yes, Mr. Bridger, I cannot dance with you *all* evening, though you dance very well." Did it please her to be fought over? She danced once or twice with Arthur Brown, too, but he was awkward; and though she held her tongue, she always looked as if she wished he were a better partner. Of the three suitors, he could be deepest hurt by her, I saw; but she appeared to care very little how he felt, and her thoughtless gaiety began to seem cruel. If she must wound, could she not do it kindly?

At eleven o'clock, Beau Nash beat his stick upon the floor, the music stopped, and as before ev'ryone gathered their cloaks and hats and began to trail out. The rain had ceased, though clouds still obscured the moon. It was a cold, murky night into which people hurried to their chairs, huddling as if the chill stabbed to their bones.

Mr. Franklin held me back by the steps. "Sir," said he to Arthur Brown, who looked gloomily askance, "walk on to the warmth of Orchard Street, if you please. Nick and I have words to say to Mr. Nash." Nodding, Brown pulled his collar about his neck and trudged off. The square was rapidly deserting. Emma had been taken away by Mrs. Valentine, Darly and Bridger were gone, Dr. Woolridge had left the assembly early. Eaves dripped whilst remnants of gay laughter melted into the night.

"Sir," said I to Mr. Franklin in some puzzlement, "was that not Mr. Nash just gone away in his white hat? If you wish to speak to him, should we not catch up?"

" 'Tis not Nash I wish to accost but another: F. J. Mossop. See the corner of that building?" He bobbed his head, and I peered into the night. Mist had begun to rise from the cobbles, so at first I could discern nothing save a projection of stone—but after a few seconds, I made out a dark shape.

"Why—"

"Mossop, no mistake," murmured Mr. Franklin, "in that coat of his; I glimpsed his face as we came out, before he hid. Confound the man—why does he spy? I mean to know; thus we shall follow him, Nick—but this way." Hailing a party of revelers, as if he intended to join 'em, he led me to the opposite corner of the stone facade. Disappearing round this, we halted whilst the revelers trotted merrily on to vanish into Westgate Street. About us Bath grew still; though there came whispers and other oddments of sound that might have been exhaled by ghosts. We peered round the edge of our building. Ev'ryone was now gone from the Assembly Room, the candles snuffed, the windows dark, the musicians trailing away, footmen closing and latching the tall glass doors. Slow-moving Isaac Hobhouse was nearly the last to depart, only now being helped into a waiting chair, which made off by the dim light of a street lamp.

"Nick!" whispered Mr. Franklin, though he need not have, for I had already glimpsed secretive movement: two men creeping in the shadows on the far side of the square. They scuttled after Hobhouse's chair, as if they followed him. They were mere black shapes, but I could not help thinking on the men who had pummeled Mr. Franklin's bed in The Cock's Crow. Up to mischief again?

And then F. J. Mossop—or the short, round shape that seemed to be he—separated like a wraith from his own shadows and crept after the two mysterious men. "A parade," said Mr. Franklin. "We must join it." With watchful caution we set out.

We went in the direction of Orchard Street—and why not,

174

for that was where Hobhouse resided. We knew little else, however, for as we descended toward the Avon, the fog grew thicker, dank and evil-smelling, so that the way dissolved to pools of yellowish light beneath the infrequent lamps. Ahead of us the darting form of Mossop entered, passed through, vanished beyond each of these pools, but we had lost all sight of Hobhouse and the two men who crept behind him. Were they still there? I shivered, for they might lurk and never be seen 'til they leapt out upon us. And how transformed was Bath! From the elegant city of day, it dissolved to a landscape of looming dark, where the poor huddled by fires like hellspouts in inky alleys, and whores thrust their painted faces into ours.

We proceeded in this manner five minutes. Then, just as Mossop was about to pass from one of the pools of light into the darkness beyond, he stopped. Had he heard us, guessed he was followed? But when he glanced back his expression said otherwise: he himself had been seen! His hand slid inside his coat.

Mr. Franklin and I must be invisible, for we were in the black zone betwixt lamps, but we could not remain there; for, crouching low, the little man began to scurry back in our direction.

"Quick!" Grasping my arm, Mr. Franklin pulled me close against the wall of a shuttered house, and we turned our backs to hide our faces. The little man puffed near, rushed by—but I had hardly time to sigh relief before more footfalls sounded, and two men burst through the misty light which Mossop had just vacated.

Their faces were for a moment clearly illuminated, grim and purposive.

Albert Noakes.

And the highwayman.

Mr. Franklin saw 'em, too, for his grip urged me to press

even nearer the dank wall. Face averted, I did so, though I wished to run.

The evil pair clattered past.

Air burst from my lungs. I had had my fill and longed to seek the barred door of Orchard Street—but Mr. Franklin was determined. "Come," said he when the noise of their passing had barely ceased. "We will know the truth."

With great misgivings, I followed him back in the direction we had traveled, behind the two men who now followed F. J. Mossop. As we returned up Stall Street, my mind was a jumble of confusion. Noakes and the highwayman? What to make of it? I recalled those moments in which Noakes had seemed to defy his master; how could a servant gain such power over a lord? And what had he to do with the man who had shot that lord?

We lost sight of the pair. They had entered a ball of light, left it—but they had not rushed on into the next. "Curse it!" muttered Mr. Franklin, halting. In our haste we had shown ourselves under one of those lamps, so that if the men had glanced back they must have seen us. Did they now watch, wait? Both knew our faces, and suddenly I felt certain it had also been Noakes and the highwayman at The Cock's Crow Inn.

Mr. Franklin drew me into a dark doorway. Gazing about, I saw where we were: at the west side of the square containing the great Abbey Church, its twin towers looming, its struggling stone souls still climbing those tall double ladders. The sky that framed its soaring bulk was ruled by a fitful moon.

"If the pair lurk," whispered Mr. Franklin, "they will expect us to retreat. Therefore we shall not. Come." He drew me into the gloom that clung to the edges of the closed shops that bounded the square. There lay the balustrade of the King's Bath, there the ghostly facade of the Pump Room. I near tripped over a beggar who held out a clawlike hand before he sank back into night. Across the flags a drunken creature reeled, fell, was sucked up by the dark. A huge brown rat darted over my toes.

Suddenly a figure loomed ahead of us. Mossop? It seemed so. The little man's arm beckoned, and we hesitated, then followed as he moved deliberately, keeping in sight yet staying distant enough so he could flee should we seek to catch him. He led us round the side of the Abbey Church.

And then he was gone, as if he had plunged into a hole in the earth.

"What—?" muttered Mr. Franklin, but the mystery was soon resolved, for when we crept to where he had stood, we found the tall north doors of the church ajar. Had he gone in? The air about us was chill, the street narrow. What to do?

Sounds at our back decided us: the scrape of urgent steps.

We slipped into Bath Abbey.

This was the ancient church of the parish, whose origins dated from the Black Monks of St. Benedict, the site where King Edgar the Peaceful was crowned in 973. Later John of Tours rebuilt it on a vast scale but, though the present edifice, dating from the sixteenth century, was constructed in the space occupied by the nave of the former building, it was still imposing. All this we knew from Arthur Brown. At first I thought we must proceed as if blind, for as we passed through the doors a smothering blackness fell over us. Yet shortly my eyes began to make out soaring walls, capped by pointed arches. High above, the clerestory windows admitted the dim starshine of a fitful sky.

About us stretched a vast, brooding space, still and waiting. The man who had seemed to lead us was nowhere to be discovered.

We groped forward, halting at the point where the transept

met the high, vaulted nave. Huddled beside one of the four massive carved pillars that demarked the center of the church, we peered back where we had come. The north portal was sunk in gloom—we could make out little—but soon enough we heard angry breaths, whispers, the cautious scrape of advancing boots.

Our pursuers followed.

Abruptly the moon shed its clouds to send beams through one of the high east windows. The light was feathery and dim but sufficient to reveal rows of pews and tombs, stone faces dreaming of Heaven.

It also showed two men hovering just inside the north doors.

We slipped behind our pillar—but we could not stay there, for the men began to advance. Had they seen us come in? There seemed nothing for it but to flee down the inner aisle, toward the main, west entrance. This we did, crouched low, creeping as softly as we could, though our ev'ry breath seemed to cry out our presence. How could we not be seen? And indeed we were, for a voice at our backs suddenly barked: *"There they be!"*—a snarl of triumph. My blood ran cold, my mind ceasing to reflect as all my concentration flowed into my pumping legs, Mr. Franklin beside me. All I could think as we scurried was that we must escape. How had an invitation to the pleasures of Bath delivered us to such peril?

We headed toward the great west doors. They might be open; we could dash into town, cry *"Help!"* But they were shut fast, inexorable, so that after wasting precious seconds, we must turn and trot on, to the south side of the church and up the dim south aisle. This gave our pursuers a greater advantage, for they crossed through the pews—with terror I saw their darting forms—so that they near cut us off. A burst of speed kept us ahead of 'em, however, and all too soon we were past the south transept and amongst the choir.

178

This proved no advantage. It was only a trap, a postponing of the inevitable, and Mr. Franklin slowed. "Run on, Nick," urged he. "Into the shadows. I shall deal with these fellows." He turned to face our pursuers, who had halted a dozen paces from him, their eyes gleaming as they crouched like predators to tear apart some panting bit of flesh. They had drawn cloths over their lower faces, but they were Noakes and the highwayman nonetheless.

I would not go on. I stayed by Benjamin Franklin's side.

"Nay, Nick," he chid. "Save yourself."

"No, sir." I had never disobeyed him, but I could not obey him now.

He looked at me. He squeezed my shoulder. "Well, we will have a better chance together. Watch your back." Lifting his ebony stick, he prepared himself, and I did too. He had taught me many tricks of fighting, which I had had occasion to test on more than one bully, and as I took deep breaths I felt a strange exhilaration. Though Noakes carried a cudgel and the other man a long-knife, we would give 'em more than they bargained for. If they sent us down 'twould not be because we did not fight.

They began to circle, to draw near. I put my legs apart, setting my back against Mr. Franklin's. Would we die?

By the side of my father, then!

Facing me, Noakes made his leap.

He was agile, and the swing of his cudgel, brushing my sleeve, startled me. I was glad I had dodged so alertly, for his grunt as he sent the blow gave no doubt he meant to crack my skull. My movement separated me from Mr. Franklin, so we became two pairs of fighters, weaving about the stalls and screens and low wooden rails of the choir. Out of the corner of my eye I saw Mr. Franklin parry his adversary's glinting knife. How long could he do it? How long could I last against

Noakes, who was taller and stronger, well-armed, too? I wished to lead him away from Mr. Franklin, and did so, back into the choir, in the direction of the great pipe organ. I knew I could not retreat very far before a wall met my back and one of his blows spilt my brains, but I had little choice. The cudgel swung, I scampered away; it swung, I dodged. I fought down terror. I struggled to think: could I find a weapon? In the dim light I searched for one, but nothing presented itself; all was fixed wood, stone, brass. Use what Mr. Franklin taught you, Nick! Noakes swung again, and I saw that at the end of each swing he tipped off balance a little, his stick tugging his right arm across his chest awkwardly.

It must be then.

I would get but one chance, and I began to watch for it, all the while aware of that other pair of shadows battling ten yards away. Dear father! If I could but disable Noakes, Mr. Franklin need not fight two if I should be done for.

"You are finished, boy," I heard Noakes sneer.

He swung again.

We were very near the tall wall below the pipes of the great organ. I could not retreat far, and I felt the wind of his stick an inch from my brow. Noakes had plainly thought to end me— but instead of retreating, as I had done 'til now, I darted under the swing, which he did not expect.

"Wot?" cried he.

With all the force I could muster I drove my right boot-toe betwixt Albert Noakes's legs.

A cry escaped him as I pulled back, prepared to run. Yet I need not have feared, for I had been more effective than I hoped. The cudgel dropped from Noakes's hand, and he reeled back like a drunken man, clutching himself, careering toward one of the stalls. The carven wooden face of a patron of the church waited. His face rushed to meet it.

The two heads butted with a jarring *crack!*

Noakes rebounded from the blow to drop to the stone floor, where he curled wormlike and lay still.

I stared, amazed at what I had effected. But I had no time to pride myself, for I must help Mr. Franklin. I turned. He had been driven into a corner, weaponless. Where was his stick? Snatching Noakes's fallen cudgel, I stumbled toward him, for his adversary pressed him hard. A darting jab of knife caused him to twist, and he seemed to trip, for I saw him slip sideways against the great pulpit. The knife raised again as I pushed my exhausted legs to save him—but I would not make it, I saw, for I was too far away. In helpless horror, I watched Mr. Franklin's awkward slide, saw the wicked knife flash.

A great sound shuddered, as if God Himself, displeased at the desecration of his temple, had struck a reverberating blow. Stunned, I fell upon the cold stone flags.

I smelt gunpowder.

A ringing filled my ears. On hands and knees I blinked, struggling to comprehend. My senses returned—sight, hearing—and I groped to my feet but could see neither Mr. Franklin nor the highwayman. I made my way forward, cudgel in hand.

A figure rose before me. I cried out, raised my weapon.

But it was Mr. Franklin, and I fell into his arms. "Sir, sir, I am glad you are well!" I pulled free. "But the highwayman—!" I looked about in alarm, in case he might attack us both.

" 'Twas a pistol shot, Nick," said Mr. Franklin. "We need fear the highwayman no more." He turned me about, to look down at a sprawled form. The cloth had slid from his face, and his staring eyes were lifeless in a shaft of moonlight. A thread of blood trickled from his sagging mouth.

I had seen death of many kinds—a London boy could not

avoid it, but it always sickened me. Fighting the sour taste that rose in my throat, I turned in bewilderment. "I did not know you carried a pistol, sir—"

"I do not. Look." He pointed, and I made out a form creeping from the church. A small man in a voluminous coat.

When we searched for Albert Noakes, we found him gone.

❧ 18 ❧

IN WHICH a pretty young woman is locked up, and dire news is cried at night . . .

The following morn marked the mid-point of our sou-journ in Bath; it was not cheering to think that the first half had ended in murder.

We came down late, past ten, to the sound of voices from Arthur Brown's rooms. His door stood open, and we walked in. The grinning skull greeted us; the musty smell of time's remains. The broad, central worktable was spread with Brown's latest in gatherings: mossy shards, crumbling stone, the *denarius* which he had dug up three days ago.

The other voice proved to have been Tom Bridger's.

The young man stood near one the many cabinets that lined the walls. As we came in Brown blinked from him to us through his thick-lenses spectacles, as if he did not quite know what to make of so many callers so early.

"Hullo, Franklin," Bridger spoke up in his easy way, poking at an old Roman seal, which Brown appeared to have been showing him. "I am in Orchard Street for the beautiful Emma—I am to accompany her to church (I worship at many shrines). But I said to myself, 'Hear, now, you must stop to see these old things, which the girl likes so much.' He pulled a face. "Tut, Mr. Brown, I do not see their interest—excepting the ones made of gold, that is."

"They are not c-cards or d-dice," replied Arthur Brown.

Bridger laughed. "You have me there. But your old Romans gamed—Christ's robe, eh?" he winked. "I thank you, sir; I only wish I had found more of profit. It is time I called for Emma."

Mr. Franklin and I accompanied the young man out upon the stoop. "Does Miss Morland look for you?" inquired Mr. Franklin.

"She longs for me!" Bridger gazed gaily at the rag-tag sky. "At any rate, she likes me more than she likes that stick, Darly."

"Can you be so sure? How old are you, sir?"

"Twenty-eight."

"She is not yet twenty. She has led a sheltered life."

"And hated ev'ry hour of it, I'll wager."

"She has romantic fancies, it is true—but that does not mean that any man ought to take advantage of 'em."

"Here, now!" Bridger frowned for the first time. "I owe you for two nights ago, when you could've kept ev'ry farthing in my purse. But you may not preach to me. I'll not have it."

"Did you know that Miss Morland is near penniless?"

"What of it?"

"Her uncle has a modest income; her dowry will be small."

Bridger's frown deepened. "What do you take me for, sir!"

"Yet her other uncle is Titus Morland."

This took the young man aback—or seemed to. He stared. "Old Morland? Of Gloucestershire? Why, I hear he's Croesus himself!"

"No profit to Emma. He gave her up long ago. He'll have nothing to do with her, do you see?"

"I see that you tell me this to assure me she has no money. To put me off? Well, sir, I have no money either, so we are well-matched—better than she and Edmund Darly."

"You have serious designs upon her, then?"

"I have no designs beyond keeping a roof over my head one day at a time; I have not the luxury for 'em. I live catch-as-catch-can, and I owe you no more answer than that." Bridger found his smile once more. "Come, sir, you have near made me angry. But I shall not be provoked. I seek only pleasure, with little thought to tomorrow, and I shall take the pleasure of accompanying a beautiful girl to church."

We watched him rap upon the door of number two. "Can any man have so little thought for tomorrow?" mused Benjamin Franklin.

But as we went up to our rooms, I could think neither of tomorrow nor today—only of last night. I could not repress a shiver at the memory of our pursuit through Bath's dark streets, the entrapment, the battle, the pistol shot—and a man sprawled dead on the cold Abbey floor. Mr. Franklin and I had whispered what to do about him. "I do not care to be seen to have had any part in it," he had said. "I must have the freedom to pursue things in my own way. Yet we cannot simply leave the man here. Let us send a boy from the inn in the square. We shall represent ourselves as passers-by: we found the door open, we heard a disturbance within—a pistol shot. The boy can carry this message to the sexton. We shall melt away. The authorities of the town can then take their course."

"But Albert Noakes?"

"He may yet lead us to some truth, so we shall leave him be—for the time. He is a dangerous man, and there must be a reckoning soon. I regret to say that in wielding my stick, I shat-

185

tered it against a pillar." He gathered the halves. "We must leave no trace." He hung an arm about my shoulders. "To Orchard Street, lad."

We had stopped by The Bull Inn, keeping our collars tucked about our faces whilst we sent a boy for the sexton. Back in our chambers, I was grateful to be behind closed, locked oak, though I still felt wary. Did Albert Noakes know we had seen his face before he covered it? Would he seek revenge against me?

Were they his boot-toes I had seen in the street?

We had talked more, before bed. "Noakes and the highwayman—" Sinking into one of the chairs by the hearth, Mr. Franklin had made a steeple of fingers before his face. "Does that mean the attack upon our coach was planned? Did Noakes bribe the coachman to take that lonely way?"

"So the highwayman could rob us?"

"Nay, there is more to it than that, for they aimed to finish us tonight, as they meant to disable me in the inn."

"Because . . . of Quimp?" asked I.

He looked at me. "Let us ask other questions. Did Noakes know that Edmund Darly would arrive at that lonely spot to save Miss Morland?"

"How could he?"

"True, though I find it difficult to believe the young lord merely happened upon us. Yet he did, flags flying. Is that, then, why Noakes is so surly toward him: he resents his master foiling his plan?"

"Yet why does Darly tolerate the surliness?"

"If we knew that we might know all. As to F. J. Mossop, did the little man anticipate the danger of our Bath journey, as Arthur Brown seemed to in his letter? Did he carry a pistol to protect us against it?"

"He seemed to try to save us tonight."

"Or did he lead us into a trap? You yourself proposed that Mossop might have been in connivance with the robbers, riding in our coach only to make a third party if a third were needed. Did he shoot the highwayman tonight for our sakes— or because of some falling-out amongst the thieves?"

"Why, then, did they follow Isaac Hobhouse?"

"Ah!" But this exclamation was a prelude only to pulling off boots for bed.

That night I dreamt on Quimp.

But this was the morrow. Back in our rooms Mr. Franklin fretted over letters that still had not come: "Why does the post bring me nothing?" Meanwhile out my window I watched Tom Bridger emerge from the Snows' with Emma on his arm. Did Mr. and Mrs. Snow know he took her? There could be no impropriety—they walked in broad daylight to church—but there seemed something wrong nonetheless. Did Emma give herself too freely? She leant near Bridger wearing her gay little smile just as Arthur Brown arrived in the street, returned from some errand. They did not see him, and he halted, a heartstruck expression twisting his face. *Is she such a fool?* it seemed to say. *Dear Emma, do you know what you do?*

Mr. Franklin and I spent the day about town, strolling the Circus, with its 324 Doric, Ionic, and Corinthian columns, taking special note, as we had been told we must, of the massive stone acorns that capped the roofs. We stopped by the coffee house too, its newspapers full of the dead man in Bath Abbey. The town buzzed about him, but no one knew who he was, though there was much speculation. We who had been there could have answered little of it; for though Mr. Franklin had searched the dead man's pockets, he had found nothing to tell his name or why he wished us harm.

He had been shot with remarkable accuracy, said the newspapers, straight through the heart.

Around two o'clock we strolled to Ham Gate, to refresh ourselves gazing over the Avon. Beechen Cliff was a picturesque rise on the far side, whilst the Mendip Hills folded richly beneath a sky of benign white cloud. I sucked in the heady air. Bath occupied a remarkable setting, and for a moment mystery and murder—the turbid roil of the human tide—sank to insignificance amidst its grandeur.

But not for long. We caught sight of Emma Morland in a small open carriage on the road below. She was with Tom Bridger, unchaperoned.

Mr. Franklin tutted. "I like a spirited woman, Nick, but there is a point at which spirit turns to folly." I shook my head. Would we be forced to leave the girl to her fate? I felt sad at that.

Mr. Franklin pursued our mystery nonetheless. Back in Orchard Street he sought out Isaac Hobhouse in his lodgings. "You were very nearly the last to leave the assembly yesterday eve," observed he when Hobhouse had lumbered downstairs to greet us, in no very friendly fashion.

"And what of it, sir? I move slow. Age takes its toll."

"I shall come to the point: two men followed you last night; my boy and I saw 'em. One of the men is the fellow who was found shot dead in Bath Abbey. Have you heard the tale?"

"How could I not?—his murder rings hourly with the bells. But, see here, why should you think the dead man is one of a pair who followed me?"

"Nick and I were about the streets last night. We saw the selfsame man enter the church's north door."

Hobhouse peered. "And why do you tell me this?"

"To warn you. Sir, you must take care."

The man's old eyes narrowed further as he stood leaning upon his stick. He was heavy with age—but he was heavy with something more, some inner burden. His expression did not say Mr. Franklin's warning was absurd. It seemed even to debate whether to yield up truth, to share his soul's burden with us. He only heaved a sigh. "I am weary, sir, and I must rest." He turned and left us where we stood.

"Would I could plumb the man," said Mr. Franklin on the street a moment later. "Yet he was not surprised to learn he was followed. If he knows the fellows who pursued him . . . why, then. . . ?" Clasping his hands behind his back, Mr. Franklin fell into a thoughtful silence.

I did not like these silences, but I knew that when they came I must be patient 'til something emerged from 'em. Meantime the remainder of the day hatched little—except that, sketching at my window, I spied Edmund Darly arriving at the Snows'. I was surprised how soon he came out again, within minutes. He had arrived smiling, but he brooded now, in his angry boy's way, kicking at stones. He had learnt of Emma's foray with Tom Bridger, no doubt, and he stalked off scowling; yet within three-quarters of an hour, reinforcements arrived in the form of Mrs. Sophia Valentine. Had he gone straight to her? In any case, sweeping in, she stayed a full half-hour, and when she came out, I heard her adjurations upon the stoop: "Your niece must be reined in, ma'am," said she to Mrs. Snow. "Her position as Mr. Darly's favorite must not be compromised. Does she know what a catch she has within her grasp?"

"It shall be as you say," replied Mrs. Snow, wringing her hands. I frowned. Why did Mrs. Valentine take such an interest in promoting Emma? Did the fact that she and her husband were close friends to Darly's father contain the answer? I thought on the old Earl of Hendon. He was far away, in London or upon his estate in Northumberland, but he had fixed ideas about how his son should act. Did he design Emma for him? Was Mrs. Valentine his agent?

This only left me more at sea, for why should he design a penniless girl for his son, and I returned to the consolations of art, where the world could be drawn as it appeared.

The remainder of the day passed calmly. I was glad, for I was rattled by last night's events, and I was happy to have time to regain my composure.

I could not know that climactic events were near.

Edmund Darly called upon Mr. Franklin in the early eve. He had traveled to Orchard Street, to see Emma, he said, but the girl had refused to come down. "She is too exhausted by her afternoon," Mrs. Snow had given out, in some embarrassment.

"I know how she spent her afternoon," Darly puffed, "she rid about the hills with Tom Bridger!" I watched him over the top of *Roderick Random*. His golden hair hung awry on his brow, his strong jaw worked. Even thwarted and angry he had a coltish charm. Why, indeed, did Emma rebuff this "catch"?

Darly stomped about. "This cannot go on." He turned. "See here, Mr. Franklin, you are a good fellow. Miss Morland trusts you. So do I. She would listen to you. Why . . . the man is a fortune-hunter!"

"Then he is an erring one, for Miss Morland has no fortune."

"He is a gamester, then. What can he be about? What can she? She would be mad to . . . my dear sir, you must see what I mean?"

"I see what you mean, but not what you wish of me."

"To advise her what is best, of course."

"And what *is* best, sir?"

190

"Why . . . why—"

"To ride in the country with you, instead?"

Darly threw out his chest. "Yes, if I must say so myself."

Mr. Franklin smiled at our young hero. He patted Darly's arm. "Calm yourself. You once told me you liked a man to speak his mind; so do I. I will consider doing as you ask—but first you must do something for me: explain your manservant, Albert Noakes."

Darly blinked. "Whatever do you mean?"

"Come, he is rude to the point of insolence. He sneaks about after you; you must know that. You do not like him, I think. Why do you tolerate him, then? That is what I mean."

The young lord sputtered. "I come to speak of Miss Morland, and . . . and you wish to talk of my manservant? He contained himself. "Very well. Noakes and I sometimes have a falling out, it is true—masters and servants do not always get on, you know. But I chastise him, and he says he is sorry, and there is an end. He is a very useful fellow, very necessary. I am accustomed to him, so there is no more to say. Now, please, sir, will you speak to Miss Morland?"

Mr. Franklin inclined his head. "I will do what I can."

"Thank you, sir!" Edmund Darly wrung Mr. Franklin's hand. Shortly, with the same hasty precipitousness with which he did ev'rything, he dashed out into the night.

When he was gone Mr. Franklin turned to me. "Noakes is 'useful,' is he? 'Necessary'?" He scowled. "For what, damn it?—striking down Ben Franklin?"

The following morn we gazed over the stone balustrade surrounding the baths. Billows of steam wafted the iron-and-egg odor of the waters to us, whilst cure-seekers and pleasure-seekers bobbed about below. In the night I had thought more on Edmund Darly's father, wondering yet more if he might be the key to it all. I searched for Emma amidst the steam-clouds, but she was not to be seen. Still "exhausted"?

A woman's voice purred, "Mr. Franklin," and we turned. Mrs. Sophia Valentine.

She wore green satin with a pale-yellow bodice under a little tight-fitting jacket. Lace bloomed at her wrists and bosom, and she was powdered and patched, though the morning light betrayed lines about her eyes and mouth which powder could not hide. She had her customary purposive air. Could such busyness give real pleasure? Were there moments when the woman grew weary of its sham?

With no hint of doubt, she went straight to the point: "Sir, I am glad to have come upon you, for there is a very serious matter upon which I must enlist your aid. Miss Morland begins to see far too much of Tom Bridger. It is wrong, misguided, impossible! I have taken it upon myself to investigate the man further, and I have learnt that he lives in an entirely disreputable part of town." She paused with great drama. "He keeps a woman as well."

"Does he?"

"A slattern." Steely triumph flashed in her eyes. "You are surprised? I am not, for I saw from the very first how he was. Why, there are a dozen like him come to Bath each day!—we know 'em well. The wonder is that he has captivated Emma."

"He captivated her uncle first."

"By gaming. Yes, I hear tales of that."

"So it is true?"

She emitted a disdainful puff of air. "You reside next door to Miss Morland. You have influence upon the girl—"

"Surely very little."

"Do not deny me, sir. She respects you. She has told me so. And you are a disinterested party. She would listen to you, Mr. Franklin. Thus you are obliged to speak to her."

192

"How can I refuse? But did you know that Edmund Darly has asked me the selfsame service?"

"Has he? Then he is wise. We shall both count upon you, then. Good day." The lady strode off with a maidservant.

Mr. Franklin watched 'em go. " 'We,' eh? Darly and she work together well, do they not? Any gentleman in pursuit of a young woman ought to have so expert a go-between." He tapped his jaw. "What, I wonder, will be her reward?"

Back in Orchard Street, we chanced upon the Snows. They huddled upon the stoop of their lodging in obvious distress.

Mr. Franklin inquired what might be the matter.

"My niece, that is what!" burst out Mrs. Snow, throwing up her arms. "O, the wicked girl! She begged off the baths this morn, and I accompanied my dear Edgar, though the waters do not agree with me. Would I had stayed at home, for our landlady has just informed us that Tom Bridger called shortly after we left, and the rebellious girl has gone with him to the Pump Room! I tell you, she shall henceforth be ruled by me! I shall lock her away!"

"Dear me," said Benjamin Franklin.

What occurred when Emma returned just past ten, we did not hear, but she was not seen to go out for the remainder of the day. Mrs. Valentine called around three, remaining more than an hour, closeted with the girl, I guessed. No doubt Mrs. Valentine wrung her heart, appealed to her sense. I did not like how Emma treated Arthur Brown, but I felt sorry for her. Yet was it not for the best? Could the likes of Tom Bridger be good for any girl?

We saw Dr. Woolridge at tea, he stopping by to report how his practice fared: "The town has many who want curing, but few who will pay." He shook his head. "Though I should like to help all the poor wretches who come to me, I must have fees to earn my keep. Yet for ev'ry man with pursestrings, there are half a dozen doctors who clamor to loosen 'em."

"They are not as good doctors as you," said Mr. Franklin kindly. "Your reputation will get round. But will you not try old Hobhouse, as I proposed?"

Woolridge shook his head. Taking up his hat, he turned to go but stopped by the door. "Dear me, I do not know why I have forgot to tell you—I saw Miss Morland in a carriage yesterday with Tom Bridger. I glimpsed 'em this morn, too, in the Pump Room. It is not good, Franklin. Eyes watched 'em, and afterward I heard disparaging words about the girl. Gossip spreads in a place like Bath, and Bridger is looked upon with suspicion. Is Miss Morland properly guided? It is none of my business, but I should not care to see an innocent girl harmed."

When he was gone Mr. Franklin mused, "How the forces gather against Tom Bridger. Is even Woolridge in on the plan?"

I sat upright in muffling dark: *smash! smash!* The webs of sleep flew free, and I realized that the pounding was no dream but real: someone struck the door below, whilst a man's voice cried, "Mr. Franklin! Mr. Brown!"

It was the dead of night. What hour? I had no idea, but hearing footfalls, I tumbled from bed, pulled my breeches over my nightshirt and hurried from my room. Moonshine lit the chamber beyond, enough to show that Mr. Franklin's bed lay empty. His door stood ajar however, and making my way downstairs, I reached the lower floor just as Arthur Brown darted from his rooms in his nightcap. In a hastily-thrown-on overdress, Mrs. Finching bustled amongst us with a candle.

Mr. Franklin stood in his maroon dressing gown in the entry-way.

More pounding sounded, and he turned and opened the door.

By Mrs. Finching's light our visitor was revealed as Edgar Snow. "Sirs, sirs, I have had a sleepless night wond'ring what to do. I meant to let be, but could not. O, is it too late to prevent?"

"Calm yourself," said Mr. Franklin. "Prevent what?"

"The duel betwixt Edmund Darly and Tom Bridger, that is what! A duel, I tell you, sirs!"

❧ 19 ❧

IN WHICH a pistol fires at dawn and a young man breathes no more . . .

The streets of Bath were as strange and ill-lit as they had been two nights ago, but now four of us wended our way through their gloom: Mr. Franklin, I, Edgar Snow, Arthur Brown. Our footfalls scraped, our breaths puffed; no one spoke. Mr. Snow had told his story quickly. There were laws against gaming, but we all knew that cards and dice flourished; the challenge had arisen at one of the small, private wagering houses that dotted the city. Mr. Franklin did not ask Mr. Snow why he had been in such a place, but in any case Edmund Darly had shown up, too. Had he known Bridger would be present? Whether or no, he was belligerent from the first, playing only a few hands of *vingt-et-un* before he accused Bridger of cheating.

Little else to tell. The duel was on. The two young men would meet with pistols on Kingsdown at dawn.

There seemed something inevitable about it—Tom Bridger and Edmund Darly must have it out. Yet there had been no doubt by Mrs. Finching's candlelight that we must attempt to prevent the thing. Mr. Franklin was grave: "Let us hope reason will prevail." Hastily throwing on clothes, he, I, and Arthur

Brown had hurried into the night with Edgar Snow.

Kingsdown was some distance west of town; we could not go on foot. An inn was our best chance of finding conveyance at this drowsy hour, so we tumbled into the yard of the nearby Lamb just as an ancient crier gave out that it was half-past five and all was well. We roused a sleepy ostler, he kicked a stableboy, and in ten minutes they had fastened two mares to an open coach that would just fit four.

We set out, Arthur Brown at the reins.

"*Was* Tom Bridger cheating?" Mr. Franklin asked Edgar Snow as we wheeled from Stall Street into Westgate in a skidding rush.

"I cannot say."

"Has Bridger in any way used your indebtedness to him to gain some special privilege with your niece?"

I could feel Arthur Brown stir at this question, but Snow replied, "He has not. I would not tolerate such a thing."

"I am glad to hear it, sir. Faster, Mr. Brown, if you can."

Rolling past King's Mead Square, we were shortly amongst open land: fields silvered by a low moon. But dawn was nigh, for when I glanced back I saw a faint brightening of the sky. Would we arrive in time? A Bath fingerpost loomed, receded. Our mares' hooves clopped. Fists clenched, I tried to imagine a duel: the pistols, the pacing, the slow turn, and the cry of *"Fire!"* Then death facing you from a small round barrel. I recalled the shot highwayman. Would Edmund Darly or Tom Bridger be the next to die in this affair? Both, if worse came to worst?

And Emma Morland the cause of it all.

After a quarter of an hour, Kingsdown Hill loomed against a sky that was no longer black: a bare crown encircled by thick woods. "As dueling is outlawed, they c-come here to avoid being seen by the law," Arthur Brown told us. "There is a clearing on the lower slope, hidden by t-trees. I have dug some f-fine old Roman implements there."

The sky had turned to pearl as Brown pulled off the earthen track onto a faint path through dewy grass. "Some conveyance has p-passed here within the hour," said he, pointing to crushed nettles and bracken. He urged our mares on whilst skylarks rose, a blackbird fluted, and cowbells began to clank in nearby fields, strangely mournful. The line of trees neared, and shortly we came upon a small chaise, pulled into a leafy hollow. A single horse stood tethered nearby.

Brown halted our mares. "Quick, gentlemen!" urged Mr. Franklin, jumping down.

As our feet touched the ground we heard a pistol shot.

We halted, as if frozen. Though the faint *pop!* was muffled by the screen of trees, it made me blanch, and I glanced at Mr. Franklin. "The fools, the fools . . . " muttered he. "Lead the way, Mr. Brown."

Brown set out through the trees, we following in a ragged line. The ground was slick with rotted leaves, and dew-wet branches whipped our faces. Twigs scratched—it was an enveloping tangle—but we burst through at last, upon a broad slope which led to a rough granite outcropping that marked the steeper rise of Kingsdown tor. The sky had achieved a pale rose, sufficient light, I thought with sinking heart, for men to bloody the earth with their honor.

Three figures stood outlined against the dawn.

One was Edmund Darly. Wearing a scarlet coat, he held a pistol loosely by his side in a solemn stillness whilst by his side Dr. James Woolridge appeared to be expostulating with him. The third man, a stranger, stood apart, rotund and shabbily long-coated, with eyes that darted like a frightened rabbit's.

He saw us. Clutching his hat to his head, he bounded toward

a far opening in the semicircle of trees. In a moment he was gone.

Wind moaned faintly. The grass was knee-high. I felt despair. Did Tom Bridger lie amongst its fresh green stalks?

Dr. Woolridge pointed to us; and, bareheaded, his blond curls catching the slanting morning sun, Darly turned. His features were as staunch and handsome as ever—but what of his blue eyes? Did they say he had shot a man?

We mounted quickly to 'em. Woolridge looked relieved to see us, but Darly spoke first. "You told 'em, did you, eh, Mr. Snow? I might've done the same." With a short, barked laugh he added: "Ha, do not look so downcast. I have shot no one. You heard a report? I merely discharged my pistol into the air. The coward, Bridger, did not show up. That was his second who ran off—Wilkes, I believe was his name. Wasn't it Wilkes, doctor? He was supposed to meet Bridger here, to stand up with him, but Bridger never came." Darly kicked a clod of earth. "Well, I am glad. I did not want to shoot him—though I should like to thrash the blackguard. He must be kept off Miss Morland, I tell you! And you, Mr. Snow . . . well, I should not game with him anymore."

"Thank God no ill has come of this," Edgar Snow murmured at this.

Mr. Franklin's brow furrowed. "You saw no sight of Tom Bridger at all?"

"Nor hide nor hair. Not since last eve," replied Darly.

"I do not like it. The man may cheat at cards, but he did not seem a coward. But how come you to be here, Woolridge?"

"Through no desire of my own. I chanced upon Mr. Darly in the street last night. He asked if I would second him in a duel. I tried to dissuade him, but he would not listen, so I yielded. A doctor's presence at such an affair may save a life."

"And what of this Wilkes?"

"Some gaming friend of Bridger's," sniffed Darly, "of the same disreputable ilk."

Dr. Woolridge was peering at the trees that hid the rise. "Let us leave this place at once, in case the law, too, has heard of our intent."

"First let me thank you, doctor," Darly said. "You bound my wound; now you have stood up with me." He thrust out his hand. Woolridge clasped it briefly, and we all moved off. Arthur Brown said nothing amidst the whisper of grass made by our boots. What did he feel in the face of Edmund Darly now? Did he wish it had been *he* who had challenged Tom Bridger for the sake of Emma Morland?

"Woolridge 'chanced' upon Darly last night, did he?" muttered Mr. Franklin so only I could hear, as we groped through the woods to our coach. "Damn it, Nick, there are too many chance encounters in this."

It was near seven when we returned to town, the sky clearing, drovers urging geese to market, shop boys taking down shutters, chairs setting out on their rounds. Darly rid in his small gig with Dr. Woolridge. Our two conveyances arrived in the Abbey square at the same moment.

We met disaster.

A group of men were gathered at the stone balustrade overlooking the King's Bath. Why? The bathing had not begun. It was an odd commingling of gentlemen and beggars, and I felt a tingle of apprehension. What brought 'em together? A dour gent appeared to be in the act of sending a boy to fetch help, and Mr. Franklin jumped down. I followed at his heels.

We approached the men. We looked over the railing.

A body floated in the steaming water. It was face-down, of

no certain identity, yet something about its form and clothing filled me with a terrible premonition. Mr. Franklin must have felt the same, for he snapped, "Quick, lad," and beckoned me at a trot toward the narrow way that led to the slips. Descending, we burst into the area of dressing chambers, deserted save for a half-dozen attendants who held out their hands with cries that Mr. Franklin must pay. He brushed past 'em.

In a moment we emerged from the dank heat of the slips upon the bath's edge.

There lay the expanse of steaming water, the stone niches, the pumps, the Bladud Tower. Mr. Franklin did not hesitate but leapt in fully clothed. He swam to the body. Turning it face-up, he tugged it to the far edge of the bath, where he wrestled it from the water and laid it upon the stone terrace just under the balustrade. I scrambled along the edge of the water. Mr. Franklin had fallen on his knees, straddling the man. He pushed rhythmically upon his chest. A spurt of water poured from the sagging mouth which in life had been so mobile and laughing, but it was a dead mouth now, in a dead body, and after a few moments, Mr. Franklin desisted, for it was plain that the breath was gone for good.

It was Tom Bridger, his black hair matted against his brow, his once-lively eyes half rolled-up in an eerie blankness that made me sick to heart. I had liked him despite his cheating at cards, and I was filled with that sinking sense of waste—of terror too at the wonder and precariousness of life—which I always felt when I gazed upon death.

I shook myself to clear my head; Mr. Franklin might need his boy.

I saw him feel about the body. Gently he turned the head to peer at something at its back. He held the hands too, briefly pushing up each coat sleeve.

And then other men were with us: Edgar Snow, Edmund

Darly, Arthur Brown, Dr. Woolridge, officials of the bath. Chief amongst these was a tall, disgruntled-looking fellow, who gave his name as Featherdown. He scowled and fretted. "We must get the damned fellow out of here before the quality arrive."

Mr. Franklin gave him a look.

Featherdown returned it coldly. "They fall in now and then. Drunk. We scoop 'em up, we take 'em away. It is no great matter."

Mr. Franklin nodded toward Woolridge. "This man is a doctor. I should like him to examine the body before any of your men lay a hand upon it."

"What?" Featherdown sputtered. "Is it not obvious what has occurred? By what authority do you ask this? Is the dead man a relation of yours, sir? A friend?"

"He is a fellow being."

Featherdown's fingers fidgeted. "Very well. Simpkins," he barked to a minion, "bar the doors to the slips 'til this is done. And for God's sake get your men here quickly, so we may carry the body away before all Bath hears of it and no one will take the waters today."

Dr. Woolridge knelt as Mr. Franklin adjured. He felt of the limbs, he examined the head. Glancing up at the balustrade, where yet more curious faces peered down, he spoke gravely to Mr. Franklin: "He seems indeed to have fallen. See the blow to the back of the head?" He indicated bloodied hair. "It is twenty feet to the stone floor—quite enough."

"To kill him instantly."

"I should judge so."

"Yet he was in the bath."

"Why . . . that is so. He did not die at once, then. He was conscious enough to crawl—"

"—into the water? Why should he crawl into the water?"

202

"I do not know. What do you suggest? Perhaps he was not entirely sensible what he did. Too, it was night. I do not think—"

"And then there are his wrists."

"His wrists?"

"Just so. See?" Mr. Franklin pushed up the sleeves, as he had done a moment ago. "They are chafed and bruised." I was conscious of Edgar Snow, Edmund Darly, and Arthur Brown leaning near, and indeed marks such as Mr. Franklin described encircled the wrists, like burns.

"But what—?" demanded Woolridge with a bewildered look.

"Strong cords, pulled tight," replied Mr. Franklin.

"His hands were . . . *t-tied*?" murmured Arthur Brown at my back.

Standing, Mr. Franklin gazed down. "Poor man. He did not deserve it." He turned to Edmund Darly. "Now you know, sir, why Tom Bridger did not meet you this morn."

Darly was white as chalk. "Damn me, I did not like him, but . . . but this . . . why, sir, he did not deserve . . . no man deserves—"

Featherstone had gone gray with dismay. "You are saying the man was murdered?"

"Who keeps watch on the baths at night?" Mr. Franklin returned.

"Why . . . no one. There is no need."

"Then I think, sir, you had better call the constable. To lay a report before the magistrate. The dead man's name is Tom Bridger, a gamester; whatever else he may've been remains to be discovered, but there is good evidence he was tied before he was thrown over the balustrade. Likely the cords were then removed, and he was pushed into the waters. I am wet; I must change into dry clothes. Mr. Snow, would you remain here to

203

convey these discoveries to the constable?"

A funereal nod.

"I shall stay, too," put in Dr. Woolridge.

"As you think best. Come, Nick, to Orchard Street. Shall you accompany us, Mr. Brown?"

Brown nodded, and the three of us set off. As we made our way along the edge of the bath I looked back. Edmund Darly stood a little apart gazing at the body as if he gazed upon his own death. How shaken he appeared! As if in premonition, I glanced up at the balustrade—and there amongst the gawkers stood Albert Noakes, staring down like vengeance upon his master and the corpse.

In Orchard Street, Mrs. Finching cried out at Mr. Franklin's state, but she was quick to build a fire to warm him, and he was soon dried and dressed in fresh clothes. She bustled off to prepare breakfast.

Arthur Brown joined us in our chambers. "What t-terrible events! When I asked you to Bath, sir, I had no idea of involving you in such m-matters."

"No?"

"Certainly n-not. But it is truly murder? I c-can hardly credit it. Who should wish to d-do such a thing to Mr. Bridger?"

"Men followed him. Perhaps he won more from 'em than they liked. Or"—Mr. Franklin allowed a pause—"it may've been one of us."

Brown stared. "We who were together this morn? But . . . we are all g-gentlemen. And we were at Kingsdown."

"Tom Bridger was dead at least an hour before we left for Kingsdown."

"How can you know th-that?"

"The warmth of the waters. The state of his body."

"You are expert in m-more than I knew, sir."

"Not enough to surmise the answer to another mystery."

"What?"

Mr. Franklin fished in a pocket. "How this came to be upon the dead man's person." He held out a gleaming disk: the golden medallion which Arthur Brown had shown us on our second day in Bath, the hideous beast's face on one side, *Vanquish My Enemy* in Latin upon the other.

Brown and I gaped, whilst his Adam's apple bobbed. "I did not know it had been stolen!" breathed he.

"Who could have taken it?"

He considered. "Anyone. That is, m-many people knew it was there: you, the Snows, Emma, Mr. D-Darly, Mr. Bridger, Dr. Woolridge, Mrs. Finching, her maid. Even Isaac Hobhouse."

Mr. Franklin made a disgruntled sound.

Two persons who could *not* know of it were Albert Noakes and F. J. Mossop, thought I.

Brown peered into Mr. Franklin's face. "You think it was p-placed upon Mr. Bridger's body by whoever murdered him?"

"I do not know what to think. But if Bridger was someone's enemy, he has been vanquished indeed." Mr. Franklin pressed the medallion firmly into Arthur Brown's hand. "Lock this away."

Mr. Franklin was accustomed to lead a life of ease at his clubs in Fleet Street and the Strand, or round St. Paul's. But when some matter came to a head, he moved swiftly; and the undoing of Tom Bridger had brought our matter to a head indeed. "We must find who murdered the young man," said he as he drew me into the street moments after his talk with Arthur Brown.

To prevent further murder? thought I.

The gentleman headed toward the center of town, but we were stopped by Edgar Snow, returning from his report to the constable. "It was not encouraging, sir," Snow told us. "The fellow plainly wished to believe Bridger had fallen—so much less trouble that way. Still he wrote down all Woolridge and I told him, and promised to lay it before the magistrate."

"We must be satisfied with that," replied Mr. Franklin. "Look you, sir; the matter is grave. Do you know anything of it which you have not told?"

"I gamed with Bridger, to my loss and chagrin. But beyond that I know no more of him than you do. You must believe me." He seemed sincere, but I wondered how much debt he had run up.

Did not murder cancel debts?

"You make for town?" Snow said. "Not yet, please. I ask you to stand by me when I tell my wife and niece what has occurred? Mrs. Snow did not approve of young Bridger. But Emma—" He shook his head. "Once I thought I knew her heart, but she has grown quite wild. I fear for her. I do not know how she will take this, but you will do me a great favor by being present. She has spoken well of you."

Mr. Franklin nodded, and we accompanied Mr. Snow to his lodging, where he called his wife and niece to the front parlor. There he told 'em of the planned duel and of discovering Tom Bridger's body. I had not seen Emma for two days. Wearing a lavender-colored morning gown, she went pale at the news, her hands leapt to her mouth, and she huddled upon her chair with broken little cries. "He sang so sweetly . . . we rid together. Why, he made me laugh." Her damp eyes searched our helpless faces. "Can he truly be no more. . . ?"

"There, Emma." Mrs. Snow stroked her hair. "It is a pity he is dead, but I knew the young man would come to a bad end."

This was heartless consolation, and Emma turned to Mr.

Franklin. "You pulled him from the water. Please say what you know of this—why . . . how. . . ?"

"I shall entrust you with the truth, child: I believe he was murdered." Gently, yet leaving nothing out, Mr. Franklin told why he thought so, including Bridger's poor chafed wrists.

"Is this necessary, sir?" protested Mrs. Snow.

"The tale will be all over Bath by noon, ma'am. Do you not think it best your niece hear it from us?" Emma looked stricken, but she thanked Mr. Franklin for his honesty.

When we were out upon the street he said, "They must all know the truth, to teach 'em caution."

"But did she love him, sir?" asked I.

"She liked him, a handsome young man, amusing, worldly, full of attentions. But love?" He shook his head as we moved on. "I can read the flirtatious girl's heart no better than her uncle."

Near the King's Bath we met Beau Nash in his huge white hat, just climbing into his chair.

"Hallo, Franklin! They have just took a body away—some drunken gamester. There is talk of murder. Pah, I do not like murder in Bath. There was one in the Abbey t'other night. There was talk of a duel, too, this morn. I tell you, when I was at the height of power, there was never a duel within a hundred miles, for they feared me then."

"Has anything more been learnt of the drowned man?" Mr. Franklin asked.

"Not that I know."

"By the by, have you recalled how or why you knew Edmund Darly?"

"Nay"—the bloated old man tapped his shaggy wig—"though I shall. But, sir," added he, leaning his head out his chair window, "why did you never tell me that pretty Miss Morland, who is your friend, is Titus Morland's niece?"

"I did not think it significant."

"She's in disgrace with him, I hear. Morland's a curmudgeon. He's hard as flint."

"Have you ever met him?"

"No. He never came to Bath. But I hear news of him (gossip flies quickest about the rich). Poor man."

"What, has he died, then? I heard that he was ill."

"Died? Nay. He was ill, it is true, but I have it on excellent authority that he is well recovered for a man of his years. No, I say 'poor man' because of his son."

"Wesley Morland?"

"The same. A base fellow. A whoring rake, of the blackest stripe! He was sent to the Indies in hopes of amending him, but it did no good and he contracted a disease. He came back to England two months ago, but died within a week."

Mr. Franklin's eyes closed, opened. "Titus Morland's son is dead?"

"Have I not just said so?"

"And near two months?"

"Do you deny me, sir? Old Morland preferred to keep it a secret, I suppose, for it was an ignoble death. But 'twas a death nonetheless; you may trust the Beau. Good day."

His chair moved off. Mr. Franklin stared after it. "Old Morland had no other son." He met my eyes. "If no other male relation stands in line, will all his vast fortune pass to Emma?"

❦ 20 ❧

IN WHICH we visit a dead man's
mistress and take the waters once
more . . .

Mr. Franklin frowned as we went on. "It cannot be that Emma shall inherit, for if there is no male heir the entire estate escheats to the Crown. A female does not inherit. Unless"—he stopped,—"unless there is a will which leaves the estate to her."

"But would old Morland have made such a will?" asked I.

He pulled at his lip. "It does not seem so, for he disavowed her long ago. Further, if Nash spoke true, Morland is cured and may live some years longer, which makes the question of who inherits moot, for now." He rubbed his brow as we walked on. "How did the death of his son affect the old man, I wonder . . . "

In ten minutes we came to Wood Street, near Queen Square. Here lay the offices of the *Bath Chronicle*, the town's chief newspaper. When I was a boy-of-work at Inch, Printer, I had derived my only pleasure from setting type or working the press, so I loved the smell of thick black ink that poured from the room at the rear of the small front office. Mr. Franklin's sally was brief. Standing before the waist-high wooden partition he addressed the thin-lipped clerk: "New arrivals in town, sir—how do their names come to appear in the *Chronicle*, if you please? I am particularly interested in Edmund Darly."

"The young earl." The clerk scratched his ear with his quill. "His manservant brought round his partic'lars, I recall."

Mr. Franklin described Albert Noakes.

"A nod. "That was the man."

"And Mr. Isaac Hobhouse. Did anyone deliver to you about him?"

"Nay, never heard of 'im. But if he is not a person of quality, I would not, for we do not print names that do not b'long to persons of quality."

"Then you have not printed Tom Bridger's name."

"No."

"You will soon, for he was murdered in the baths this morn. Good day." Out on the street Mr. Franklin said, "Was there any profit in this? Fortunately there are other paths to follow." Pulling a scrap of paper from his coat pocket, he held it out.

It proved a dunning letter, from a haberdasher of Tunbridge Wells.

It was directed to: *Tom Bridger, Bow House, Bath.*

In a badly misspelt scrawl, it demanded seven pounds nine-pence for three linen shirts and a green velvet waistcoat. "I took it from the same pocket from which I pulled the medal-lion (I did not care to leave it for some constable to misuse). I pray this Bow House proves to be Tom Bridger's lodging."

Asking directions, we skirted town by the Borough Walls, heading toward Avon Street. This was the most sordid precinct of Bath, home to doxies and gin houses; as we walked, it dis-played a rag-tag collection of human flotsam: limbless beggars, tattered children, lewd slatterns who eyed us from shadowed doorways. We sought out Cropper's Mews halfway down, a short stub of an alley smelling of rot and despair. Its pavement was jumbled and sunk, and only three gray, leaning buildings occupied it, but Bow House was one, obvious from its bow window, which poked out like a swollen eye.

Tom Bridger's rooms were on the second floor, a surly old man who sat on the stoop informed us. We mounted narrow, creaking stairs.

A knock delivered a small, white face through a tentative cracking of the door. "We are friends of Mr. Bridger's," announced Mr. Franklin. "May we enter?" The face hesitated. Then the door was wordlessly opened and we walked in.

The chamber proved cramped, overlooking the mews. It contained a single bed, two broken-seated chairs, a deal table, a shabby wardrobe, some worn rush mats upon the floor, a basin, a ewer—that was all. It smelt musty, but it was neat; someone had sought to make it home. A half-dozen wilted peonies made an attempt to cheer the place in a glass upon the table. A well-worn deck of cards lay next 'em.

"Tom tries to teach me to play," said the girl who had admitted us, perhaps sixteen. She had a thin, reedy voice. "I am no good at it, I fear."

"What is your name?"

Large eyes of a watery blue turned shyly up. "Nellie Blessing."

"Pleased to meet you, Nellie. I am Benjamin Franklin. This is my boy, Nicolas. You live here with Mr. Bridger?"

She colored. "I do." She was small and delicate-looking, with the whitest blonde hair I had ever seen, like wisps of flax upon her round, childlike head. Her dress was plain but clean, and she had a faintly desperate air, as if she would do anything to please us.

My heart sank to think what we must tell her.

Gently Mr. Franklin asked how long she had known Mr. Bridger. "Two months, p'rhaps," answered she in her reedy piping, "since just after he come to town." How had they met?

211

She colored more at this, gazing sidelong. Mr. Bridger had been kind, she murmured, saving her from some trouble with another man. He had kept her since then, fed her. She glanced at the bed. "I please him how I can." Her eyes shone with gratitude: "No one has ever treated me so well!" She might love him, I saw, and I felt even worse about what we must reveal. With a little show of bravery she trailed a finger along a chair back. "La, he will go someday; he will leave me . . . but 'til then . . . " 'Til then she had this little room, safe, whilst she waited for her keeper.

Mr. Franklin asked a few more questions. Her replies told us that Tom Bridger had indeed been a gamester, making his way by cards and dice. Did she know Mr. Wilkes, too? "O, yes, one o' Tom's friends. I can tell you where t' find him, if you like." She did so.

Mr. Franklin sat her down. Not speaking of bound wrists or murder—his words made it a quick and painless death—he told her Bridger's fate. He clasped her hands as he did so. "And so he is gone, I am sorry to say, my child."

It wrenched her; her whole little body seemed to writhe— yet she made but one sound, a sort of mew. She forced back tears, she bit her lips. The streets had taught her fortitude. Necessity too. Pulling her hands free, she rose to draw a thin shawl about her shoulders. She put on a bedraggled little hat. "Then I must go," said she.

Mr. Franklin stood too. "But where?"

"I must earn my bread." She pasted upon her lips a smile of awful coquetry. "May I earn some of you, sir? I know how to please a man."

He started. "My dear child, no—!"

A shrug. "Then elsewhere." She made for the door.

Mr. Franklin held out a hand. "But let me help."

She turned. "How? Will you keep me?" A resigned look, without anger. "I see you will not. Then I must keep myself—that is, until . . ." She gave a terrible look. *Until I can bear it no more,* she meant to say, and I thought of the bodies of women, young and old, which were washed up ev'ry day from the Thames. Many flung themselves to death when life grew too hard. I stared into Nellie Blessing's plain, set face. Was she even sixteen?

And then she was gone. I stared, shaken, whilst Mr. Franklin stood with a hand upon the jam of the door through which she had left. His back was to me, and he did not move for a long while. My eyes found the little flowers in the glass.

At last Mr. Franklin turned. Drawing a hand across his brow, he said with hard determination, "Come, Nick, we will find the murderer who did this thing!"

We trudged down the street, to the gin shop where Nellie Blessing had said we might meet Wilkes. The Pirate's Bones proved to be a dank den filled with spirit-soaked air and rough laughter. There at a low plank bench against the far wall huddled the furtive-eyed man who had fled Kingsdown. He was adrinking with cronies, but at sight of us he leapt up, as to flee. Mr. Franklin was at his side with remarkable quickness, fastening an iron grip upon his arm. "We are not the law." Propelling him to a table, he sat him down.

"Bartram Wilkes, Esquire, sir," confessed the man when he had been bought a glass of gin. He wiped his chin with the back of a hand. "I have known Tommy Bridger three year or so. Has he marked ye, took ye down? Ha!—well, if ye play, ye will sometime lose. Play him again, I say. His luck cannot hold."

"Luck? He is dead, Mr. Wilkes. Murdered, I believe."

213

Wilkes paled. "I have nothin' to do with his game!"

Mr. Franklin bent near. "And what game is that? Best to tell us all you know."

Gulping more gin, the man poured out what he knew of Tom Bridger. He was the impecunious son of a country squire. "That's how he larnt his fancy ways." But he was the second son; so, when his elder brother, who despised him, had inherited both the land and the rents, Tom was tossed out to fend for himself. "He were clever, he did not wish t'soil his hands. So he turned to cards and dice."

"Cheated?"

"Well, sir, he may've helped fortune along."

"As do you?"

"Here, now!" Wilkes protested that Bridger was a noble soul, however he made his way in life. "As for this Emma Morland you talk on . . . I saw him with her once. What a s'prise! But when I asked about her, he only laughed. He could not b'lieve his luck, he said—but he had no hopes; t'was only a passing fancy, for he knew he must move on someday. (The gulls was beginnin' to tip to him, y'see.) As for Nellie, he were kind to the girl, he did not beat her. So they did tip to him, did they? And drowned him? Poor Tom. I shall shed a tear for him, Mr. Franklin."

Bartram Wilkes shed that tear into another glass of gin.

" 'Noble,' was he?" said Mr. Franklin when we had left The Pirate's Bones. "I would not give him so much. But he was not deeply wicked; he did not deserve to die."

We returned under a clear sky, past the gentry in their peacock finery. Back in Orchard Street, Mrs. Finching said that two letters had come.

"I hope and pray—" Mr. Franklin broke off and carried 'em eagerly upstairs.

214

I waited a little apart as he read the pair by his window—yet not so far that I could not see from their covers that one came from Northumberland, the other from Butcher's Cross, the obscure village which James Woolridge had lived in. Who writ to Mr. Franklin from these places?

The gentleman let the letters drop to his side. "I must think on this—though if what I suspect is true, one person is in especial danger."

"Who is that, sir?" asked I.

"Isaac Hobhouse," answered he.

I was let to read the letters. One was from the Reverend Samuel Oakes, rector of Butcher's Cross Parish Church. It bewildered me, for I could hardly credit what it implied.

The other letter, from Northumberland, appeared to imply nothing pertinent that I could see. It was writ by a gentleman Mr. Franklin knew because both were staunch Whigs; they had met in London. It touched on political matters. "So you have met the young earl who comes from my parts," it went on. It described Darly's father, the Earl of Hendon: "He treats his tenants well; he is not reprehensibly Tory." It spoke well, too, of his son and daughter, Edmund and Caroline. I could not tell what Mr. Franklin made of it, for he fell into silent reflection. "There is one more letter to come," he murmured out of the funk in which he sat for three-quarters of an hour. "Let it arrive soon."

He went out around two. "Take care, sir," said I as he took up his hat.

"O, I shall." He seemed to have some plan.

Gazing out his window, I noted that he turned into Isaac Hobhouse's lodgings first. Hobhouse in danger? Why? From whom? Mr. Franklin stayed only a short while before strolling on with his bamboo stick. At loose ends, I sank into his chair.

215

What a strange chain of events. The pursuits, the attacks, the death of Tom Bridger could not be random—but what forged the connection? Mr. Franklin had left the two letters on his desk, and I poured over 'em again, to no end. I thought on Wesley Morland's death, his aged father's surprising recovery. I thought on Arthur Brown, too, and such was my pitch of suspicion that I continued to wonder if the scholar were as harmless as he appeared. I had not glimpsed F. J. Mossop for two days. Did he still lurk? He had shot a highwayman, but what had brought that selfsame highwayman to the lonely ambush on our path to Bath? I shivered knowing Albert Noakes was still at large. In deepest puzzlement, I recalled Edmund Darly's pale grimace as he gazed down at Tom Bridger's body, Noakes hovering over him like some incubus. Was Noakes the source of the evil we sought to plumb?

And then there was Emma Morland. Wayward innocent or shrewd schemer? And the Snows. Was Mrs. Fanny Snow as blindly naïve as she appeared? Was Edgar Snow's only lapse into gaming?

I sketched Bath's denizens from Mr. Franklin's window: a girl yoked to water pails, an oyster-seller. At half-past two, Edmund Darly made another pilgrimage next door. To tell Emma that, though he had meant to fire a pistol at Tom Bridger, he regretted his rival had drowned? Saying so without seeming hypocritical might prove some trick, but Darly's honest blue eyes must help. Nonetheless, he appeared ill-at-ease, tugging at his coat before he presented himself at their door.

He departed some half an hour later, and like a clockwork Mrs. Sophia Valentine arrived. No qualms were writ on her brow as she breezed in; and twenty minutes later her blandishments (whatever they were) succeeded in persuading Emma to step out with her. The girl wore a dress of somber gray, and my glimpse of her beneath her severe little hat showed ashen cheeks. "Fresh air will do you good, child," I heard Mrs. Valentine chirp as they clopped off in her gig, as if it were only a cat which had drowned.

Mr. Franklin returned at half-past five. "We take the waters tomorrow morn, Nick," proclaimed he with a glint in his eye. "How I long to swim in 'em once more!"

The gentleman continued to weigh matters in his silent fashion the rest of the day. Not wishing to interrupt his thoughts, I left him alone, but his ruminations did not prevent him giving Arthur Brown his full measure of discourse after supper. Cheerily, as if nothing could be wrong, he elucidated the principle of his famous stove. He also urged Mrs. Finching to erect a lightning rod upon her rooftop: "It may save your life, ma'am."

When Brown's turn came to talk, his deep-set eyes burned with determination. "I tell you, I *will* write Bath's t-true history some day!"

"O? And shall you write its dark side too? Tales of murder?" Brown looked dismayed at such talk on a day when murder had actually occurred, but Mr. Franklin was not abashed: "Come, is not wickedness a part of the true history of any place? It, too, needs to be revealed. Perhaps I shall write of it myself. Or you, Nick, eh?"

I woke betimes next morn and was dressed when Mr. Franklin tapped upon my door at a quarter to seven, and by a quarter past, we were in the broad square betwixt the Abbey and the King's Bath. The air was crisp, a clear sky held the field. Making our way down the steep passageway, from thence to one of the cramped, dank chambers, we paid our fee, changed clothes and were shortly in the bathing slips. I looked forward to stepping into the famous waters 'til I recalled that they had taken

217

Tom Bridger's life. I peered at the soft greenish waves. *Come, Nick, it is not they which murdered the young gamester but an unknown villain.* Still, many heads bobbed amongst the malodorous steam, and I could not help wondering if the villain paddled before me even now.

Mr. Franklin and I descended into the great King's Bath.

Its warmth assuaged me, the lapping heat. Here all was public, all safe save from gossip, which could never wound Nick Handy. I felt grateful to have no name, for I could freely watch, listen, make drawings and notes. Would that be all my life?

Philosophy was banished by Emma Morland, who appeared beside me in billowing yellow linen once more. Her hand gripped my arm to steady her. "Thank you, boy." Her voice was subdued and grave, with none of its former delight, and again I was reminded of a flower floating upon the waves, but a wilted one this time. Her remarkable green eyes were downcast.

Mr. Franklin came near to speak soft words; and as she turned her face up to him, smiling wanly, I recalled the many times I had seen him cheer others, and I understood why my dead mother had loved him.

Edmund Darly took the waters too. He swam to us. "My dear Emma, it is at Mr. Franklin's suggestion that I am here. You want cheering? I should be grateful to supply it. May I take you about?" She consented, and the way she leant against him as they pushed through the chest-high waters reminded me of the way she had leant against Tom Bridger when she walked to church with him. Were her affections so fleeting? Yet perhaps she had never truly cared for Bridger, only used him to pique the man she really sought. If so it had been a bold game, but she had won, it appeared, for Darly was plainly smitten, stroking Emma's hand. Watching 'em go about, I seemed to see a pledge betwixt 'em. And was he not best for her? He was no cynical town lord. Bred to freer ways, he could elect a girl for herself alone. He had his faults, but he was golden-haired, titled, a catch indeed.

Mr. Franklin seemed to think so, too, for he made a point of making his way to the couple and speaking to 'em with a pleased air, as if he knew the good news they must announce soon—though as he turned to leave he slipped a little and had to cling to Darly's arm to right himself. This lasted but an instant before he moved off with a grave little amendment to his smile. Did this new look have meaning?

O, yes, for in that moment Benjamin Franklin had solved our mystery.

❧ 21 ❧

*IN WHICH a young woman vanishes
and a pistol fires once more . . .*

We were dried and dressed and in the Pump Room at the stroke of nine. There mingled the Bath persons-of-note: marchionesses and reverend doctors and colonels bowing over their glasses of cure. Wags gossiped. Eyes roved. Bosoms heaved. The Snows were not amongst us, I noted. Nor was Edmund Darly. But old Isaac Hobhouse was here, trundling on his servant's arm. He caught Mr. Franklin's eye but circled warily, as if there were some unspoken communication betwixt the men.

What had they talked on yesterday?

We departed before ten. "Where does F. J. Mossop keep himself these days?" mused Mr. Franklin as we strolled. "I should sorely like to speak to the man." Back in Orchard Street, we learnt that Arthur Brown had gone next door to pay a call. "And Mr. Darly has just left the Snows'," Mrs. Finching informed us, for there was little she did not know about her neighbors.

"Let us call upon 'em too," said Benjamin Franklin.

We found a strained air of anticipation when we greeted Mr. and Mrs. Snow and Arthur Brown in the front parlor. Emma was in the back garden, we were told in whispers. Mr. Darly had took her there upon his arrival, and she had remained when he left, though no one save a maidservant had seen him depart.

She was there a long time, and we looked mutely in the direction of the garden, awaiting her return as if all discourse must cease 'til she revealed the result of Darly's call. A proposal of marriage? Mrs. Snow plainly thought so, for she could barely contain herself as she toyed with her fingers as if she counted banknotes. Mr. Snow pulled soberly at his mustaches. As for Arthur Brown, his resigned look said he still meant to make the best of it if Emma married another.

And then the girl came into the room, flushed, agitated. She forced herself to meet her aunt's expectant eyes. She was brave, she knew what must tell, and she told it with all the courage she could muster, though her chin trembled. "He has asked me to marry him. I have refused."

Silence crashed. "Wha-at?" bleated Mrs. Snow.

"Foolish, willful girl," muttered Mr. Snow.

Emma was pale. She spread her hands in an eloquent plea. "I . . . I thought he might ask me, and until a quarter of an hour ago I truly did not know what I should reply. But when he put the question . . . I could not. He pressed my obligation to him: 'I saved you from the highwayman,' said he. 'But a debt must not be paid by marriage,' said I. O, he is a good man, kind; he loves me, I believe. But he is an earl, and I am only a poor orphan girl. Too, I do not think our natures are compatible. He is honest and straightforward, whilst I—"

Arthur Brown went to her. "Are you certain, Emma?" He grasped her hands, peered into her face. "He is a g-good m-man. You would w-want for n-nothing if you took him."

Emma's eyes lifted incredulously. "*You* urge me to this?" She tore her hands free. "Mr. Brown, you almost make me be-

221

lieve that I was wrong to refuse him." Eyes brimming, the girl ran from the room.

Brown stared aghast whilst Mrs. Snow leapt up. "See how you have upset her! O, she will change her mind. She must!" She rushed after her niece.

Sounds drifted from Orchard Street as Bath went on its way. The remnants of a fire crackled in the grate. Mr. Franklin turned to Edgar Snow. "Did Darly ask you if he could make this proposal?"

"He did, this very morn. He wished to do all in the proper way. Naturally I gave my consent." Mr. Snow pounded a fist into a palm. "She would have learnt to be happy!" He gazed after his willful niece. "What can the mad girl mean?"

I did not know either, and on the street Mr. Franklin frowned into his own thoughts. "It is too short a time," grumbled he.

"T-too short?" asked Arthur Brown, still plainly shaken.

Mr. Franklin nodded. "Darly has known the girl but a dozen days. What young earl proposes in less than a fortnight— makes an earnest proposal of marriage, I mean? His sister has not met Emma. Why not wait 'til she has? His father has not met her either. Nor has the old earl met the Snows. Can Darly be so impetuous? So sure of his heart? So certain the thing will be approved?"

"He has acted impetuously before, sir," I reminded.

"Damn the man! He carries it to folly now."

We strolled to the Abbey garden after luncheon, to clear our minds. Isaac Hobhouse was there; he came to us where we stood looking out over the Avon. "She has turned him down, I hear," puffed he.

"She has," replied Mr. Franklin. "Is her heart elsewhere?"

Something stirred deep in the gruff man's eyes.

Mr. Franklin surveyed him. "Do you keep well?"

"I keep watch, that is what I do. Good day, Franklin." The old man trundled off.

I continued to wonder at Emma's choice as we walked back to our lodgings. Where *was* her heart?

We met yet another on our way: James Woolridge, just leaving number two, Orchard Street. Mrs. Snow had summoned him about a nervous attack which had sent her to bed with the megrim. "It is her niece's decision that afflicts her, I am sure," said the doctor. "Why should she turn down Edmund Darly?"

"You, too, think Miss Morland should marry him?" asked Mr. Franklin.

Woolridge stared. "Who could not think so? I am a practical man. Necessity has taught me to view the matter but one way. A young woman in her position must see to herself. This is a great chance, which cannot come again. She is fond of Darly—she has seemed so, at least. He dotes on her. He has a title and wealth to boot. She could buy a fine future with a yes."

"Perhaps she does not wish to buy anything with herself."

Strong feeling shook Woolridge. He had always been the calmest of men. Now bitterness—or some kindred feeling—welled. "Is what she wishes important when she is so young? Should not wiser heads prevail? Why, if I had such a chance—!" As if he dared not trust his tongue, he wheeled away.

"Dear me!" exclaimed Mr. Franklin when he was gone. "Yet he makes a point. Wealth, title, a doting husband—and the silly girl throws 'em over. What say you, Nick? Is she mad?"

"Many women must settle for less," replied I, thinking on Nellie Blessing. Yet I also thought on Woolridge's fit of pique. What had moved him so?

* * *

223

Mr. Franklin left me at Orchard Street at three, whilst he went to see what he might draw from Edmund Darly. Would he meet Albert Noakes at Darly's lodgings in the South Parade? I was ill at ease 'til he returned, around five. "Mrs. Valentine called too, Nick," said he when he sat himself down to make his report. "I met her and Darly in that big drawing room. What a deal it must cost to let that house! What do you think?—Darly insists that Emma did not absolutely refuse him. O, she made some cavil, he allows, but she did not say no for a certainty."

"But she told us—"

"—in quite plain terms. So, who lies? Or mistakes? I asked Darly why he proposed marriage so soon. Was this not a great rush? He threw out that heroic chest of his. 'No hurry when you have found a girl like Miss Morland,' said he. Can one credit such boldness? What of his father? asked I. 'O, I am certain he will approve my choice!' As for Mrs. Valentine, she purred like a cat. 'Emma is coy,' said she. 'We are quite certain the girl will be persuaded.' "

"Then it will all turn out well in the end?" I said doubtfully.

Mr. Franklin's mouth compressed. "For whom, Nicolas?— that is the question." He looked grave. "I pray Emma's caprice does not drive her in the wrong direction when Darly presses his suit once more, as he seems certain to do."

I asked about Albert Noakes. "He was about," replied the gentleman—but just then a knock sounded. It was Mrs. Finching's maid, with a letter. "Just delivered, sir."

Mr. Franklin snatched it. "So," said he when he had perused it at the desk by the window.

"What is it, sir?"

He looked up. "News of a man who does not exist." He scratched a corner of the letter against his chin. "I must think

224

on this." Folding his hands, he fell silent as Abbey bells chimed the hour, and out about the city society wended its way home to prepare for evening pastimes. I took up *Roderick Random* but could not read. A man who did not exist? Yet I was not surprised, for I found that I had harbored suspicions of just such a man, ever since I had observed the solicitude with which a certain old gentleman bent near Emma Morland. I had dismissed the idea as too fantastical. Was I proved right all along?

As afternoon sank to evening, I did much thinking of my own.

After supper Arthur Brown excused himself betimes, making his way from the dining room with a bewildered air. Should he be encouraged that Emma refused Edmund Darly? "Poor fellow," said Mr. Franklin. Drawing me upstairs, he sat me with him in the two large chairs by the fireplace. A light glimmered in his deep brown eyes. "You have been patient, Nick. Shall I now say what has been afoot?"

"I am all ears, sir."

The murmur of Bath accompanied him through the casement. "Let us start with the letter I received this afternoon. It came from the town of East Cornford, Gloucestershire, near which Isaac Hobhouse gave us to believe he lives. He has evaded revealing how he came by his wealth, but he is plainly a man of some prosperity; thus he must be well known about this town. I writ to an alderman there, on some pretext (its nature does not matter). My letter proposed questions about Hobhouse." He paused. "My answer is that the alderman has never heard of Isaac Hobhouse."

"The man who does not exist," murmured I.

"And yet he does exist. And so—"

"—and so he is someone else." I felt sure I knew who that was. "But that means that there are two men who do not exist," said I.

Mr. Franklin nodded. In his letter from Butcher's Cross the Reverend Samuel Oakes, rector of that parish for nineteen years, had informed us that no Dr. James Woolridge had ever practiced thereabouts. What man, then, was Woolridge? And how did this knowledge relate to Isaac Hobhouse?

"I have felt from the start," continued Mr. Franklin, "that the mischances and suspicions which have puzzled us must have some simple genesis. They do, Nick, as simple as a man changing his mind. For—"

But a sudden rapping upon our door stopped this speech.

Mr. Franklin opened.

Arthur Brown stood outside, wearing an agitated look. " 'Tis Mr. Snow. Downstairs. Emma w-went out with Mrs. Valentine around two, he says. She was to r-return by four, but she is not b-back, and it is near nine. He has g-gone about town these sev'ral hours—his servants have searched as well—but no one c-can discover hide nor hair of her. Nor of Mrs. Valentine either. Emma is d-disappeared, Mr. Franklin. Emma is g-gone."

In half a minute we had pulled on our coats and were clattering downstairs behind Brown. Just inside the open front door we found Edgar Snow crushing his hat in his hands. Quickly he confirmed all that Arthur Brown had told us. His eyes pled. "You are level-headed, Mr. Franklin. Tell me what I must do now."

"Did your niece say anything, behave in any way, to suggest she had plans other than to return at the appointed hour?"

"No, though truth to tell she has not been herself since Tom Bridger's death; she has been quiet, withdrawn. She refused Mr. Darly—is that not evidence of her strangeness? We

226

had hoped she would come round. We hoped he might ask again. We hoped—"

"Yes, yes. 'Twas Mrs. Valentine who took her out?"

"The same. Emma appeared grateful to see her. She was glad the woman forgave her for refusing Darly."

"How admirably condescending the woman is. Naturally you inquired at Darly's?"

"Twice. His house was dark and shut."

"No servants answered?"

"No."

"I do not like it. To your lodgings, then. I must speak with your wife."

We were there in a moment, finding Mrs. Fanny Snow in the small, tidy parlor. Her eyes were fixed upon a paper by candlelight, and as we came in, she shook it at us with an air of triumph. "This! This explains it all! It is no scandal, Mr. Snow. Marriage will come of it."

"What do you say?" demanded her husband.

Mr. Franklin took the letter. "She has eloped with Edmund Darly."

I was struck dumb, and a shuddering by my side told me how Arthur Brown took the news. Yet he looked brave even while he was cast down. He had always wanted the best for Emma; now she had it: a fine lord. It was by elopement, true—and a precipitate one (by what means had Darly persuaded her?)—but she had longed to run away to romance and now her desire was fulfilled.

Yet I was not entirely at ease. I glanced at Mr. Franklin.

"How did this come?" he asked Mrs. Snow.

"By a boy. From the coaching inn." She beamed round. "Well? Can we not be happy that Emma has changed her mind?"

Mr. Franklin had given the paper to Arthur Brown, and I read it with him:

> Dearest Uncle and Aunt:
> I love Edmund Darly. I was wrong to refuse him. He has asked again, and I have said yes. He urges me to go with him now, to marry, and I have agreed. It is what I wish. I am safe and well; you need not seek me. We shall return within the fortnight.
>   Your Loving Niece,
>   Emma

"What time was this delivered?" asked Mr. Franklin.

"A moment ago."

"Why, then we may be able to catch 'em!"

Mrs. Snow drew herself up. "Why should you wish to? In any case, you cannot, for the boy told me the note was given him at half-past three. He was instructed not to bring it 'til now."

Mr. Franklin sank back. "They planned well, then. She has been spirited away, I tell you. See how she makes a point of saying she is safe and well? It is surely to put us off."

Mrs. Snow stood firm. "You merely wish to spoil her happiness, sir! And mine."

Mr. Franklin took the letter. He held it out. "Is this your niece's hand?"

The woman faltered. "Should it not be?"

"Come, there is no time to lose. Her journal—does she keep it in her chamber?"

"Customarily," said Mr. Snow.

"I pray she did not take it. See if it is there."

With a look of growing doubt, Mrs. Snow went upstairs, returning in less than three minutes with Emma's small leather-bound book.

"Is it not odd that she left this? More evidence." Mr. Franklin opened the pages. "Privacy must give way to necessity." Holding Emma's letter near, he frowned from one to the other. His balding head lifted. "It is not her hand. I am expert in these matters. It is a good semblance, but someone else wrote the note."

"Why do you persist in looking for trouble?" cried Mrs. Snow.

"They plotted long against her. You could not know that," Mr. Franklin turned to Arthur Brown. "When you writ asking me to watch out for the girl, you meant only in the most general way. But now—"

"We must s-save her, then!" asserted Brown.

"We must try." Mr. Franklin tucked both letter and journal into a pocket.

Mrs. Snow began to wring her hands. "Save? Why, surely she is safe with Mr. Darly."

"She is least safe with him, I cannot explain now. Come gentlemen, to the coaching inn. We may discover what direction they have took."

"O, Emma, Emma!" moaned Mrs. Snow as we rushed to the door, Arthur Brown taking the lead—a new Brown, who plunged ahead as recklessly as ever Edmund Darly did. It was nearly ten o'clock. The lone street lamp shed sufficient light to reveal the curve of Orchard Street leading toward Southgate—but our hurrying steps got us only to Isaac Hobhouse's lodging when we heard a sharp *crack!* and I jerked to a halt.

I had heard a similar report only two days ago: a pistol shot.

The others halted too. We all peered at the looming shape of the house. "O, I pray—!" murmured Mr. Franklin. Two of the three upper windows showed light, but the ground floor was dark. Stepping to the front door, Mr. Franklin tried it. It proved unlatched, and he pressed the oak.

"Take care, sir," said I.

"I shall. Stand back." Hinges faintly creaked as the black rectangle of the interior came into view, and when after sev'ral heartbeats no consequence befell, Mr. Franklin cautiously stepped in, we following. A glow rose to diminish the darkness, and Isaac Hobhouse's landlord, a little grizzled man, crept from belowstairs carrying a candle, his manservant huddled behind him. Both men appeared terrified. "O, what is it? Do not harm us!" cried they at sight of Mr. Franklin backed by three shadowy followers.

"We are no robbers. Where did the pistol shot come from?"

The landlord lifted a quavering finger. "Above, I believe."

Six pairs of eyes turned toward the stairs, which bent out of sight. I smelt the sharp odor of gunpowder.

Mr. Franklin placed his foot upon the first step. "Mr. Hobhouse. Are you well?" called he up into the gloom.

"Mr. Franklin?" came a voice after a moment, shaken. "You may come up."

He did so, I close behind him, Edgar Snow and Arthur Brown upon my heels. The stairs made a turn, and shortly we were crowded into the upper corridor.

Two candles flickered in sconces. By their light we saw a smear upon a door jamb: blood. Wigless, old Hobhouse leant against this jamb in a long white dressing gown. He was death-pale.

F. J. Mossop stood by him, his smoking pistol in his hand.

✣ 22 ✣

*IN WHICH we meet a man of two
names and pursue a stolen girl . . .*

A t sight of Mossop and his pistol, I drew back. Might he
have reloaded?

"Nay, Nick, do not fear," said Mr. Franklin as the
little man's eyes peeped over the collar of his voluminous coat.
"You found need to save another soul, sir, eh?" said he to Mossop. "I have had no opportunity to thank you for saving ours in
the Abbey. Do I guess aright: Albert Noakes has struck
again?"

"He has."

"Would you had shot him with the highwayman, for then
Tom Bridger might still be alive. Nonetheless, you have
served your master well." Mr. Franklin turned to Isaac Hobhouse. "You *are* his master, sir?"

A curt nod. "And fortunate to have a man like F. J. Mossop."

"But, you are wounded."

Hobhouse peered at his hand. "A trifle." He made a face as
he wrapped the cut in a handkerchief. "If old age has not done
me in, an ill-used dagger cannot. I only regret that my man's
ball did not finish the blackguard."

"He is still at large, then?"

"I do not usually miss," muttered Mossop, "but the dim light, the suddenness ”

"I am sorry to hear the villain is not stone dead."

"He was rifling my things when I came upon him," said Hobhouse.

"To make it appear a robbery, no doubt."

"He must have believed I had retired early. But I read by a candle in my bed; thus I heard him in the antechamber. When I came upon him he made no bones. He meant to slit my throat."

"He is cold-blooded," said Mr. Franklin.

Blinking like a mouse caught in a housewife's candleglow, Mossop completed his master's story: "I followed him from the street. I watch there each night." (*Boot-toes!* thought I.) "I found him with his knife out. I fired, but I missed, curse the luck, and he fled through that back window before I could close with him."

"You would have fought him hand to hand?" asked Edgar Snow.

"I have wrestled more than one brute to a fall."

Mr. Franklin clapped the little man upon his shoulder. "Sir, I should like you with me in any fight! But I hope your wound is sufficiently stanched, Mr. Morland?"

There was a silence. "M-Morland?" echoed Arthur Brown.

"O, quite." Mr. Franklin gestured at the man we had known as Isaac Hobhouse. "Meet Titus Morland, Emma's other uncle."

Once more I found myself wedged betwixt Mr. Franklin and Arthur Brown in an open chaise, speeding from Bath. 'Twas a trim carriage, just what was wanted.

232

Edgar Snow, Titus Morland, and F. J. Mossop rid in a slightly larger conveyance just behind.

Our mares' hooves clopped, leathern straps creaked. In the blackness stars pricked out an icy design, whilst silvery mists curled about hills that loomed and fell like the slow waves of an oily sea. The air was cold (I had pulled my collar to my chin), and only now and then did a glimmer from a passing farmhouse hint that other souls lived near. It was eleven now; we seemed the only travelers on the road.

I thought what had led us here. We all would have fit into a larger coach, for one had been handy at the inn, but such a vehicle would have gone too slow, and we must move fast if we were to rescue Emma Morland. Could we do it? In Orchard Street, upon learning that his niece had been abducted, Titus Morland growled, "I *will* come with you, sirs! I must!" F. J. Mossop must come too, and hurrying through Bath's dark streets we had found luck at the inn. The ostler had cocked his head at the coins old Morland clinked in his bandaged hand. Ye-es, said he, he remembered the handsome young gen'leman who had hired a chaise about three o'clock. That young gen'leman had been in a hurry, he had paid handsomely. Aye, there was a pretty young thing with him, too. "But she did not seem well."

"N-not well?" asked Arthur Brown.

"Sleepy-like," said the ostler. "Sick, p'rhaps" He tutted. "Th' waters does not cure 'em all."

"They have drugged her, then," said Mr. Franklin, "as they did me. Were there any others with 'em?"

"A fine lady."

"Mrs. Valentine, no doubt."

"And another man, too," added the ostler.

"Describe him."

The ostler did.

"But that is Dr. Woolridge!" exclaimed Edgar Snow.

Mr. Franklin smiled grimly. "Do not be surprised. Who better to know what to slip into a man's beer, to render him unconscious in an inn on the way to Bath? Or how to drug a girl so a marriage ceremony may be done against her will? Your niece has been ringed with conspirators, sir, and they will have the way well-prepared: a chapel, a tractable parson, witnesses to say the bride stepped happily to the altar, the parish clerk to set the joining down in the official register; last, some bower where Darly can have his way with the girl."

Arthur Brown shuddered. "We m-must s-stop this from h-happening!"

"You take great interest in a girl you have known so little," Titus Morland said to him.

"I have known her m-many years. I know her heart, her m-mind."

Morland waved a hand. "Enough, man!"

Darly and Emma had rid off alone, the ostler told us—yet many roads left Bath. Which had they took? The ostler winked. "I heard the older woman and the young man awhisp'rin'." He hooked a thumb. " 'Tis west they went, toward Bristol."

"Thank you, sir!" proclaimed Mr. Franklin. "By the by, has anyone else hired a horse or gig this last hour?"

"One fellow took a horse—Mr. Darly's; it were stabled here." The ostler's description fit Albert Noakes.

I felt a sinking, and Mr. Franklin looked grave. "Curse the man. He rides to warn Darly that he failed to finish you, Morland—all the more peril to your niece." He clambered in beside me. "Make our mare fly, Mr. Brown."

* * *

234

Our mare did not fly, but she made brisk progress over the packed earth of the Bristol Road, and as the minutes crept toward midnight I was grateful we met no bogs such as had slowed our journey to Bath. This meant Darly and his prisoner had made good time, too, but Mr. Franklin was hopeful: "Even if they ride late, they must stop at some lodging. Darly will not expect us to pursue him." I harbored doubts. What if Darly did not halt? What if he traveled on? What if the chapel and parson and witnesses had been near, and he and Emma Morland were man and wife already?

"Please, sir, why should an earl's son go to such lengths?" asked I.

"He is not an earl's son."

Arthur Brown's great beak of a nose gleamed in the starlight. "You m-must explain it all now, sir."

"I shall. It began when someone unsealed your letter to me. I would have paid little heed had the wax not been so artfully resealed (there is such a thing as being too clever), but my suspicions were fanned by events on the way to Bath. There was F. J. Mossop with his odd, secretive ways. There was the highwayman, too, who was interrupted by the fortuitous arrival of a handsome young hero. Was such chance credible? And was it merely luck that we had a doctor along, to bind his wound? (It was only later I recalled that it had been James Woolridge who urged our driver toward that lonely place.) Albert Noakes compounded my suspicions. He was openly insolent to his master. Why did Darly tolerate him?

"And then we arrived at the White Hart, where I was drugged so that I would make no difficulty. How convenient that Woolridge was gone from our chamber when the villains set upon my bed. They failed, but their intent was clear: I was to be prevented from proceeding. By whom? Who but him who secretly read your letter to me? Yet why go to such lengths, opening then resealing the letter, setting bludgeoners on me? Some significant prize must be at stake."

Quimp, thought I. *Always and ever Quimp.*

"What prize?" Mr. Franklin went on. "Wealth, surely. But whose? Edgar Snow was well-to-do, but hardly worth such elaborate plans. And Emma's other uncle, though rich, had dismissed her years ago. True, he had seemed to love the child, but was not that love long dead?

"Before I say more, I must tell you of a man named Quimp. He has no other name, to my knowledge—yet he has a thousand, for he is the villain behind much crime that plagues London. John Fielding, the principal magistrate for Westminster, is my friend; he has told me of Quimp: how the villain's net grows. Whore-masters, robbers, highwaymen, receivers of goods, smugglers, counterfeiters, all manner of petty cutthroats who will murder as well as wink—all are at Quimp's beck and call. Lawyers and Parliament men, too. So when I discovered my letter had been opened, I guessed it might be his hand behind the deed."

"B-but why should he pay any m-mind to you?" asked Brown.

"Because he has crossed my path before—or I have crossed his. I have foiled him more than once. Nick thought he saw him at the White Hart. I believe he did see the man. I also believe he is behind the plot against Emma Morland. He has kept watch many weeks. He knew Miss Morland came to Bath, to take lodgings near you at your arranging. What better place to spring his trap than Bath, the freest town in England, where an impressionable girl might easily be ensnared? Mrs. Snow told me unknown persons asked about her niece in London, surely Quimp's spies. They learnt her heart; they learnt her naïve desire to meet a highwayman. Thus was a play set in

236

motion upon Hounslow Heath. Nothing was left to fortune (Quimp has not gained power by mischance), so as a friend of the Snows you were watched too, your letters noted. How surprised Quimp must have been to learn that one had been posted to Ben Franklin. He could not allow any possibility that I might spoil his plans as I have done in the past, so he arranged to have me stopped at the White Hart."

Brown stared. "And Dr. Woolridge played a part in that? But he is a d-decent man. He came to Bath to help the infirm; he told me so. How can he be in this w-wicked fellow's employ?"

"A letter from Butcher's Cross informs me that no Dr. Woolridge ever practiced thereabouts," said Mr. Franklin.

"Dear me!" Brown sat in numb silence a moment. "And Edmund Darly was in it too? But he was shot."

"Was he? There have been many deceptions, yet I did not truly suspect Darly of being in on 'em 'til the luncheon at his lodgings at which we first met Mrs. Valentine. What a show was put on! Yet an error marred it: upon being reminded he had been wounded, Darly winced—and clutched the wrong arm. It was but a moment's lapse; he quickly corrected himself, and at first I wondered if I had mistook. No one else seemed to have noticed, yet it roused my suspicions, for if I had seen aright it meant that he and Woolridge were in collusion, for it was Woolridge who tended Darly's arm."

"B-but there was b-blood."

"A chicken's. A pig's. In a concealed bladder. It has been done before."

"But how could Darly know the highwayman's b-ball would go astray?" Brown stared. "You m-mean . . . the highwayman was in on the conspiracy, too?"

Mr. Franklin nodded. "Men go to great lengths when a prize is at stake, and one was now, tens of thousands of pounds: Titus Morland's whole, vast fortune. To obtain it, Quimp's plan was to marry Emma to a man whose soul was in thrall to him (by English law a husband gains power over his wife's dowry). We do not know what hold Quimp has on Darly—it must be terrible—but in any case the girl longed for a handsome hero, so Quimp gave her one, with a show of bravery upon Hounslow Heath to stamp his glory upon her heart. With Quimp's resources, it cannot have been difficult to manage. Too, he is bold; he prides himself on clever tricks. And he has a theatrical turn of mind. Not that he eschewed cruder means." Mr. Franklin described our battle in the Abbey. "I have no doubt it was the highwayman and Noakes who first tried to do me in at the inn. Seeing a second chance, they set about it—but they did not take F. J. Mossop into account. Thank heaven for him, eh, Nick?"

"Thank heaven, sir," said I.

"Days before that I had writ letters to Butcher's Cross and Northumberland, seeking to know if what I was beginning to suspect were true. When I saw Isaac Hobhouse's ways, how he paid close attention to Emma, yet would tell little of himself—and how conveniently near the Snows he lodged (I mistrusted that coincidence too)—I writ also to Gloucestershire, where he claimed to live. Truly I began to doubt ev'ryone—even you, Mr. Brown."

"I?"

"What did I really know of you? I am glad to discover you took no part in the plot."

"I would never d-do anything to harm Emma! But you will not t-tell me that Tom Bridger was also in the thing?"

"No. He merely stood in the way, poor man. He threatened to lure Emma from Edmund Darly. He must therefore be stopped."

"Dear God."

"I am sure it was Albert Noakes who did him in."

"And Mrs. Valentine—?"

"Another conspirator, to take Emma in hand to deliver her as often as possible into Edmund Darly's company. As for Darly's 'sister,' she does not exist, though she provided one of those touches which Quimp delights in. As I told you I have studied the quirks and quiddities of handwriting. Having examined Darly's from the letters which I posted for him, I compared it to the 'reply' from Caroline. It was the same hand; therefore Darly himself had writ Caroline's letter, likely on Quimp's orders, little thinking anyone would look close at it. Quimp was too clever in another particular, for he chose to disguise Darly as a real peer instead of an invented one. He settled upon a man far from Bath, a Northumberland earl with a reputation for reclusiveness. He must have thought Emma would be entrapped long before the deception came to light. But I have a friend in Northumberland. I writ to him, begging a prompt reply. Yet even if his letter had not arrived, a final proof came yesterday, in the King's Bath. Pretending to slip, I grasped Darly's arm. Bathing garments are loose-fitting; thus it proved easy to slide up his sleeve. He had no scar."

"And thus no wound," breathed Arthur Brown.

"Quite."

And all because a man changed his mind, thought I whilst Brown flicked the reins; for as Titus Morland had told us as we waited for our carriages to be readied, he had made a new will.

"I settled everything upon my niece," he said. "I always meant to leave my fortune to my son, but he fell from bad to worse; he took pleasure in degrading all about him. I tried ev'rything to amend his ways—bribery, threats—but he was mired in wickedness. As a last resort I packed him off to India (I have interests there). But he fell into even worse ways. The reports I got from Chandrapoor! A wracking disease was the price of his sins, and he came home to die, unrepentant to the end. He spat upon me, can you imagine?—I, the only soul in the world who loved him! I stood by his bed, I watched him gasp his last. He was my only son, and I wept when he was gone; but I was glad to close his eyes, for he had pleased neither himself nor anyone else in his wretched life. I began to think on Emma, the babe I had held in my lap. I had always loved my niece. What a fool I had been! Pride had made me cast her from me, but time had taught its lesson, and I longed to make up for my error. I heard she grew into a fine young woman (I have always received secret reports of her). To whom else should I leave my fortune? My son's death had made me ill—there were rumors I would die—but I must alter my will. I did so, only two persons besides my lawyer knowing. One was Mr. Mossop, the other my doctor, a man named Flynn. I trusted Flynn, yet he had a friend, another doctor, an apparently respectable practitioner, though poor and unsuccessful. I met him once. What was my surprise when I seemed to meet him again, in Bath. At first I thought I was mistook; now I know that I was not. Flynn must've let slip to him the story of my will, little thinking it mattered. The other doctor's true name is James Reed, but he gave himself to you as James Woolridge."

"So that was how Quimp learnt of your changed will," murmured Mr. Franklin.

Quimp dangled hooks about wealthy men, thought I. He had caught a doctor with one.

"How affrighted Woolridge must have been to see you here when he expected to hear of your death," mused Mr. Franklin. "For that matter, how the news that you were Morland rather than Hobhouse must have affrighted all the conspirators. No wonder Woolridge evaded you. And no wonder Noakes and his accomplice followed you that night. 'Twould have been made out a robbery, but they meant to cut your throat, for you must be dead in order for Emma to inherit. But why precisely did you come to Bath?"

"My son's failings taught me a hard lesson. I must see Emma for myself. Should she prove unworthy, I would not hesitate to change my will once more."

"And *is* she worthy, Mr. Morland?"

The old man glanced at Arthur Brown in a peculiarly speculative fashion before he replied. "Some might say she has too much spirit. Yet, damn me, had I lacked spirit, I should be a poor man! Her heart is good, Mr. Franklin, and I find her most worthy. Pray God we save her!"

We arrived at our first posting stop to change horses past one. Dogs barked, the stars gleamed down. A sleepy ostler told us that a fellow of Darly's description, with a young woman, had changed horses here; we were on the right road. We were not pleased to learn this had occurred at five in the afternoon, more than eight hours ago. The ostler had no news of Noakes. "Let 'em not reach the coast," murmured Mr. Franklin. "Let him have no plan to fly with her to Ireland."

"But what use is she to them if Mr. Morland is still alive?" asked I as fresh steeds were strapped into the traces.

"Much planning has gone into Quimp's scheme; he will not give over at this stage o' the game. He knows Morland's feeling for his niece. He knows that to save her name—perhaps even her life—the old man will pay much. Count upon it, the marriage will go through. She will then be Darly's—and Darly is Quimp's."

We plunged once more into the night.

241

❧ 23 ❧

IN WHICH we attend a wedding
and confront an enemy . . .

I n two hours, we reached our second posting stop, March-
ford; it was 3:00 A.M. We roused a maidservant to fetch the
landlord, who came downstairs. Yes, said he, a young man
of Edmund Darly's description had hired fresh horses just past
seven. He and his companion—his sister, he had called her—
had eaten a cold collation in the dining room. "Whether she
were his sister or no, she looked desperate to fly from him,
though there was little chance o' that, for he kept his hand
tight upon her all the while."

"She is alert enough to flee?" said Mr. Franklin. "The drug
has worn off, then."

"Hurry, man," growled Titus Morland to the landlord. "We
want fresh horses. I will pay what you ask."

Within twenty minutes, we had set out again under glinting
stars. We had an extra spur, for the landlord had also told us
that a man, plainly Albert Noakes, had rid in half an hour ago
on a mount near dead with whipping and had sped off on a
fresh steed. "We follow the right road, then," said Mr. Franklin, but I felt fresh doubts. Signposts began to point north
to Gloucester, south to Glastonbury. Beyond Gloucester

242

stretched Wales. Below Glastonbury lay Devon and Cornwall and the great Atlantic Sea. Were we right to continue west?

As the morn crept toward dawn, the road rattled my bones. I had not slept, and a great tiredness crept upon me. I thought on Emma Morland. I was glad to learn she was no conniving fortune-seeker. The girl knew her heart; she had the courage to follow it, and she would not marry a "catch" if she did not love him. I glanced at Arthur Brown. How earnest he looked with his beaky nose as keen as some old Roman's. Could I doubt he loved Emma? Had he been bolder, would she already be his affianced bride? I turned to Mr. Franklin. He wore his beaver hat low over his ears, his collar up. His hands rested upon his lap, whilst his round face turned quizzically up to the sky as if to seek guidance from the stars. He had discovered the plot against Emma when no other could have, but that made me fearful, for his great enemy must be reckoned with.

I prayed Quimp did not lie ahead.

I must have slept, for when my eyes fluttered open Mr. Franklin was peering at his watch. "Near five-thirty," murmured he. I shook myself. A faint glow lit the sky ahead, but it could not be sunrise; that would come at our backs.

Mr. Franklin read my thought. "Bristol," he said.

The glow was only a tiny brightening just above the horizon: the streetlamps and early candles of the town (had there been the least mist we should never have noted it). I squinted. The port was about a mile away, I judged; and, as we started the long descent to it, its jumble of houses and wharves gradually stood out before a convocation of ship masts like thin, stiff fingers praying against the night. I could smell the sea. Had Darly arrived long before? Had he taken Emma to wife? Had he secreted her in some lair we should never discover?

"Do not lose hope." Mr. Franklin patted Arthur Brown's arm. Yet we all knew the pair might have turned off some other road, might be in some far place. Brown's hands snapped the reins but did little good, for our mare had pulled near three hours and could pull but weakly now. "We must stop," said Mr. Franklin resignedly. A sign proclaimed the village of Green's Ford, and we halted before a posting house attached to a small, unprepossessing inn. Titus Morland, Edgar Snow, and F. J. Mossop drew up just behind us.

"Our horse is near done in, too," grumbled Morland when we had all got down.

"We must continue to search," replied Mr. Franklin though he frowned toward Bristol. How many inns were in the populous town? Further, how would we ever find Darly if he had been alerted by Albert Noakes?

We pounded at the posting house door, a candle flared behind a window, and we were admitted by a drowsy potboy. He rubbed his eyes. Aye, he would fetch the master. This man came down, ill-pleased to be wakened. "What? You seek a handsome young man? With a pretty girl? Describe 'em. Aye . . . well, then, you are in luck, for they did not merely stop to change horses, they sleep upstairs now, in my very best chamber."

This caused a sensation, and my heart leapt. Had we saved Emma after all?

Arthur Brown looked ready to dash upstairs at once.

"Beggin' yer pardon, but you are not the first to seek 'em," piped up the potboy before anyone could act.

"What?" demanded the landlord.

The boy ducked his head. "I did not rouse you, sir, b'cause the man told me not to. No need, he said. He come about three-quarter of an hour ago. He said he were the servant of a man who stopped here—had a message for 'im what could not wait. Give me a florin, he did, if I would say where t'find 'im, and seein' no harm I did, second door on th' right." A wary peering. "Was I wrong t'do it?"

Arthur Brown was at the stairs in a flash, but Mr. Franklin gripped his arm. "Let us not give up the game so near to winning. At the very least, Noakes has a knife; Darly may be armed, too. Noakes cannot know we followed—they may think we were fooled by Emma's 'letter'—so let us do nothing to spoil our advantage." He spoke in a low voice to the boy. "Has anyone come down?"

"No. I heard some sounds just after the man went up, but I fell asleep soon after. Nothin' woke me 'til you knocked, sir."

"Mr. Mossop?"

The little man had already drawn his pistol. "Shall I go up first?"

"If you please."

The landlord blanched. "See here, sirs . . . !"

Mr. Franklin turned to him. "The young woman has been abducted. We intend to save her."

"But they are to be married by Parson Widford."

This gave us fresh reason to pause. "How do you know that?" demanded Edgar Snow.

"B'cause 'tis all arranged. The chamber has been waitin' since Monday—a man from London come and paid for it, said he were the girl's father."

"So that is how Noakes knew to stop here," murmured Mr. Franklin. "Quimp has planned well. Come, what more?"

"Parson Widford met 'em in the public room last night, when they arrived," replied the landlord. "They sat together, the girl betwixt 'em, and he and the young man talked on the wedding, which is to take place this very morn at the chapel."

"This morn?" gasped Arthur Brown.

"How near is this chapel?" demanded Mr. Franklin.

"Why, just at the bottom of the street."

I recalled a stark Norman tower looming against the sky in the direction of Bristol. "Upstairs at once, Mr. Mossop!" barked Mr. Franklin, and Mossop obeyed, pistol in hand. Did Noakes wait with his knife? I did not like how closely Mr. Franklin followed upon Mossop's heels. Arthur Brown went, too, and the three vanished in gloom, whilst Titus Morland, Edgar Snow, and I craned our necks in anticipation, but no commotion ensued, no pistol shot sounded.

Mr. Franklin's face appeared above, solemn as an icon. "They are gone. To the chapel, eh, Mr. Brown? That is where we must fly."

In less than a minute, we had set out.

Old Morland could walk but slowly. "Go on," urged he, wheezing. "I shall follow."

Edgar Snow hung back to help him as Mr. Franklin, F. J. Mossop, Arthur Brown, and I pressed at full speed along the road. Dawn was just breaking, light seeping into the sky. Somewhere a cock crowed as Bristol awoke to day half a mile downhill and the sea shed her nighttime veils. "A back stairs," puffed Mr. Franklin to tell how Darly and Noakes had ferreted their captive from the inn. "They will have obtained a license under the fiction that they live in this parish. They will have waked their parson. Sent Noakes, perhaps. Waked witnesses too. And the parish clerk. They will try to get the thing done quickly, I believe."

Green's Ford was little more than a line of buildings along the Bristol Road: a smithy, a corn chandler, a sailmaker, and two dozen dwellings of unadorned wood and stone, one sporting a mournful plume of smoke. Hurrying behind Arthur Brown's long, storklike strides, we were at the churchyard in moments, at the very edge of town, with its wicket gate and jumble of lichened headstones. It was still only half-day, the old Norman edifice looming against the dawn sky like a great beached ship. No person other than ourselves was in sight. Grass sighed and twigs ticked in the salt breeze that came up from the sea.

"Your pistol, sir," said Mr. Franklin, but Mossop already held it ready.

"Could we be wrong?" murmured Brown. "Can they have g-gone on to B-Bristol?"

"We must see. Come, gentlemen. Nick, you are to take up the rear. Under no circumstances put yourself in danger, do you hear?"

"Yes, sir." I crept to the church portal behind the three men. We found its pair of heavy wooden doors shut, but they were not locked, for when Mr. Franklin tugged at one of the great iron handles the left door swung out. I winced, for its groaning hinges must warn anyone inside.

We peered obliquely into the narthex. All was dark and silent.

And then there came a violent sneeze, echoing.

"Emma!" cried Arthur Brown.

A silence.

"Arthur?" came Emma Morland's voice, small and startled.

Before Mr. Franklin could prevent him, Brown had rushed into the church. He was swallowed by the darkness, but we heard his questing cry: "Emma? Emma?"

"Foolhardy . . . " muttered Mr. Franklin, hurrying in, too. I glanced at Mossop. His eyes were hooded, and he hung back. Why? In spite of Mr. Franklin's adjuration I could not stay where I was when my father might be in danger.

I followed him into the church.

Chill, it filled my nostrils with the flinty odor of stone and hallowed eons. This was no many-windowed edifice like Bath Abbey—it was a long, austere rectangle—but its row of clerestory panes let in enough of dawn to make out a group of persons gathered about the chancel at the far end. Their intent was obvious: marriage, but they had turned to face down the central aisle, where Arthur Brown stood with his back to me. Mr. Franklin had stopped a few paces behind him.

"Mr. Brown—" murmured Mr. Franklin, lifting a hand. Brown seemed not to hear. "Emma!" he burst out.

"O, Arthur, you are safe!"

"Come no nearer, sir!" warned Edmund Darly. "Emma is now mine." He stood beside her, his hand gripping the girl's wrist so she could not flee. Behind 'em hovered the rector in his black broadcloth and white bands, frowning deeply. Nearby waited an old couple, startled-looking (it must have been she who sneezed, for she did so again, loudly). To the right of 'em stood another man, thin and grave, with a book in his hand, the parish clerk, I guessed.

Darly's words made my heart sink. The wedding was over then? Had we any right to wrest a man's bride from him, however he had won her?

But the rector fixed his puzzled gaze upon Darly. "Nay, sir, she is not yours yet. You roused us to do at six what was meant to go forth at ten. Now comes a man who . . . well, sir, why do you come?"

Brown's voice quavered with hope: "The m-marriage is not yet d-done?"

"It has not even begun."

Brown drew himself up. "Why, then, it m-must n-not be!"

The rector frowned. "You have some objection?"

Darly flicked an impatient hand. "Continue with the ceremony, reverend. He will say nothing."

"He may, and I am obliged to hear him. Speak, sir. You had better have good reason for this."

Albert Noakes slid from shadow at the side of the nave. He

248

was at Arthur Brown's side in an instant, his long, sallow face as insolent as ever. And as determined. I heard him mutter a warning as he thrust an object against Brown's breast, and I groaned, for it was a pistol, though Noakes used his cloak to conceal it from the six in the chancel.

"I await you, sir," called the rector down the aisle, his sepulchral voice echoing.

Brown's hands worked at his sides, and he trembled so that I thought he would burst. For my part I longed to fling myself upon the hateful Noakes, but I dared not, and even Mr. Franklin stood still.

A flickering smile crossed Darly's lips. "Did I not tell you he would say nothing? Proceed, I tell you," drawled he to the churchman.

The rector remained troubled. "Sir?" called he to Brown again. I looked at Emma. She was as beautiful as ever, pale and staring. Poor girl. This was how her longing for romance had rewarded her: she must watch her oldest friend, the man who loved her best, silenced whilst she was forced to marry another, for though she could not see Noakes's pistol, she must know he promised death to Arthur Brown if he spoke.

"One last time, sir," came the rector's demand, "have you some objection to this union? No? Very well, then, I must proceed."

What to do? Charge upon Noakes myself? But I need not, for help arrived from another quarter. I did not know whence he came (he must have crept behind me), but as if he were compacted out of air, F. J. Mossop suddenly stood two feet from Albert Noakes. Mossop was short and round; he appeared comically unprepossessing next to the tall, lank villain. But Noakes had scant reason to smile, for with his stubby arm Mossop pressed his own pistol squarely and with no concealment against Noakes's right temple. "I shall discharge this into your

249

brain if you do not let your pistol drop, sir. Count upon it, I will."

Noakes turned with a look of black, seething fury.

Mossop shook his head. "Nay, sir, believe me, I should like nothing better than to shoot you. Give me the slightest reason, and you are dead. Come, shall I scatter your brains?"

"You had best do as he says, Mr. Noakes," murmured Benjamin Franklin.

There was a silence, during which my heart pounded.

Noakes cursed. His weapon clattered upon the stone flags.

"Arthur!" cried Emma. She made as if to run to him, but Darly held her back—and in that small distracting moment Noakes flung up his arm, striking Mossop's pistol. Quick as a flash he had bent, scooped up his own weapon, and in what seemed less than a second turned and began to level it. Would he shoot F. J. Mossop? Might he hit Mr. Franklin instead? I made to rush forward, as if I could stop what must come.

There was no need. Mossop had been jarred but little, and he aimed his pistol well. Coolly he fired, the *crack!* multiplying in a thousand reverberations, as if the walls of the church had been shattered. An explosion of cloth and buttons leapt from Noakes's breast, his whole body jerked, his pistol flew, his feet stumbled, and he fell back, bounced, rolled upon his belly. He twitched thrice upon the footworn flags before he moved no more.

Emma screamed, the old woman fainted, the parish clerk dropped his book.

Arthur Brown dashed toward the front of the church.

He leapt over Noakes's body as if it were nothing. He was gangling, but his long legs had trod many a hill about Bath; he took no wrong step. Emma had made to flee again, but Darly still prevented, thrusting her back against the rector, who

250

stood aghast at what was done in church. Darly crouched to await Arthur Brown.

Brown leapt upon him.

Brown was thirty-five, a bookish man. Darly was younger, taller, broader; surely he must quickly win the encounter. But I had not reckoned with those long hours in the air which Brown had spent, how they had toughened his sinews and strengthened his wind. Too he fought for the woman he loved; that gave him heart. Darly had been trained in fisticuffs, and at first he dodged Brown, driving blows into his face, darting jabs that soon had that great nose bleeding. "No . . . stop!" cried Emma as Edgar Snow and Titus Morland arrived at our backs. Snow looked like he might try to stop the fight, but Mr. Franklin held him back. "Let 'em have at it. I wager for Mr. Brown."

Old Morland smiled wolfishly. "I believe I do too, sir. I believe I do too."

More blows were struck. Darly had the greater skill; yet he seemed to flag whilst Brown appeared tireless. Though he was struck often, Brown only blinked, sniffed a breath, and came on again in his flailing way. And he learned. Seeing Darly's method, he began to imitate it with sharp blows of his own, so that Darly began to bleed, too; an eye began to swell. They circled, they struck, they grunted whilst Emma huddled in terror. "Gentlemen, I beg you!" the rector found his voice. "This is God's house!"

It must come to an end. Darly stumbled against the front pew. Brown came for him, but Darly stretched out his hands, palms up. He was gasping, and his golden hair lay damp with sweat across his brow. Brown stopped warily whilst Darly drew himself up to gaze at Emma with a peculiar shattered solemnity, and for a moment, despite his bruises, I saw the fine young gentleman he had once seemed: rash but honorable.

251

"Well, sir?" demanded Brown, ready to spring once more.

"Nay, sir, I am done," panted Darly, pushing back his damp hair. "Why should I fight you? To what purpose? Our plan is defeated—you have saved Miss Morland, and I am glad. I have not liked my part in the thing. I did it only to . . . to save my honor from a wicked man." His mouth twisted bitterly. "I have lost that honor instead, but at least I can say that I am sorry." He looked at Emma. "I *am* sorry, dear girl. I have wounded you, in more ways than one, but I hope someday you can forgive me. The truth is, I am fond of you in spite of what I have done." He gazed round. "I want you all to know that I had no part in the murder of poor Tom Bridger. *He* did it, that vile creature." He pointed to Noakes's crumpled body. "Dear God, how he kept his thumb on me."

"For Quimp?" asked Mr. Franklin.

"You know the devil, then? He told us you might provide much trouble."

"Where is he?"

"Long gone, back to London (he prefers to manipulate affairs from afar, so the law may not touch him). At least Albert Noakes can trouble no one any longer; you are well rid of him." Darly straightened his coat. "And now I shall rid you of me, too." Brushing past Arthur Brown, he started down the aisle.

Mr. Franklin had picked up Noakes's undischarged pistol. He faced the disheveled young man.

Darly stopped. He cocked his head. "Sir, you must let me pass, or I shall force you to shoot me. I have a score to settle, you see."

"With Quimp?"

A nod. "I have nothing to lose—and perhaps a little to gain: some measure of lost honor."

Mr. Franklin pursed his lips. He stepped aside. "I wish you the better of him, sir."

Edmund Darly—or the man we had known by that name—strode from the church.

Arthur Brown rushed to Emma. He clasped her. "Miss Morland. Emma. Thank God you are safe! Now hear me well: you shall marry no one if you do not marry me."

She looked up at him palely. "O, how long you have been in asking, Mr. Brown."

❦ 24 ❧

*IN WHICH two uncles decide the fate
of one girl whilst Mr. Franklin decides
the fate of another...*

We traveled unimpeded on the road back from Bristol, all save F. J. Mossop, who must stay behind to explain to the local justices why he had shot a man. But we had no doubt he should easily acquit himself; he had witnesses aplenty to say he had acted to save his life. "No need for him to confess to shooting that wretch in Bath Abbey," murmured Mr. Franklin quietly to me when we stopped to change horses at noon.

As we rid I wondered: would Arthur Brown and Emma Morland truly wed? Other persons held the girl's fate in their hands—they might not approve, and it did not seem to portend well that these persons, her uncles, had snatched her from Brown before we left Green's Ford, so that Brown must ride with us whilst she sat tucked betwixt Titus Morland and Edgar Snow in the other carriage that came behind. I could understand old Morland's wish to have her near at long last, but might he turn her against her scholar? Who was Brown after all but an odd, reclusive fellow who kept his great nose buried in the past? Poor Brown. He sent many a troubled glance backward as we rattled along, torn between joy at finding his love safe (Darly had made no attempt to touch her at the inn, she had told us) and terror at wondering if he had lost her despite his brave show.

When Emma had learnt that Isaac Hobhouse was Titus Morland, she had burst into tears. "Can you ever forgive me?" "Whatever for, my dear?" the old man had grasped her hands by the doors of the church. "O . . . O . . . you must think me a wicked, flirtatious girl." Morland shook his head. "Nay, I am the wicked one. All these years . . .? You must let me make up for 'em now."

Falteringly, Emma had told us how Mrs. Valentine had taken her to a teashop. "The woman must have dropped some compound into my drink, for I grew so drowsy that I hardly remember meeting Mr. Darly and being handed into a carriage with him." When she regained her senses many miles later, Darly had attempted to persuade her that she had eloped of her own accord: "I asked you, Emma, and you said yes," he told me; but when I said I was sure I could never have done so, he pressed the romance of it upon me, his love, his wealth, my great good fortune. Still I denied him, demanding that he return me to Bath. He changed fearfully then. He said he would not go back and that I must marry him or dreadful things would happen to you, Uncle; and to Aunt; and to Mr. Brown." She searched Brown's face. "He said he had confederates. He said they had taken you, Arthur. He said they held you in a secret place and might *murder* you if I did not comply."

"It was all for my fortune," Titus Morland told her, "for I give it all to you, dear niece." He gazed deep at her, at which she burst into tears once more.

We rid on. Though all danger to Emma seemed over, there remained Quimp. He hated to be thwarted. Yet I found I could not worry about him, for I was drained of worry. I gazed at the world with longing eyes: spring! How bright and green the day, with its smell of loamy fields. Meadows grew thick with buttercup, slopes sprouted clover, hawthorn flowered, cuckoos called, lapwings plunged, and ash trees sent out their reddish buds under a clear blue sky.

We had engaged to stay no more than a fortnight in Bath. We rescued Emma Morland on the thirteenth morn of that sojourn; thus we must depart the following day. Mr. Franklin had business in London—there were the Penns to deal with, the Board of Trade. Too, he longed to meet with the Royal Society and his beloved Honest Whigs. Our great affection for Mrs. Stevenson and her daughter drew us to the safety of Craven Street, where we might undertake a more regulated life. And Mr. Franklin fretted over William: his elder son pursued the pleasures of town—but did he pursue his studies?

But that was tomorrow. Upon arriving at The Bull Inn round about three, we chanced upon Beau Nash, returning from a convocation of the town's aldermen, where, he told us with much slashing of his stick, that he had railed against the lax morality that threatened Bath. "But, Franklin," he tapped his old, white-hatted head, "I have recalled where I met that Darly rogue. It was in Tunbridge some two or three years ago—but he was not Darly, he was Pepperel, I'll swear he was, and he gamed like a knave and chased all the ladies."

"O?" Mr. Franklin told the King of Bath more of Pepperel, enough to make the old fellow's eyebrows fly up in amazement. "B'god, man, do you say true? He was *not* the son of an earl? What imposture!" Nash urged his chairmen to take him straightaway to an alehouse, where, he said, he would down three bumpers to make him blind to the perfidy of the world.

Emma and her two uncles set off for Orchard Street. Ashen, the girl went willingly, which seemed to bode even worse for Arthur Brown, though as she was tucked into a chair at old

Morland's bidding, she sent him a heartfelt look. But she vanished soon, and Brown trudged beside us down Stall Street. "Cheer up, man," urged Mr. Franklin. "She is safe and well." A question had puzzled me. "What of the medallion which you found upon Tom Bridger's body?" asked I. "Bridger himself must have stole it. It was gold, and our young gamester was not overscrupulous." Hands behind his back, Benjamin Franklin squinted at the sky.

Back in our rooms, we began to pack our boxes and bags. "Is it not a great satisfaction to see a thing well completed, Nicolas?"

"*Is* it well completed, sir?" asked I.

"Brown and Miss Morland, you mean? But I have her journal." He patted a pocket. "In the course of glancing through it, I could not miss her sentiments on Mr. Brown, for they appear on ev'ry page. She loves him, Nick. She has not seen him much in recent years, yet she has her memory of him—the kindness he showed when she was young. Letters from him, too, in the hundreds. How assiduously he wrote! She has a romantic soul, but we have misjudged its quality, for love for a philosopher has flowered in its soil. The girl's brain has been fired by Brown's studies, which she has come to delight in through him. They are an unlikely pair, the staid scholar and the sprightly girl. Yet I think they may be happy—if they are allowed. Dear me, I hope Morland's fortune does not spoil 'em! Did I tell you his worth?" He named a sum which caused me to gasp. "No wonder Quimp went to such lengths to get the girl in his power. Shall we next door, so I may return her book?"

We found Titus Morland seated in the front parlor of number two with Edgar Snow. Their glances at one another said they had been deep in talk. "Emma is resting," Mr. Snow told us, "watched over by my wife. She is greatly relieved to learn her niece has not been ruined. This is in large part due to you, Franklin. How can we ever repay the debt?"

"By allowing your niece to wed Arthur Brown."

This forthright response produced a weighty silence. Edgar Snow glanced at Titus Morland. Titus Morland returned the look. "As to that—" Morland began.

Abruptly a commotion rose in the entryway, the landlady's voice was heard, then Arthur Brown flew into the room with a wild look. His hair was ruffled, his great nose gleamed. He glanced only briefly at Mr. Franklin.

"Mr. M-Morland, Mr. S-Snow," burst out he, "I know that as Miss Morland's parents are d-deceased, you stand in their stead. You have authority over her, and I assure you I have m-made n-no understanding with her behind your backs. I would n-never do so. But circumstances have . . . that is . . . I care n-nothing for your fortune, Mr. Morland. Settle it all upon Emma if you wish, or part, or none; I do not care. But I l-love her and I believe I may make her happy. She seemed to say she l-loved me too, and would have me, and I am c-come to ask you to let me wed her if she does n-not change her mind. I know I have little to offer in the way of goods, but I have a t-true heart, and—"

Morland cleared his throat. "Come, sir, calm yourself. Mr. Snow and I have just been talking upon this matter, and he assures me you have a sterling character. I have observed it myself these ten days past. Emma has been tempted by scoundrels, but a decent man is what she needs, and plainly you are that. A scholar, rather than a courtier? All the better! (Dear God, save us from courtiers.) And so, sir, if she wants you she shall have you, do you hear? Now that you know this, you may close your mouth, for it has hung open far too long. Be seated.

The landlady brings tea. Join us. When Emma wakes, she will see you if she wishes."

"I do wish," said Emma at the door. We turned, and there she stood, more fetching than I had ever seen her, in a rose-pink dressing gown, her aunt behind her. "What a fuss you made as you came in, Arthur; how could anyone sleep? Was that a second proposal? You wait much too long to make the first, and then you make more than you need, for I have already said yes."

Brown could only stare.

Emma came near him. "When shall we be married, then?" Slipping her arm through his, she gazed up into eyes filled with the dawning, joyful knowledge that she was truly his.

Mrs. Sophia Valentine played one last scene in our drama. Mr. Franklin, having stepped out in the late afternoon to read some newspapers, came upon her in High Street, "dressed for business," he reported to me half an hour later. "She greeted me in that politic way of hers. She had no way of knowing Quimp's plan was foiled. 'Have you heard, Miss Morland is to wed Arthur Brown?' said I. 'They are just now at her lodgings, making plans.' I thought I heard whalebone crack, and she paled, but to give her her due she preserved her dignity. 'But how?' inquired she. 'How not?' replied I. I did not stay to tell her more."

I smiled at the story—but I also reflected on Mrs. Valentine. Did her husband even exist? Perhaps she was alone. Perhaps she kept herself how she could, supplying what services a woman with no fortune could provide.

As for James Woolridge, we saw him no more in Bath, and to my knowledge no one of our party ever saw him again. How had he been entrapped by Quimp? We did not know, nor did we learn if Quimp took vengeance upon him for being a party to failure. (He had punished failures before.) I could not entirely condemn Woolridge. Nor the man we had known as Edmund Darly. There had seemed a streak of decency in both, and it was not they who had murdered Tom Bridger. Truly I feared how Darly's sally against Quimp would fare. Quimp was powerful, and it was likely Darly, rather than his enemy, who would be found floating in the Thames—if Darly were ever found at all.

A fine supper was laid out at Titus Morland's that last eve, marked by much joy. The old man had indeed kept his eye on Arthur Brown. No doubt he compared him to his unruly son, who had succeeded only in grinding his advantages into the mud. Arthur Brown might not be a man of the world, but he was no fool; Morland must see that. In short, there were no reservations in his approbation of Emma's choice, and so we drank more than one toast to the affianced pair, Mrs. Fanny Snow flushing so red that I thought she might faint away in amazement that her niece was settled so well.

But one thing remained to be seen to before our departure, and it was a measure of Mr. Franklin's character that he did not neglect it: Nellie Blessing. Since our interview with the girl, I had often thought on her. Could she be saved?

Yes.

Mr. Franklin spoke to old Morland on the matter before we left his lodgings that eve. The amazing Mossop, who had by then returned from Bristol, was sent to find the girl, and he delivered her to Morland's lodging the following morn before nine. She came in peeping warily, seeming to believe that Mossop sought her favors, if not for himself then for some other; and when she heard that the wealthy Titus Morland offered her a respectable place as a housemaid in his grand house in Gloucestershire, she could hardly believe her fortune. Mr. Franklin persuaded her it was true, at which she sobbed and fell on her knees before him. "Serve Mr. Morland well, child," said he, making her stand. "Nick, we must go."

We departed Bath by the 11:00 A.M. coach; tomorrow eve we would be in our familiar rooms in Craven Street. We said our farewells. Arthur Brown prayed he and Mr. Franklin would discourse again on matters old and new. Miss Morland kissed Mr. Franklin's cheek—and mine: "Good-bye, boy." We caught one last glimpse of Beau Nash in his white hat as our coach moved through town.

Ten minutes later, we were out upon the Great Bath Road.

"All is well which ends well, as someone once observed," said Mr. Franklin, though his faraway expression proclaimed that his mind already turned upon future business. Quimp lurked in the "great, smoky house," as Mr. Franklin called London. Would he learn the part we had played in thwarting him? But Albert Noakes could not reveal it, and perhaps Quimp never learnt; at any rate no consequences befell. Not that Quimp did not cross our path again, as subsequent adventures proved; but for the time being, Mr. Franklin was safe.

As for me, Nick Handy, I made the best of what had occurred. The world was full of perfidy, but I had learnt that in my hard life at Inch, Printer. Yet though life dealt blows to crush the Tom Bridgers of this world, it delivered good, too. Emma Morland was saved; and though I could not help thinking with some longing on her fine green eyes, I was thoroughly happy for Arthur Brown. Thus as we rattled back to London I sat content next to Benjamin Franklin, his stubby fingers quiet in his lap, his beaver hat low on his smooth, broad brow.

Taking out my little book, I drew our fellow passengers beside the best and wisest man whom I have known.